Mina did not waste another thought on either of the men she had married. . . .

Perhaps her father had done her a favor, saving her from wedding a weakling. But then her son might have lived and she'd have that joy. Perhaps not. Who could understand the vagaries of fate?

The one favor her father had definitely done for Mina was to outlast Sparrowdale. Now she was wealthy beyond counting, with no husband to claim her fortune as his, no trustee other than Mr. Sizemore, her solicitor. Lady Sparrow was twenty-three, a countess, an heiress, a widow.

She placed a small bouquet of flowers on the grave of the son who was not her husband's. Now, she told herself, now she had to spread her wings.

Lady Sparrow

Barbara Metzger

A SIGNET BOOK

SIGNET
Published by New American Library, a division of
Penguin Putnam Inc., 375 Hudson Street,
New York, New York 10014, U.S.A.
Penguin Books Ltd, 80 Strand,
London WC2R 0RL, England
Penguin Books Australia Ltd, Ringwood,
Victoria, Australia
Penguin Books Canada Ltd, 10 Alcorn Avenue,
Toronto, Ontario, Canada M4V 3B2
Penguin Books (N.Z.) Ltd, 182–190 Wairau Road,
Auckland 10, New Zealand

Penguin Books Ltd, Registered Offices:
Harmondsworth, Middlesex, England

First published by Signet, an imprint of New American Library,
a division of Penguin Putnam Inc.

First Printing, August 2002
10 9 8 7 6 5 4 3 2 1

Printed in the United States of America

PUBLISHER'S NOTE
This is a work of fiction. Names, characters, places, and incidents either are
the product of the author's imagination or are used fictitiously, and any
resemblance to actual persons, living or dead, business establishments, events,
or locales is entirely coincidental.

To Mamie

Chapter One

*H*e would have been four, her son, had he lived. Mina thought of him nearly every day.

Her husband had been dead for seven months. Mina thought of him as rarely as possible.

Her dead husband was not the father of her dead son.

Mina, Minerva Caldwell, as she was then, had not wanted to marry Harold Sparr, Earl of Sparrowdale. What young woman of eight and ten summers would wish to wed a raddled old man of so many winters? Why, Sparrowdale's son from his first marriage was older than Miss Caldwell. Father and son shared beaked noses, black hair, and a bent toward debauchery. Minerva had declared she'd never share a bed with either of them.

Her father had thought otherwise. He'd hired the best governess, sent Mina off to the best schools, all for one purpose. He wanted a title for his only child, and he wanted the government contracts such a connection could bring to his shipbuilding enterprise. The Sparrowdale son was a wastrel, and promised since birth to a duke's daughter besides, but the earl was in need of a fresh young wife to warm his old bones.

Mina would rather warm her hands at Satan's stewpot. No, she was going to marry Ninian Rourke, a handsome, fair-haired youth with a promising future.

"Wed my assistant foreman?" her father had bellowed. "Like hell you will!" He'd gone on planning the nuptials the way he ran his business and reared his daughter, with no dissent, no delay, and no one deciding anything but himself.

So Mina and Ninian had eloped.

They'd changed horses and carriages and names and directions, to throw off any pursuit on their mad dash north. They'd finally reached the Scottish border long after dark, long uncomfortable days after setting out. They'd found an inn, declared themselves husband and wife in front of the innkeeper and his wife, and gone up to the slant-roofed attic room provided for their wedding night.

The whole affair had lacked the romantic touches a girl dreamed about for her marriage. There was no beautiful dress, no flowers, cake, or champagne toasts. The inn did not even offer a hot bath, only a can of lukewarm water and a basin, and a narrow bed with a faded cover. Mina was too tired to care. She did care—too late—that the room had no lock on the door.

"But we are already married!" she'd cried when her father and Lord Sparrowdale and his son burst into the attic chamber. An avowal in front of witnesses made it so in Scotland, Mina was sure. "Tell them, Ninian."

"We are—" Ninian had begun, only to have his words stopped by her father's fist.

"Like hell you are!" Malachy Caldwell had shouted, pulling Mina from the bed and shoving her toward Lord Sparrowdale. Shivering in her shift, Mina had pleaded, but the earl pushed her and a bundle of her clothes behind the privacy screen, while his son ogled her bare legs and licked his lips.

Sobbing, Mina got dressed, still hearing the sound of fist against flesh. She also heard the clink of coins when her father tossed a pouch at Ninian Rourke. "There, take it and get out, and never come back or I will see you rot in hell. You never knew my daughter, d'you hear? Say it, you cur, say it out loud. You never knew Minerva in the past and never will in the future."

And Ninian said it. And meant it. He forgot she ever existed.

"And you'll do the same, my girl," her father had ordered, "if you know what's good for you."

Like hell she would. How could Mina forget her lost love when she might be carrying his child?

Sparrowdale had wanted to marry her despite the possibility, so great was her dowry, so deep his debts. Mina had even fewer choices then, after her father nearly broke her jaw. She could run away and starve in a ditch, or she could marry the earl. She was ruined either way, but if there was going to be a child, her child, she had to protect it.

So Miss Minerva Caldwell and Harold Sparr, Earl of Sparrowdale, were wed under the auspices of the church and the crown and the accountants.

Mina's second wedding night was almost as awful as her first. Lord Sparrowdale found as little pleasure in this marriage bed, with a weeping, wan bride threatening to cast up her accounts at the first touch of his cold, gnarly fingers. If the earl could not enjoy his young wife in the country, he was more than content to enjoy her dowry in London with its gaming hells and houses of convenience. Part of his bargain with Moneybags Malachy, though, was to see Minerva established among the *beau monde*. Sparrowdale dragged his new countess to town with him and to a couple of balls and breakfast parties, then delegated his son to accompany Minerva on the social rounds. Having her escort fall down drunk or start a brawl was part of her introduction to so-called Polite Society. So was hiding in the ladies' withdrawing room, cowering behind her fan, and pleading headaches, which were all too real.

The *ton* dubbed her Lady Sparrow. Like her namesake, Mina was commonplace in appearance, brown-haired, small of stature, and plump. Of course she was plump; she was, in fact, breeding. Mostly what she was, in the eyes of the gossipmongers and the matrons, the gentlemen at their clubs and the dowagers at tea, was common, as common as dirt or the little birds who pecked for seeds there. Her mother might have been an

Albright of Lincolnshire; her gowns and jewels might have cost a king's ransom; but her father was in Trade.

Mina was never going to be accepted in London society, nor in the smaller circles of Berkshire, when Lord Sparrowdale finally let her return to his estate before her pregnancy became too obvious. The countryfolk surrounding Sparrows Nest already despised the dissolute lord and his profligate son. Rumors of Mina's prior elopement convinced her neighbors that she was no better than the rest of the family, and no better than she ought to be.

Mina was so miserable that she did not care. She was having a difficult pregnancy, and despaired of her future with the earl and his shifty-eyed son, Harmon, Viscount Sparling. Luckily the Sparrowdale gentlemen—if such a word could be applied to the two—were too busy in London spending her father's money to bother her much.

Lord Sparrowdale did return when Mina was close to term, along with his son and nephew, and other hard-drinking, high-stakes-betting cronies. They were carousing in her parlor while Lady Sparrowdale was suffering through childbirth above. Mina had no mother to help, no aunts or married sisters to give comfort, no experienced neighbor ladies to lend support. She had the disapproving servants, the physician the earl had sent for along with his none-too-gentle nurse, and her cousin Dorcas.

Her mother's cousin, actually, Dorcas Albright was a spinster gentlewoman of a certain age and uncertain nerves. She was afraid of thunder and sickness and horses and men. If she had not been more terrified of poverty, she'd have left Malachy Caldwell's home years ago, and Lord Sparrowdale's when he returned from London. She clutched her vinaigrette when Mina's contractions began. She clutched her heart when the water broke. She clutched the bedpost when Mina moaned. Then she fainted altogether, thank goodness.

When Mina would have cried out with the pain, the physician dosed her with laudanum. "We would not want to disturb the gentlemen, now, would we?"

Mina would gladly have disturbed them with her

screams—and her father back in Portsmouth, too, and that lily-livered Ninian Rourke, wherever he was. But then, after hours that felt like years, the physician announced that she had a son.

She heard him wail. "Let me see him," she managed to say.

"No, he is too weak. The nurse has him. We cannot be too careful with these early births," the physician told her.

"But he is not early. He is—"

A strange-smelling cloth was placed over her nose and mouth. "All you have to do is rest."

When she awoke, they asked her to name the infant, for his funeral. "Robert," Mina said through her tears, for her grandfather Albright. She would have called him Robin in private, a trespasser at Sparrows Nest. Robert was enough.

They kept her drugged through the ceremonies and the condolence calls, then she poured her own laudanum rather than face her grief, so she would not hear that one loud wail forever in her mind.

Her husband, thankfully, had no interest in a befogged, forlorn female, so he returned to London, where the sickness that was already in him worsened. Without Sparrowdale's scant influence, his rakehell son grew more reckless over the course of the next few years until he was killed in a knife fight after being caught cheating at dice.

Sparrowdale returned to the country then, perhaps thinking to father a replacement heir, but he was too old, too ill, and Lady Sparrow was too embittered now to let the foul-breathed relic come near her. No longer a trembling girl, she had been managing Sparrows Nest in the earl's absence, learning to run a profitable estate, keep accounts, and handle servants and tenants alike. Mina was her father's daughter after all, and she had nothing to lose by closing her bedroom door—and making sure it stayed locked this time. The earl had her dowry and a competent chatelaine. That was all he was going to get.

Mina did nurse Sparrowdale in his last months. She had given her vows, through sickness and health. Cousin Dorcas was no help, naturally, and the servants regarded the old man and his disease with equal fear. The earl called Mina by the name of his first wife, and she did not care.

Now they were all dead—her husband, his son, her father. Malachy had contracted a congestion of the lungs on his way to Sparrowdale's funeral and died in the same bed as his son-in-law had. Mina had nursed him too. She'd have done the same for a sick dog.

For all she knew, Ninian Rourke was dead too, and she did not care about that either. She barely recalled his looks, only that he had taken her father's purse. Well, he had his money, the same as the earl had. Mina did not waste another thought on either of the men she had married.

Perhaps her father had done her a favor, saving her from wedding a weakling. But then her son might have lived and she'd have that joy. Perhaps not. Who could understand the vagaries of fate?

The one favor her father had definitely done for Mina was to outlast Sparrowdale. Now she was wealthy beyond counting, with no husband to claim her fortune as his, no trustee other than Mr. Sizemore, her solicitor. Lady Sparrow was twenty-three, a countess, an heiress, a widow.

She placed a small bouquet of flowers on the grave of the son who was not her husband's. Now, she told herself, now she had to spread her wings.

Chapter Two

"Where do you think we should go, Dorcas?" Mina asked her cousin and companion. "To London, to my father's house in Portsmouth? Or should we simply move to the dower house here? Or somewhere entirely different?"

Dorcas put down her tatting. She was one of the few women Mina knew who made lace, with the finest spun yarn and what seemed like a jackstraw jumble of needles. Every surface in the morning room was covered with doilies or antimacassars. Every black gown each lady wore was trimmed at collar or cuff. Every one of Miss Albright's silvered curls was hidden by a wispy cap of gauzy lace. So were Mina's brown locks, as befitted her new matronly status.

"Oh, my, I am sure I do not know. Wherever you decide will be best, dearest."

Since Mina had never made such a decision in her life, she thought her cousin's confidence was perhaps misplaced. "Well, I would like to see the sights of London that I missed the only time I was there, and attend the opera, visit the museums and galleries. That kind of thing."

"Oh, I should not think you would enjoy London at this time of year, with the warm weather nearly upon us. The air, you know, and the dirt. And everyone who matters will be leaving for their country homes or house parties."

"I was not thinking of socializing." Not after Mina's

last experience among the *ton*. "I am in mourning, at any rate."

"But that will not stop the Town bucks from ogling you and gathering around you like flies on a fallen peppermint drop. Half the gentlemen in Town are perpetually mourning their missing fortunes. Yours would be such a tempting morsel." Dorcas straightened out a loop in the needlework in her lap, then quickly added, "Not that the gentlemen would not admire you for your pretty looks and pleasing manners, of course."

"Of course," Mina echoed with sarcasm, recalling how no one took a second glance at Sparrowdale's little countess, the one time she was in London. She definitely did not wish to be pursued by fortune hunters now or by those who thought a young widow was fair game for a bit of dalliance. "London is out, then. What about Portsmouth?" Her father had built himself a fine new mansion on the outskirts, away from his shipyards, befitting a visit from his daughter the countess. Mina had never gone there, and she felt no emotional attachment to the house or the neighborhood. Still, she owned the property, until she decided to sell it.

Dorcas recalled living under Malachy Caldwell's heavy hand, and she wanted no reminders of it. "But recall how the army is using Portsmouth as an embarkation point. The town will be overrun with red coats. And the rest of the area is full of rough sailors and their haunts."

"And Bath is filled with half-pay officers and rheumatics sufferers. Brighton will soon be aswarm with the Prince and his rackety set. What's left? Travel?"

"Oh, no, my dear Minerva. You know how long coach rides make me bilious. Heavens, you were not thinking of sailing somewhere, were you?" Dorcas reached for her smelling salts at the very idea of open seas, barechested seamen, and storms.

Mina frowned. "Perhaps we should take up residence in Sparrows Nest's dower house after all."

"With Roderick Sparr taking up residence here?" Dorcas went as pale as the white yarn in her lace.

Roderick was Lord Sparrowdale's nephew and heir,

the new earl. Thirty-some years of age, he had the dark
hair and prominent nose of his family, but not their reputation for dissipation. He had not turned to profligacy—
not in public, anyway—but that might have been due
to lack of funds, not desire. Now, though, he had the
wherewithal to cut a swathe through London society. He
had Mina's wherewithal, from her dowry and from her
careful management of the estate, so he no longer had to
augment his income with gambling. The gossip columns
Cousin Dorcas read religiously had the new peer paying
court to his deceased cousin's fiancée, not hell-raking the
way the previous heir had done. He was staying on in
Town to see about his seat in Parliament, like a respectable, responsible titleholder, unlike any Sparrowdale in
recent history.

Roderick had assured Mina that she was welcome in
his home, mouthing all the correct phrases, and yet . . .

"There is something about that man I cannot like,"
Dorcas was saying.

There was something about every man that Dorcas did
not like, but Mina knew what her cousin meant. Roderick's dark eyes were too close together, and he rarely
looked at the person he was addressing. His platitudes
were too glib, his handshake too soft, and his dress too
fastidious. He might not use weighted dice as the previous heir had, but Mina would never trust her nephew-
by-marriage with a deck of cards, a secret, or the keys
to her jewelry box—or to her bedroom door. No, Mina
did not wish to live in such close proximity to the new
lord of Sparrows Nest.

She tapped her pencil against the page of the ledger
she was examining, trying to think where she and her
cousin might go.

"I know," Dorcas said, brightening. "We can ask Mr.
Sizemore's advice."

The solicitor never failed to bring Cousin Dorcas the
latest book and the newest gossip from Town, along with
a box of comfits. He never raised his voice, and he never
made suggestive remarks. After living as a poor relation
at the untender mercies of Malachy Caldwell and Lord

Sparrowdale, Miss Dorcas Albright found Mina's man of affairs a relief, if not a friend.

"I think I might write to Mr. Sizemore at that," Mina said, closing the ledger she was attempting to decipher. "I can make neither heads nor tails of these figures. Perhaps he can do so."

Cousin Dorcas picked up her needles again, now that the uncertain but bound to be uncomfortable future was not quite as imminent. Carriages and packing and inns—why, all that was enough to give anyone palpitations.

"I thought you had the accounts all in order, dear," Dorcas said once she had her yarns and bobbins spinning and whirling.

"So did I, but there is a sum taken from every quarter, it appears, going back for years. The unspecified withdrawals started long before I took over the bookkeeping, as far back as I have researched, in fact. I would like to resolve the matter before Roderick or his agent takes over, lest they find some impropriety in my accounts."

Dorcas clucked her tongue. "There would be no accounts to speak of without your dowry."

"Yes, but Lord Sparrowdale always found the monies he needed for this expense, whatever it was. The amount kept increasing over the years, but at odd intervals. I cannot help but wonder what the money is for. It is not an outlandish amount, merely considerable, since he let his tailor and his vintner go unpaid."

"Gambling debts." Dorcas was positive. "Sparrowdale's and that son of his."

"No, for my father paid them all off at the time of the marriage." Malachy Caldwell had had to pay a great deal more than he'd first intended, since what he was trading, his daughter, had become soiled goods. The earl's outstanding vowels were redeemed, the family portraits and heirloom jewelry reclaimed from the moneylenders, the mortgages on the London town house and Sparrows Nest satisfied.

"Hmpf. That did not stop either of them from wagering away every shilling they could."

"Yes, but those new debts were all itemized in the ledgers." Sparrowdale had kept decent records, so no one could charge him twice. "This has to be something else."

"Perhaps he was buying contraband. You know how Lord Sparrowdale enjoyed his spirits."

Those bills from the wine merchants proved it. The earl had no need for more. "Every quarter? I doubt it."

Dorcas looked around to make sure none of the servants could overhear. "Perhaps he was keeping one of *those* women."

Mina had to smile. There was not a soul or a servant for miles who did not know of Lord Sparrowdale's lechery. "She was a very expensive bit of baggage, in that case. And why would the sums increase twice in the last five years?"

"Perhaps he had more than one mistress," her cousin whispered. "A harem of harlots he kept in furs and diamonds."

"Lord Sparrowdale?" Mina asked with a laugh. She could not picture her late, unlamented lord parting with sixpence, not when he could have wagered it on a race or a mill or a cockfight. Besides, he'd been paying for years. Sparrowdale was no Prinny, loyally bearing affection for an aging mistress. Mina doubted he cared for anything but his own pleasure, and that could have been bought for a great deal less than the missing monies.

"Gentlemen do have their . . . needs, you know." Dorcas was nearly blushing at the direction her thoughts were taking.

Not Sparrowdale, not in the past few years. Mina knew that to her certain knowledge, although she would swallow the pages of the dusty ledger she held before admitting such to her spinster cousin. Sparrowdale's . . . potency had withered, yet the withdrawals had continued. Mina could not imagine him continuing to pay for services not rendered, yet he had written bank drafts for the unspecified expenses until he was too incapacitated to hold a pen, at which point Mina had taken over the accounts. Sparrowdale never ordered her to send money to anyone, or to make deposits into another account. It was all very strange.

"Do you think—" Dorcas began, only to pause. "That is, Lord Sparrowdale was not everything a person could wish, if that is not speaking too ill of the dead. And his son was certainly no saint, caught with weighted dice. Could the earl have been paying blackmail to someone?"

"That was my first surmise," Mina admitted. "But why should the fee jump twice since I have known him?"

"Prices of everything have gone up, dear. Why, the cost of silk is nigh double what it used to be."

"I do not think extortion works that way. Moreover, Sparrowdale was not one to hide his vices." Indeed, he wore them on his pockmarked face. "What could he have done that was so terrible he was willing to pay for it all those years?"

Dorcas shivered. "I cannot imagine." Quite to the contrary, Cousin Dorcas had a well-exercised imagination. "Perhaps he murdered an older brother to gain the succession and a servant saw him commit the foul deed. Or he could have been selling state secrets to the French and had to buy his way out of hanging. Or he might have written incriminating letters. That's what blackmail is usually about, in the novels, you know." She finally ran out of speculations. "But to think of us living under his roof while he . . . while he did whatever it was he did, is dreadful. You do not suppose anyone can accuse us of complicity in his crimes, do you?"

"We do not know there were any crimes, silly, and the payments start at least fifteen years ago. No one can find us guilty of anything, except curiosity."

"But what if the blackmailer comes after us, for the money he is owed?" One of the yarn bobbins dropped to the floor.

Mina got up to retrieve the tiny spool. "Now that is foolish beyond permission, Cousin. You might as well start worrying lest Sparrowdale's ghost starts walking the halls to haunt us."

"Oh, my, perhaps we ought to remove to the dower house after all."

Mina could have bitten her tongue. Now she'd be up half the night reassuring her cousin that the earl's specter was not lurking in the corridors. No, it was his son who used to do that. "I'll write to Mr. Sizemore. Perhaps he knows something of the matter, although he has not been employed by the earl all that long. Sparrowdale might have confided in him when they rewrote the earl's will after the viscount's death."

"That's all right, then," Dorcas said, her needles resuming their clicking. "Mr. Sizemore will know what to do."

"But Mr. Sizemore is an honest man. He might not have knowledge of whatever nefarious dealings Sparrowdale had."

Mina returned to her desk and opened the ledger again. She had marked her place with a scrap of paper cut out of one of Cousin Dorcas's London journals. The small advertisement had a simple black border around it. *Discreet inquiries made,* was all it said, along with a name, *Lowell Merrison,* and care of the newspaper's address.

Chapter Three

*M*r. Sizemore was not much help, although the box of candied violets did take Cousin Dorcas's mind off bogeys and blackmailers. As for relocating, the be-wigged and beefy solicitor did not approve of ladies going jaunting off by themselves without masculine es-cort. London with no father, uncle, brother, or husband was no place for gently reared females of whatever age or circumstance, he believed, no matter how many men-servants they employed.

"Forgive me, my lady," he told Mina over tea and poppyseed cake, "but for all your years of marriage, your business acumen, and estate-management experience, you are still a green girl when it comes to opportunists and importunists. Who would make sure your name was not bandied around the clubs by the rakish element?"

Mina recalled the gossip the last time she went to Lon-don. Sparrowdale had not protected her from being grist for the rumor mills.

"Who would keep the fortune hunters from your door?" Mr. Sizemore went on.

Her father had welcomed one with open arms.

"An unscrupulous scoundrel might even try to steal what was not offered, with no one to gainsay him." Mr. Sizemore was trying to be euphemistically polite.

Her stepson had not been as courteous, euphemisti-cally or otherwise, groping at her with his father cupshot beside him. Mina thought London could have no worse dangers for her.

The solicitor did. Heiresses were in danger of being kidnapped or compromised, robbed or ruined. No, Lady Sparrowdale and Miss Albright should stay right here in Berkshire, he told them, under the protection of the current Earl of Sparrowdale. Roderick Sparr seemed a vast improvement over the previous titleholder, if the countess could forgive her well-meaning solicitor's frankness. He was neither a wastrel nor a womanizer. The new earl, in fact, having put his past behind him, now seemed more interested in restoring the family name than in dragging it through more mud and muck. He would keep rumor and disreputable suitors at bay, especially since he vied for the hand of a priggish duke's proper daughter.

The idea of leaving her fate to her nephew-by-marriage left Mina cold. She pulled her black shawl more closely around her shoulders, despite the fire in the hearth. She did not want to be subject to any man's authority, not to protect her reputation or her riches. Freedom was too new to Mina for her to relinquish it so readily. London was looking more appealing.

As for the missing bank funds, the thickset solicitor was even less helpful.

"No, his lordship never disclosed such transactions to me, nor did he make any unusual stipulations in his latest will, beyond the pensions for his valet and the London butler. My unfortunately deceased partner had handled the Sparrowdale accounts before that. We never discussed such matters, of course. Client confidentiality, you know." He accepted the fresh cup of tea Mina poured out for him while he deliberated on the cash withdrawals. "Why, Lord Sparrowdale must have been donating to charity," he finally suggested. "I myself contribute anonymously to several worthy causes."

Mina almost spilled her own tea, and Cousin Dorcas choked on a slice of cake.

"Charity? Lord Sparrowdale?" Mina asked after patting her cousin's back. "I'd swear that was the first time I have heard the two mentioned in the same sentence. Why, the only man less charitable than the earl was my own father, who believed the poor deserved their misery for not working hard enough. He'd risen above his own humble beginnings by the sweat of his own labors, he said many times, and saw no reason others should not do the same. Give a man a free meal, my father was used to saying, and he would only ask for dessert."

Mr. Sizemore drew his hand back from reaching for a second piece of cake, wondering if he'd be invited to dine with the ladies after all.

Mina went on: "The earl was almost worse, except he never had funds to contribute. No, the only tithing Lord Sparrowdale did was to the cents-per-centers, to pay his gambling debts. My cousin and I have been wondering if the withdrawals were for something immoral or illegal."

"There, you see. Just what I meant," Mr. Sizemore said, deciding to take the piece of cake in case it had to last until he reached an inn for supper. "You should not have to be fretting over such havey-cavey vexations. The new earl can deal with the situation. In fact, by rights he inherited Lord Sparrowdale's dirty linen, if such it is, along with the title and the properties. You may rest assured that, with his new goal of respectability, the earl's nephew will handle the matter expeditiously."

"Yes, I have been thinking of writing to Roderick about the funds, to see if he knows aught of the situation. I was simply curious in the meantime. It amounts to a substantial sum of money over the years."

Sizemore pulled at his straining waistcoat when he heard the figure Mina had calculated. "Yes, I can see where that total might have piqued your interest and your suspicions, but I doubt if we shall ever know the truth of the matter. Dead men keep their secrets, don't you know."

"Then you agree this reeks of hugger-mugger?"

The solicitor gave up on his girth and reached for yet another slice of cake. "If it were anything aboveboard, we would have heard by now. A legitimate debt or annuity payment gone missing would have drawn a query well before two quarters had passed. Usually the claimants creep out from under their rocks before the departed is underground. Honest ones come first, with their unpaid bills in hand, hoping the estate or the family will make good on a gaming debt or a merchant's invoice. The Captain Sharps come later, hoping to cheat unsuspecting widows or grieving children out of their inheritances with fake claims on the loved one's fortune. I've had merchants waving outstanding bills with fresh ink, and females with outstanding bellies claiming the deceased as father. I've seen forged gambling chits galore, and a few long-lost relatives seeking their share of the bequests. If any such come to you, my lady, especially at this late date, refer them to me. I'll send them off with a flea in their ear, you may be certain."

"Has anyone like that approached you about Lord Sparrowdale's estate?" Mina wanted to know. "Anyone who might have been receiving money in the past?"

Mr. Sizemore thought a moment while he chewed. "I believe my clerk mentioned chasing off some ragtag boy who said he was the earl's son. As if the Sparrowdale succession could sprout a new limb at this date. The lad must take us all for fools."

"I do not suppose you got his name, did you?"'

"What, a street urchin taking a holiday from begging or picking pockets? The boy should be glad my clerk did not have him arrested. Get his name, indeed."

The boy's name was Peregrine Radway, and he arrived at Sparrows Nest the following week, but before he did, a letter arrived at Merrison House, Mersford Square, Mayfair, London. The letter was included in a package of mail recently delivered from the newspaper office. The paper was of high quality, the script was neat, the style was polite—and it piqued the interest of the Honorable Lord Lowell Merrison, second son of the Duke of Mersford, as nothing had in ages.

"Mother, what do you know of a Minerva, Lady Sparrowdale?" Lord Lowell asked the handsome woman who sat across the breakfast table from him, sorting through her own pile of invitations, announcements, and correspondence.

The dowager Duchess of Mersford put down her lorgnette and perked up her ears. "I know she is now a wealthy widow, Lolly. Are you interested in her?"

The hope in his mother's voice brought a frown to Lord Lowell's brow. "In a professional capacity only, Mother. I have never met the woman."

"Botheration." Her Grace went back to the letter from her sister in York, holding the looking glass first one way, then the other. "I cannot make out your aunt Agatha's handwriting, as usual. Either her husband is suffering from the gout, or he is acting like an old goat."

"Likely both, knowing Uncle Edgar. Do you wish to borrow my spectacles to find out?"

"Heavens no. It is enough that I have three grandchildren—not that I am not wishful for more, of course—but I absolutely refuse to don spectacles."

Lord Lowell replaced his own glasses with a sigh.

Hearing that sound, Her Grace hurried to say, "Not that you are not handsome in yours, Lolly. Very dignified, don't you know. But on a lady of my years, they are a concession to decrepitude, not a mark of distinction."

"You will never grow old, Mother," her son dutifully replied. "And if you do, you will never look it."

"Dear, dear boy. You always know the right thing to say, don't you? No wonder the young ladies are always asking if you are attending this party or that balloon ascension. I swear half the invitations I receive have your name on them too. In fact, I doubt I would be asked to half these come-out balls if I did not have such an eligible bachelor in residence. I only wish you would—"

"Lady Sparrowdale, Mother?" the duchess's son interrupted, knowing full well what lecture would follow if he did not redirect his mother's thoughts. Once the word "grandchildren" was mentioned, she was like a filly at the races, champing at the bit.

"Faugh. If your interest in the countess concerns your business, go find what you want to know. You style yourself a private investigator, do you not? Go investigate."

Lowell sighed again. He had been doing that a lot recently, it seemed. "We have been over this ground before, Mother. There is nothing untoward about my line of work."

"It is work, which you have no need to do. You have a neat competence from your father."

"Which barely covers my cattle and my clothes." He looked down at his striped silk waistcoat, admiring the soft grays and blues. "I refuse to live at my brother's expense. Bad enough that I live like a princeling in his house."

"Your brother can afford to keep any number of relations in comfort, and heaven knows this barracks of a place could house King Henry and all eight of his wives."

"I still dislike the idea of being my brother's pensioner." Lowell would have taken rooms at the Albany, well within his budget, ages ago, if not for his mother's pleas.

"You are not thinking of moving out again, are you, dear?" she asked now, ready with her handkerchief to dab at damp eyes, if tears became necessary. She would never get the gudgeon wed, she feared, if he set up housekeeping in a bachelor fastness. "What would I do without you, with your brother and That Woman spending so much time in the country? Why, I would fall into a decline, I am sure, alone in this vast pile by myself."

"Nonsense. You would fill Merrison House with even more of your card parties and musicales. And That Woman is your daughter-in-law Margaret, who would spend more time in London, I daresay, if you were not forever telling her how to raise her children."

Her Grace sniffed. "I did a good enough job on you and your brothers and sister, if I say so myself. Speaking of jobs"—the duchess could turn from an uncomfortable subject as easily as Lowell could—"a gentleman, even one with a mere courtesy title, is not expected to dirty his hands with such unsavory work as you pursue. The law, the church, the military, even politics, which is unsavory enough—those are acceptable careers for the son of a duke. Not dabbling in criminal mischief or foolishness like redeeming Lady Carstair's family diamonds from that ivory-tuner."

"You are not supposed to know anything about Lady Carstair or her diamonds, much less ivory-tuners."

"How not, when she shouted your name through the Finsters' ballroom, applauding your efforts? Everyone knows of your odd little profession. I swear it is a good thing you are so handsome and well spoken, else I could never find a woman willing to—"

Lowell pushed his chair back, ready to leave.

Now it was Her Grace's turn to sigh. "What was it you wished to know about Lady Sparrow?"

Her son resumed his seat, one golden eyebrow arched.

"That's what they called her, the one time she came to Town, right after her marriage to that loose screw Sparrowdale, if you'll forgive my language. It was about five years ago, I think. You must have been traveling that Season, after university. A sweet little dab of a thing, she was, flighty as a baby bird. And who could blame her for being anxious, with a husband like that? Her birth might not have been the best, despite good blood on her mother's side, but she was far too gently bred for that pox-ridden old poltroon."

"She married him for the title, didn't she?"

"I recall that it was her father who wanted the connection, not the poor little chit. There was some talk at the time, I cannot remember what, but Malachy Caldwell, of the Caldwell shipyards, never cared. Sparrowdale, of course, needed the gel's fortune to pull himself out of River Tick."

"What happened to her after that? I have never seen her in Town, nor heard her name mentioned."

"She retired to the country to breed, I believe. As far from Sparrowdale and that dirty-dish son of his as she could get, to no one's surprise. Now that I think on it, her child must have died, too, or Roderick Sparr would not have inherited the earldom. He might not be much, but Roderick seems an improvement over the others."

"I wonder why she did not go to him with whatever hobble she thinks I might solve."

"Who cares? Write back to her."

Lowell folded the note. "I thought you did not approve of my career."

"No, but I do approve of wealthy young widows."

"Just remember I am going to work, Your Grace, not a-wooing."

"A mother can hope, can she not?"

Chapter Four

*W*hen the boy who claimed to be Sparrowdale's son arrived at Sparrows Nest the following week, he looked even more like a ragamuffin, having traveled from London by cart when he could, or on foot when he could not, with nothing but a mud-covered mongrel for companion. Thirteen years of age, the youth had the Sparrowdale nose and the Sparrowdale dark coloring. He also had a black eye, from trying to visit the new Lord Sparrowdale.

The butler would have sent the lad on his way, after boxing his ears for bothering his betters, and using the front entrance to do so besides, except that Lady Sparrowdale herself was coming down the stairs and heard the heated exchange on her doorstep.

Mina did not hear the boy's foul language or the dog's growls. She heard him say he was the old earl's butter stamp, and wanted what he'd been promised. She did not see the filthy child or his ragged clothes or his mangy dog. She saw a son. Not her son, of course, and no legitimate claimant to the Sparrowdale succession, but a son, nevertheless.

"I will see Mr. Radway," she told her stupefied servant. "In the, ah . . ."

Harkness made a recovery, proper butler that he was. "I suggest the orangery, my lady. The dirt will not be noticeable among the plants."

"Quite. And you will see that refreshments are brought. Lemonade and bread and butter, to start." At the boy's eager nod she added, "To be followed by that meat and cheese we had for nuncheon. And something for the dog."

"I am certain Cook has some rat poison left."

"I am sorry, Harkness, I did not hear your reply."

"I said, Cook must have some rabbit stew left."

"That will be fine. Now follow me, Mr. Radway, and tell me your mission."

"What I'm missing is the blunt for my grandmother, what looks after me," the boy said as he followed her down the long corridor with its thick carpets and silk-hung walls. His head swiveled from the statues in their niches to the portraits in their gilt frames. "But you can call me Peregrine, my lady. Or Perry, like my granny does."

"And where does your granny live, Perry?" Mina asked when they reached the glass-walled conservatory. She led the boy to the table where she and Cousin Dorcas liked to take breakfast on dreary mornings, so they could be surrounded by greenery. The dog raised his leg on a potted palm tree, and Mina pretended not to notice when Perry's face turned as red as the roses blooming in the corner.

"We've got rooms in Kensington. That's outside London, ma'am. For however long we can make the rent."

"I see. And Lord Sparrowdale was in the habit of paying your bills?" She also pretended not to notice her butler's affronted sniff when he delivered the tray.

"Nah, he just gave us blunt on the quarters," Perry said around a mouthful of buttered bread once Harkness had left. "Now he's gone, and Granny's extra brass, too. She can't see to sew anymore, and I can't earn enough on my own to keep us in such prime digs."

Mina watched as the pile of slices dwindled to a few crumbs. She was going to offer the boy an orange from one of the trees, if Harkness did not arrive back with more substantial fare soon. "What is it you do, Perry, to earn your share?"

"I used to run errands for the governor."

"The governor?"

"His lordship himself. Lord Sparrowdale. My father."

Perry's chin jutted out in the same belligerent way the earl's had when Mina asked about his gambling debts. This was Sparrowdale's son, all right. Someone had to make sure he did not follow in his father's footsteps down the path to perdition. The boy needed a proper education, or an apprenticeship to a trade. He could not be left to make a living on the streets of London. Mina recalled those scenes of abject poverty on the fringes of the *ton*'s pleasure seeking. One was supposed to ignore them, the same way she ignored the dog's lapse of good manners, her butler's forgetting who paid his salary, and the boy's slipping two slices of bread into his pocket.

"How much did you say his lordship paid your grandmother?" she asked after a footman, not the butler, had brought a tray of meat and cheese and two plates, one for the boy, one for the dog.

"Twenty pounds, on the quarter."

Mina's bonnets cost more. She would gladly pay four times that much out of her own funds to see Perry clean and fed, but she still had questions. For one thing, the sum did not begin to cover those missing amounts from the earl's accounts. For another, why?

Why would the earl, who had less warmth in his heart than one of those marble statues in the hallway, continue to pay for a by-blow's upkeep?

She must have spoken aloud, for Perry grinned. "Granny says the governor had an icicle where his heart should of been. But he paid on account of the marriage license."

"The license? Your mother was married to the earl, then? How could that be? His first wife would have been alive still."

"Oh, it weren't a proper license. That was his rig, you ken."

Mina did not understand, not at all. A man did not marry his mistress, and certainly not when he was already wed to another.

"My mum was a decent girl, Granny swears it on her

Bible. They worked as seamstresses together, they did. Only Mum caught his lordship's notice. They did not know he was a flash cove, of course, or they'd never of been taken in. But he married her all right and tight. Only he gave another name. That license wasn't worth the ink to write it."

"I still do not comprehend why he went to such lengths. There must be hundreds, nay, thousands of girls in London willing to . . . to pleasure a man, without a marriage."

"He wanted a virgin, a' course. Thought it could cure what ailed him. Willing ones that didn't reek of the country were as rare as hens' teeth, unless he had a gold band in his hand." Perry kept eating, as if the depth of his sire's depravity was just another fact of life. Mina supposed it was, to him.

"So the marriage contract was invalid," she said. "Because he gave a false name. Then why did he continue to support your family? It was the proper thing to do, of course, but I cannot see Sparrowdale suffering any compunctions to take the honorable course, not after such scurvy actions."

"I don't know about any 'punctions, but he was suffering at the tables, for sure. He was trying to get more money out of his wife's father, we figure. The governor's first countess was an heiress, too," Perry informed Mina, as if she did not know. "But that old man was not forking over another farthing if he got wind of a breach-of-promise suit. Righteous he was, the governor's father-in-law. So the earl, he paid my mum to keep quiet, and my granny after."

"After . . . ?"

"After my mother passed on. The dirty dish left her with more'n a full belly."

"Oh, I am so sorry, Perry."

Perry shrugged his thin shoulders. "The pox took most of the others that way, too."

"The others?"

Mina sank back against the cushions of her chair while

Perry kept eating. Of course there were others. There was all that money. Heavens. How many others? She was not ready to ask.

She'd known her husband was a loose fish, in the servants' vernacular, but this? This went beyond the realm of lax morals and straight to wickedness, if not outright evil. "You are saying that Lord Sparrowdale plied his foul machinations on other innocent young women?"

"He plied something, at any rate. It were a game with him, like. He had more'n one dodge he used, and the silly morts believed him, or believed they'd get rich off him when he died."

"And he paid them not to go to the authorities?"

Perry narrowed his eyes. "I never kept tuppence meant for any of the others."

"No, no. I never accused you. I am simply trying to understand how he got away with this for so long."

"He was a swell. Females like my mother knew no one would take their word against a nob, if they could have afforded a lawyer in the first place. It was better to take what he offered. At least they had something then. And he never went near girls what had fathers or brothers to look after them."

Or Mr. Sizemore to warn them against going to London. "But once his wife died, why did he have to continue with this charade?"

"A'cause then he was looking for another rich cit's daughter, and he couldn't do that trailing a passel of bastards, could he? Any nodcock could see that."

Mina supposed she could not object to being referred to as a nodcock, much less a rich cit's daughter, not when Peregrine Radway called himself a bastard. A spade was a spade, after all. And even her merchant-mogul father, desperate for a titled son-in-law, would have drawn the line at a bigamist, a perjurer, a despoiler of virgins and begetter of bastards. She hoped.

Once the meat had disappeared, Perry started on the cheese. Between mouthfuls, he explained further. "He would of let the little ones starve most likely, after their mums cocked up their toes, with no one to threaten him with proof except for my granny. She found out about some of the others and made sure he paid up, else she was taking everything to the magistrate. And she made sure the governor knew her papers and such were hidden away, in case she met with 'an accident.' "

Sparrowdale would have stooped to murder? After today's revelations, Mina would put nothing past him. For the first time in her life, she wished she had Cousin Dorcas's vinaigrette. "Your grandmother is a courageous woman."

"Who's too old to be out on the streets, where we'll be if you don't pay," Perry said. "But you seem a right 'un. Wouldn't let no nippers go hungry, not after feeding my dog and me."

"Of course I will not let any children starve. But things are not that simple."

Perry pushed his plate away, even though a wedge of cheese remained, as though her words had stolen his appetite. "They never are, when it comes to you toffs parting with your brass. I should of known. Now that there's no call to hide the governor's crimes, with him dead and all, you see no reason to pay his toll." He stood and whistled the mongrel to heel. "Me'n my dog thank you for the meal. It's more'n we got from the new earl or your solicitor chap."

"Oh, sit down. You've proved you have enough pride for a nobleman's son, now show some sense. I did not say I would not help you, but this is a bigger problem than I can solve in a moment's work. If it were up to me, I would have the children brought here, to be cared for and educated." Her fingers were itching to wipe the crumbs off the boy's bellicose chin and see his dark hair cut, his ragged clothes replaced. She wanted to hire him tutors and buy him books and feed him until the bones at his wrists did not show. She could not, of course, do any of those things. Not yet. "But that is a decision for the estate, one the new earl has to make. The same goes for paying out sums of money to support my husband's, ah, progeny." She remembered Mr. Sizemore's warnings. "I need proof, for one thing. How do I know the other children even exist? Who is to say you are not some charlatan who happens to resemble Lord Sparrowdale?"

"I'm no charman. I told you, I run errands, like a footman."

"A charlatan is a fake, a fraud, an impostor trying to get money out of me. How can I prove to the earl or his solicitor that they have a moral duty to establish guardianship of you and the others?"

"What, become wards? Like in the foundling homes?"

"I do not know all the legal ramifications, but, yes, that's what it would be, I think. The earl would be—should be—trustee."

"I wouldn't trust no blasted earl."

"And neither he nor his man of affairs would trust the word of a scruffy schoolboy—who has not had enough schooling, it seems—nor entrust him with payments for the other children."

Perry raised his chin again, crumbs and all. "The governor trusted me."

"Lord Sparrowdale had no choice. Your grandmother could have seen him embarrassed in the scandal sheets at the very least. If there were any justice, she could have had him imprisoned or transported."

Perry looked at that last piece of cheese, then down at his dog, who was wagging his short tail. He used his sleeve to swipe at his face. "What kind of proof?"

"Names, dates, places. Copies of those false marriage certificates. The identities of the women themselves if you know them, or of whoever cares for the children. There must be thousands of orphans in the country. Prove to me which ones were fathered by my husband and I swear they will be cared for."

"I'll have to ask Granny."

"Of course. I will give you carriage fare to return home, and whatever cash I have on hand to take with you for now. You will get the rest when your story is proved, even if you decide not to accept Lord Sparrowdale's guardianship."

Mina could sense the boy judging her, pricing her lace-trimmed gown and matched pearls. Everything about her bespoke wealth, from her elaborately styled brown curls to her smooth hands to her silk-stockinged feet to the very room they were sitting in; Peregrine Radway had been taught by experience that rich people had no consciences.

"You will simply have to trust my word. After all," she told him, "I am trusting you with a great deal of money, with no guarantee you will even return."

Perry thought a minute, then nodded. "Right. I'll leave my dog here to prove I'm coming back."

Chapter Five

*M*ina had the dog bathed and trimmed and fed until his ribs did not stand out, and she trained him not to use the ornamentals as scent posts. Having a dog was not the same as having a boy of her own to raise, but the short-haired white mongrel was good company on walks and on visits to the tenants. When the dog wagged his bushy tail, the farmers and their wives were more friendly to her than they had been in the nearly five years of her residency at Sparrows Nest. After they patted the friendly mutt, they would try to guess the silly creature's ancestry, for once not treating the countess like an interloper in their midst. The village folk, too, stopped to chat when the dog sniffed at their packages or waited for Mina outside the shops.

Perry had refused to take the dog with him, claiming that besides standing as surety off his word, the creature would slow his journey considerably. Most drivers, he said, would not take up a dog to bark at the horses. The boy also refused to accept a ride further than to the nearest coaching house, certainly not all the way to London. He might trust the countess with his dog, it seemed, but not with his grandmother's address. For the same reason, most likely, he had turned down Lady Sparrowdale's offer of a servant to accompany him and his now heavy purse.

"Who's going to 'spect a poor chap like me of having two shillings to rub together?" he had argued, gladly taking the hamper of food instead of the footman.

"Indeed, madam," Mina's butler had agreed. "Persons

of discernment are more likely to assume Mr. Radway is the cutpurse, not the victim." Harkness was all for stripping the boy naked to see if any of the Sparrows Nest silverware hid in his pockets.

Unfortunately, Peregrine had left without telling Mina the dog's name. She decided to call her temporary pet Merlin, because his white beard reminded her of a wizard's. After all, a merlin was a sparrow hawk, wasn't it?

More unfortunately, Perry did not return in the sennight he said.

Mina went for walks, avoided her butler's eye, and wrote letters.

The first response she received was from Mr. Sizemore, who arrived back at Sparrows Nest almost before the ink was dry.

"But if you wish to remove to London, my dear lady, you have only to send word to your husband's nephew, the earl," the solicitor said when Mina reiterated her wishes. "Lord Sparrowdale would be more than pleased to have you act as hostess for him, I am certain."

Mina was equally as certain that Roderick would definitely not be pleased to turn his town house into an orphanage. And she did not mean to put any man's wishes above her own, again. "No, I do not wish to batten on the new earl. I understand Roderick is searching for a bride. Whichever young lady he chooses will not want another woman ensconced as mistress in the household."

"Very well, but where am I to find you a house for lease in London while the Season is still going on? The Quality will not leave for their country estates until the close of Parliament, when the heat of summer is upon us, if then. You cannot mean to spend August in the City."

"No, I mean to move this month, if possible. If you cannot find me a house to rent, then buy one. I want a big place, with a large garden for playing."

"Pardon, madam. Did you say for playing?"

"That is correct. I am thinking of establishing an adoption home. The children need room to run and shout, where they will not bother the neighbors."

"I see." The solicitor obviously did not see, not at all. He cleared his throat. "Ahem. That is very noble of you, my lady. However, while many gentlewomen espouse such good causes, they do not do so in their own homes. I am sure we can locate a private orphanage that will be gratified by your patronage, without your needing to bring the unfortunate children into your home and hearth. You can do as much good for the urchins, ah, orphans from the comfort and protection of Sparrows Nest."

"I misspoke, sir. I said adoption home when I should have said adopting home. I intend to take in my husband's children, as soon as I locate them."

Mr. Sizemore wiped at the beads of sweat dripping from under his brown wig. "I fear that your recent bereavement has disordered your thinking, my lady. That and the sad loss of your own infant. I realize you were deeply affected by that sorrow, but it was many years in the past. We must all rise above our grief and—"

"My husband's illegitimate children."

Cousin Dorcas was already laid on her bed, with a cloth soaked in lavender water over her eyes. She'd staggered to her chamber when Mina announced her intentions of taking in Sparrowdale's bastards, and had not come out since. Mr. Sizemore looked about ready to join her. Not in Miss Albright's bed, of course, but in the same state of appalled dismay.

"But—"

"My husband was taking responsibility for his ignoble actions," Mina said, having decided that the fewer people to know the whole truth, the better. Let Sparrowdale look like a hero. He was already rotting in hell. "I can do no less than fulfill his wishes."

"He never mentioned any such wishes to me. I am sure he would have—"

"I have concluded that he must have confided in your partner, then forgot to pass on the details to you when he transferred his business into your capable hands. You have done admirably, sir, with the mare's nest he made of his accounts and obligations, and now you must continue to serve his memory."

Since Sizemore's memory of the earl was one of utter repugnance, he shuddered. "But you were the one who convinced me the earl was so uncharitable."

"So I believed at the time. There is that money he kept withdrawing, however, and there are the children."

"Surely the new earl"—who had not retained the services of Mr. Sizemore's office—"will make arrangements."

"I have written to Roderick. No matter what he decides to do, however, I have decided that I will no longer be a spectator, watching as others govern my future. Caring for those children is what I want to do with my life, with my money."

The solicitor shook his head, almost dislodging his wig and setting his jowls to flapping. "This is what comes of giving women their independence."

Mina ignored the older man's outdated notions. "I will fill the London house with cast-off children no one wants because it is the right thing to do, and because I want them. I will fill the Portsmouth house too, if I wish. My father's money bought him the title he wanted. Now it can buy me the family I always wanted."

"But when you are out of mourning and wishing to marry again, any prospective husband will be frightened off by such a . . . an unconventional burden."

"I understand that and do not care. No, and not for the scandal either. I do not wish to marry again, so my reputation matters not." She held up her hand. "I know you are going to tell me that I will change my mind in time, that tomorrow I will regret destroying my chances today. You and Cousin Dorcas have more in common than a love of sweets. She has already enumerated the ramifications of my chosen course endlessly. I have not changed my mind in the slightest, so you may as well save your breath."

The solicitor rose and pulled his plain gray waistcoat down to try to cover the evidence of his love for sweets.

"Then I might as well be on my way, Lady Sparrowdale, to find you a London residence suitable for your new venture."

"Thank you, sir. I knew I could count on you."

And she could count on Satan going ice-skating before Mr. Sizemore wrote back about a house.

Perry did not return, and the solicitor did not locate an appropriate dwelling. Mina did, however, receive a prompt and courteous answer to her note to Mr. Merrison, regarding his advertisement.

The fellow appeared to be a lord, by the signature, which was odd considering the vocation, but not off-putting. Indeed, Mina was pleased to see a member of the peerage actually earning his bread and butter, not simply inheriting it.

Lord Lowell's reply was as circumspect as Lady Sparrowdale's inquiry. What, should she have written to an absolute stranger about what a cad her husband had been? No. And no, the detective wrote, he could not supply references, for that would betray his clients' confidences. No, he could not estimate expenses until he knew the nature of the countess's investigation. Usually he accepted a percentage, if an item of monetary value was involved. And no, he did not accept every case presented to him, especially those where he might be expected to commit illegal activity—which Mina had not mentioned. On the other hand, Lord Lowell's services were not currently engaged, his reputation for integrity could be easily ascertained at almost any gentlemen's club, and he would be pleased to meet with her, in strictest privacy, of course, at her convenience. He remained her servant, et cetera, at the end of his letter.

Mina had originally conceived of asking Mr. Merrison to assist her in discovering the reason behind her husband's bank withdrawals. The amount was never staggering, simply troubling in its secrecy. She had vaguely thought to hire someone to interview the earl's old gambling cronies to see if any of them had an inclination toward extortion or whatever. There was nothing illicit

about that—and nothing she could ask a gentleman to
undertake on her behalf, for a fee or not. Sparrowdale
and his son had frequented the lowest of dives. Lord
Lowell's letter was much too polite, the handwriting too
precise, the grammar too refined to assume that he would
be comfortable in such a milieu, much less be successful
at gaining the confidence of its denizens.

Now she knew where the money had gone, and her
investigation went far past curiosity. She needed to find
the children. Perhaps it was the loss of her own infant
that made her so determined to locate Sparrowdale's,
but her heart and her head both ached with the need to
see them safe, even if they all had black hair and beaked
noses like the man she despised more every day.

Mina was determined to find Lord Sparrowdale's leavings, with or without young Peregrine Radway's assistance. A gentleman such as the author of the note she
held just might know where another lord could have
gone to find gullible women, or corrupt clergymen willing
to put their names on faulty marriage lines. Perhaps
there had been rumors of Sparrowdale's doings in those
gentlemen's clubs where Lord Lowell was so well known.
He might even be a contemporary of the earl's, familiar
with the ancient gossip. Mina had no way of knowing his
age, of course, but she hoped he was old—old enough
to remember jokes Sparrowdale might have made about
foolish females. Then Lord Lowell would be ideal for
that line of inquiry.

She did not have to tell him about all the bastards.
She could claim that her husband had been supporting
some distant relations, but the names had been lost with
his demise. He did not need to know that all the children
were born on the wrong side of the blanket, or how
Sparrowdale had wronged their mothers. Thinking of
what the earl had done made Mina ashamed to bear his
name. Lord Lowell, of impeccable breeding and unsullied
reputation, did not need to know any of that.

No one did, not the solicitor or her cousin, not even
Harkness, who seemed to know everything. The butler,
predictably, believed that Perry had been spinning Lady

Sparrowdale a tarradiddle altogether about the other brats, and that she had exchanged a handsome purse for an ugly dog. The halfling may or may not be the earl's get—Harkness was willing to concede the family resemblance—but he would never be back. The downy butler was willing to wager a month's salary on it.

In that case, if Mina had been taken in, she wanted to find Perry, to give him a piece of her mind—if not his dog back. Surely this gentleman detective could find one lad in London's outskirts.

Mina thought she could find the boy and his grandmother herself, unless Perry had used a false name, given a wrong direction, invented a fictitious relative, and taken her money with him to Ireland or the Antipodes. Then she would need help, if only to find out the truth about her unlamented husband and his licentious ways. She could not rest easily, wondering if there were children waiting for coins that never came.

She would give Perry another few days before hiring the aristocratic investigator.

The next day, though, brought Roderick.

Chapter Six

Roderick was not appalled at Mina's plans. He was angry, aghast, and at her doorstep—his doorstep, actually—in a towering rage. Not only had he received her letter, but he'd also had a visit from Mr. Sizemore, who was hoping the head of the Sparrowdale household could talk the countess out of her latest start.

Roderick did not talk. He shouted. He did not even wait for the drawing room door to close behind Harkness, saving the butler from having to put his ear to the wooden panel. Cousin Dorcas had fled at the first curse, which happened to be Mina's, when she heard who was calling.

"How could you, Minerva?" the new earl yelled, using the given name she had never given him permission to use. She might be ten years his junior, but Mina was still Roderick's aunt by marriage, and a countess.

"Good day to you also, Roderick," Mina replied, purposely not giving the new earl his recently acquired honors either.

"It is not a good day. It is raining, if you bothered to look out the window, and my clothes are ruined, thanks to that obnoxious creature." Roderick took great pride in his appearance. His nose was not quite as prominent as his uncle's and cousin's had been, and his dark eyes were not quite as closely set. In fact, many a woman might find him handsome. Mina did not, those familiar features too reminiscent of his reprobate relatives. Roderick did pay a great deal more attention to his apparel than the stained and spotted earl had, or the dissolute, disheveled viscount. Today he wore buff pantaloons with a hunter-green coat and a figured waistcoat, all liberally splashed with mud and short dog hairs, from Merlin the mutt's greeting. The dog quickly decided—after narrowly avoiding a kick—that such a surly, stomping stranger was up to no good, and he took to snarling as loudly as the earl.

"Call that beast off or I will shoot it, I swear. This is a gentleman's residence, not a kennel, by George."

It was also her residence, Mina thought, but did not say so. There were larger issues here than one little dog, a dog, moreover, that did not even belong to her. She shooed Merlin out of the drawing room, and asked Harkness, where he hovered at the door, to bring tea and a decanter of the late earl's cognac. She, at least, could act the lady, despite her company's boorishness.

Neither the hot tea nor the spirits had a soothing effect. Roderick was still irate. "How could you think to haul the family skeletons out of the closet, madam? I am doing everything in my power to restore my family name to respectability, and you would see it dragged through the mud of yet another scandal. I will not have it, do you hear?"

Harkness heard from outside the door, for sure, and so did the dog there too, whose growls increased in volume with the threat he perceived to Mina.

Mina refused to feel intimidated. She had lived with overpowering, obdurate men her entire life. This one had no authority over her. She would move to the dower house on the morrow.

"What precisely is it that you will not have, Roderick? Cream in your tea? Wine that bears no excise stamp?"

"You know exactly what I mean, so do not come the innocent with me. You have never been innocent a day in your life. I mean this notion of yours to gather Uncle Harold's bastards together. How lovely," he said with a sneer. "Uncle's legitimate whore and his illegitimate children playing in the park—for all London to see. I can imagine the party the scandal sheets will have with that."

Mina ignored the slurs. Sparrowdale's son, Viscount Sparling, had been witness to her interrupted elopement. He had been so often in his cups, he could have told the world, much less his cousin. Roderick had also been present at the house party on the night Mina had given birth, and lost her own son. "I take it, then, you were aware of your uncle's backdoor dependents?"

"Of course I was. The old bounder boasted of his prowess often enough, in earlier years. That jackanapes Sparling was set to follow in his footsteps when the old man gave up the sport."

Some sport, Mina thought, despoiling young women and creating society's unwanteds. "Did you also know about the wedding certificates?"

"This is ridiculous, Minerva. It is all history, and must remain so."

That was no denial, Mina noted, no query about what wedding lines, or whose. The blackguard knew all along and had done nothing to stop the earl's evil pastime. "Knowing, you were going to look after your young cousins without my prompting, were you not?"

"You must be dicked in the nob to think I would waste good blunt on a dead man's baseborn brats. Or else your working-class sentimentality is coming to the fore. No true lady even mentions such creatures." He tossed back another glass of brandy and sneered. "In case you have forgotten, Minerva, you are a countess now, and countesses do not have dealings with the bar sinister. Real ladies ignore the existence of birds of paradise and their droppings. They do not parade them in public."

"You did not answer my question. Are you or are you not making provision for the children?"

"They've had more provision than they deserve. Most bastards end in workhouses or orphanages. Their mothers were light skirts, for heaven's sake."

"So that is your answer? You are not going to make your uncle's by-blows wards of the earldom?"

"I would sooner name your mutt my heir. Those brats—if any of them still live—are nothing to me. I did not create them. I did not keep them in style above their station, and I sure as Hades will not spend a farthing on them."

"Then I will."

Roderick slammed his glass down, nearly shattering the fragile crystal. "By Jove, you will not! I am head of this household, and I insist you cease this mad notion at once. Damn if I don't have enough evidence to have you declared incompetent over this absurd bee you have in your bonnet."

Mina gasped. "You would not!"

"Do not tempt me, madam. All I would have to say is that you were deranged since the death of your own child. People will believe me; you have disappeared from society, after all. I can say I need to have you incarcerated for your own safety." He rose and started pacing in front of the mantel.

"You dastard." Mina was shaking so hard she could barely speak. She took a calming sip of tea, then another, watching him tread back and forth. "You would never get away with it," she finally said. "Recall that I am the one with the funds to finance a court battle. I can hire every barrister in the land. In fact, I can use my funds to ruin you, Roderick, before you file a single paper. Most of your income derives from the shares in the Caldwell shipbuilding industry. My father was too canny to give a hardened gambler such funds outright, so he paid off Sparrowdale's debts and settled the mortgages, but he paid the rest of my dowry in shares that the earl could not touch, only the income from them. Father always held the controlling stock. Now I do. I could give the company away tomorrow, deed it to charity, or see it dismantled from woodpile to wharf, if you do not cease your threats."

"Oh, give over, Minerva." Roderick retreated, coming closer to her seat on the couch and pasting a sickly smile on his thin lips. "I was merely quizzing you. A public trial would be exactly what I do not wish. I am trying to polish up the family name, I told you. With any luck, and your cooperation, Westcott might be convinced to give me his daughter's hand. The duke promised Lady

Millicent in the cradle to Viscount Sparling, but now she is grown up, unspoken for, and ready to be presented at court—and to be snatched up by some lucky devil. I mean that devil to be me."

The devil part Mina could well imagine. She pitied the poor duke's daughter, another female who was to be bartered for fortune and title.

"Think on it, Minerva. If I wed the Westcott chit, I would not be dependent on you and your cursed shipyards. The duke could help me move up in the party, too. Who knows how high I might rise in the government with his backing, if he does not get wind of the stench at the root of our family tree."

"I wish you luck with your plans, Roderick," Mina lied. She wished him to perdition. And she wished Lady Millicent to a man who might love her, instead of her father's wealth. "However, those children will not go away."

"Deuce take it, you do not even know how many there are, your letter said. And the only evidence you have of their existence is the say-so of a thieving waif, likely put up to the scheme by Gypsies."

"You knew of the children. You said so yourself."

"An old man's braggadocio." Roderick shrugged his padded shoulders, then leaned against the back of the chair he'd been sitting on. "If he was so virile, how come his first wife had but the one son, and he never impregnated you?"

Before Mina could comment, although Lud knew she did not wish to speak of such intimate things, Roderick held up his hand.

"No," he said, "do not bring up the cuckoo bird you dropped in Uncle's nest. It's a blessing we do not have *that* brat on our hands."

A blessing that her baby was dead? Now Mina set her cup down so hard the tea spilled onto the table. "He was my son."

"And if he had not been taken, he'd have been another botheration."

"He would have been the earl in your place, you mean."

"Hah! As if I would not contest his birth, rather than see your love child inherit the earldom."

Mina used her handkerchief to blot at the spilled tea. "You would have no grounds. Your uncle acknowledged Robert."

"On his gravestone. When it no longer mattered. And then only to save your good name, and because your father insisted. They both knew the infant was not Sparrowdale's. With Sparling waiting in the wings, though, the brat's paternity made no difference. Did you really think Sparrowdale would have let your lover father the future earl? Despite his faults—and I admit they were legion—my uncle still had respect for his name and title. As do I. I would have contested your son's succession to the fullest."

"Bringing down on the House of Sparr the same scandal you hope to avoid now. Westcott would slam the door in your face."

"And if your son were earl, do you think he'd have opened it in the first place? To a plain Mr. Sparr?" He pounded on the chair back. "Hah. I would be out on my ear."

His laughter was not a pleasant sound. "You would be right where you were before Sparrowdale's son died."

"No, never that. Your Robert could not have been earl. His birth date and your wedding day do not calculate correctly."

Mina set her soiled handkerchief to the side. "The earl anticipated our vows." That was the Banbury story they had concocted for the servants and the scandalmongers.

"Fustian. Irrelevant fustian, at that. The boy is gone. It is this Peregrine Radway and his ilk we are discussing—and forgetting."

"I will not forget."

Roderick came around to stand in front of Mina, looming over her. "You will, I say. You will have nothing to do with that street urchin or his tales."

Mina sat up straighter. "You do not command my obedience, nephew."

Her resistance seemed to infuriate Roderick further.

A woman was supposed to be docile, subservient. "You are not even lady enough to know your place, by damn!" he shouted, grabbing her by the shoulders.

"You forget yourself, sirrah!"

"No, I never forget. I am the Earl of Sparrowdale, madam, and you would do well to remember that. Or else—"

"More tea, my lady?" Harkness asked from the doorway.

Chapter Seven

She was leaving. There was no way in heaven Mina was staying at Sparrows Nest, and no way in hell she would go to Sparr House in London. She would not spend another fortnight under Roderick's roof, not even when it was her funds that had put new tiles on both of them.

The dower house was hers for her lifetime. She would not go there either. It was too close. Mina wanted to expunge every Sparr thing from her life, including the despicable name. The only way she could do that, however, was to remarry. Bind herself to another man? When pigs sprouted wings.

She was going to London, and she was going to find Perry Radway, and she was going to uncover the truth about those children. Mina would go on her own if she had to. She'd find someone to help her, even if she had to pay him. Hiring that investigator might be the best anyway, for then she might be assured of loyalty, and someone who cared about her wishes. Lud knew, no one else seemed to.

Cousin Dorcas was terrified of leaving. Two women on their own? Without Mr. Sizemore's advice? Why, the solicitor had not even found them a house to rent yet.

"We can stay at a hotel," Mina replied. "Or we can buy one. It makes no nevermind. If you would rather go live with your sister in Lincolnshire, with her twenty-five cats and her husband who believes he can teach his horses to count, then I will hire a coach for you and three outriders to make sure you arrive safely."

London was not quite as unappealing.

Harkness believed the Countess of Sparrowdale belonged at Sparrows Nest. In London she would be at the mercy of untrained servants and unscrupulous tradesmen. Hadn't she been taken in by that young Radway riffraff? On her own, who knew how many dogs madam would have foisted on her?

"Very well," Mina conceded, "you can come along. Heaven knows what you will do if we find a house that already has a butler, or how Sparrows Nest will go on without you, but I cannot blame you. I do not wish to live another day under Roderick's rule, so why should you? We've both seen his true colors, and they resemble a snake's."

They could not leave in a day, or even two, for all that needed doing. Mina did not wish to leave any of her personal belongings strewn about Sparrows Nest, for she never wanted to return. Everything she could not take with her was boxed up and carted to the dower house, to be locked in the attics until she sent wagons for it. The senior footman had to be instructed in the butler's duties, and the estate agent had to be given the ledgers. Horses had to be hired, and rooms bespoken at inns along the way. Mina needed a few more mourning gowns, and Cousin Dorcas needed a few more bottles of tonics, restoratives, and sleeping potions.

Mina bade good-bye to the few neighborhood acquaintances who cared whether she stayed or left: the vicar whose church was no longer falling down around the congregations' ears, the schoolteacher whose students had books, the Sparrowdale tenants whose cottages were recently rethatched, and the farmers who had the latest equipment, all thanks to Lady Sparrowdale. She hoped they fared half as well under the next countess, if Roderick managed to snare the duke's daughter.

Then she placed a last bouquet of flowers on her son's grave. ROBERT CALDWELL SPARR, the small marker read,

BELOVED CHILD. "This is not farewell, my sweet Robin, for you will always be in my heart wherever I go."

Mina's final chore was to sort through the Sparrows Nest safe. She had to separate her own jewelry, plus her mother's collection of gems and her father's valuables that he had brought with him on his last, fateful visit, from the few entailed heirloom pieces that Sparrowdale had not managed to pawn. She made both Harkness and the replacement butler, Vorpohl, watch, so Roderick could not claim she had removed anything belonging to the earldom.

"The diamonds my father gave me on the occasion of my marriage." Mina had never worn them after the trip to London. "My mother's diamonds." They were in a heavier, old-fashioned setting, not good enough for Malachy's daughter, the countess. "Her rubies." She showed the servants the miniature of her mother wearing the parure. Again, Mina had worn them only once, in London. She had taken them with her on her flight to Scotland, though, thinking to sell them so that she and Ninian Rourke could make a new life for themselves. Now Mina placed the rubies with the sapphire set and the diamonds. She did not have time to dwell on those memories and might-have-beens.

"The tiara my mother wore for her presentation." She held it up next to the smaller, duller Sparrowdale tiara, with stones missing where the earl had pried them out to sell.

There were brooches, earbobs, three priceless snuff-boxes that Malachy Caldwell had started to collect, thinking they made him appear more like a gentleman, his costly fob watch, and a black pearl the size of Mina's thumb that he was used to wearing in his neckcloth. Mina's pile grew until the velvet pouches and lined boxes filled a small trunk of their own. And that was in addition to the trinkets and baubles she had in her jewelry case upstairs.

The Sparrowdale stack was pitifully small, Roderick having already claimed his uncle's signet ring and pocket watch. Mina pulled the emerald engagement ring that

the earl had given her off her finger and tossed it onto
the desk with the rest. The ostentatious piece had been
bought new with her father's money, Mina knew, but she
did not want to own the thing. The gold wedding band
had been her mother's. She would not part with it, despite its unfortunate history. Embarrassed, Vorpohl insisted he did not need to see the inscription inside the
ring.

"That is that, then," Mina told the servants, as she
started to put the Sparrowdale pieces back into the wall
safe. Her hand brushed against the far wall of the vault,
dislodging a folded paper.

"Per'aps it's the map to some hidden treasure," the
new butler offered. "Lost for centuries, like in them novels Cook reads." Harkness kicked him.

"No, it is merely a list," Mina said, studying the page.
"And not very old, judging from the dates. It is in the
late earl's handwriting, don't you think, Harkness?"

"Yes, I believe so, my lady. It—"

"Must be nothing, or the solicitor would have taken it
when he gathered the deeds and such to place in the
London vault. We do not have time to decipher the thing
now, at any rate." Mina quickly refolded the paper and
put it in her pocket. "I'll bring it to Mr. Sizemore when
I get to Town."

Once upstairs, Mina told her maid to finish the packing
later, for she needed to lie down a moment or two before dinner.

She bolted the door behind the girl, and sat at her
dressing table with the list spread in front of her. There
were two columns of twelve entries each, one row of
initials, one row of dates. Four sets of initials had been
crossed through. Approximately halfway down the first
column were the initials P.R. The corresponding date
was some thirteen years ago.

Peregrine Radway, thirteen years old.

Here was the list of the children her husband had
sired, not counting his rightful heir. Mina could not be
sure, but she thought the increases in the withdrawals
that had so troubled her corresponded closely to the

dates written here. Twelve. Lud, Sparrowdale had not
lost his virility through age and illness, he had worn it
out.

If she had been troubled before, she was horrified now.

Then one date in particular caught her eye. One familiar date, that she'd just seen on her son's gravestone.
Robin's birthday, the date of his death. There it was,
second from the bottom, R.S. Robert Sparr. The initials
had no line drawn through them.

Had there been an increase in the withdrawals after
the baby's birth? Mina thought so, within a month, possibly. Certainly that year, and another increase the following one. She itched to go check the old account books,
but they were all at the estate agent's now, where he
could study them. Let him make of them what he
would—Mina needed the time to think.

Was it possible? The very idea seemed so far-fetched
that Roderick would certainly have her locked in Bedlam
if he suspected. The thought of Roderick reminded Mina
of a phrase he'd used, one that kept nagging at her like
a persistent toothache: he'd said it was a blessing that
her son had been taken. She'd been bothered by the
"blessing," but it was the "taken" that jangled now.
Taken, not lost, dead, departed, demised, passed on.
Taken. She understood taken aloft, taken with the
angels—but what if Roderick simply meant taken . . .
from her.

No. No one could be so heinous as to steal her baby!
Not even a Sparr. And yet what had Roderick said, that
her love child could never be permitted to inherit the
title? And he had been there at her husband's house
party the night of the infant's birth. She shivered, as if
someone walked over her grave. No, she had to put such
evil thoughts away from her. No one could be that cruel,
that ambitious. Could he? Perhaps.

Mina remembered Roderick's words, and she remembered that one cry from her newborn infant, a sound
forever in her memory: a loud, healthy wail. Her Robin
was not born too early. He was not sickly.

He had not died.

Unless they killed him later. But then his entry on this vile list would have been scratched through, would it not?

Roderick had to know—and that was why he was so adamant about her not prying into Sparrowdale's past. The earl *had* claimed her son. Robin would be earl.

The notion was so staggering that Mina felt sick and light-headed, and like spinning in circles. Her son might be alive! She would not permit herself to celebrate, though—not yet, not yet.

But why had Sparrowdale kept paying for his *wife's* bastard? There was no indignant grandmother, no faked marriage lines as evidence of his perfidy. No one was extorting support for this particular illegitimate son. Children were left at foundling homes all the time, dropped at church gates or poorhouses. No one would have been the wiser if Sparrowdale had spirited her son away to one of those places, to survive or not, in anonymity.

The answer was on the list, in Sparrowdale's pride at having so many children before the disease stole his manhood. He could have arranged the death or disappearance of any of them—and of their complaining mothers and grandmothers, too. Mina did not think Perry's granny's threats would have caused a stir in the *ton,* no, nor in legal circles either, not with the old woman conveniently and permanently silenced. Yet he had kept paying for their upkeep, even when his own funds were so below hatches. Perhaps he had a spark of human kindness in his diseased soul after all, or perhaps he simply drew the line at murder. Possibly they were a threat to hold over his heirs' heads. Maybe he just liked children.

Then why had the earl made no provision for them for after his death? Mina wondered, her thoughts swooping around like swallows after gnats. His lordship was too ill at the end, his mind deteriorating as fast as his body, but his death came as no surprise to anyone, certainly not Sparrowdale. Half the dates on the list were older than Perry, so he might have felt those children were adults, on their own. But the younger ones? He must have told someone to continue the support. Of course. He had to have made arrangements with someone who could disguise the expense, someone who understood the nature of legacies, someone who had died unexpectedly. His old solicitor, Mr. Sizemore's partner, came to mind. So did Malachy Caldwell, her father, who might have had an interest in keeping his only grandchild alive.

That could have been part of their marriage settlements, the cost of Sparrowdale's acceptance of a possibly *enceinte* bride. Yes, it fit. The information she needed to find the children, including her son, had to be in the London vault, or with her father's papers in Portsmouth, if she could not locate Perry.

Everything fit, and so did Roderick's anger. The other baseborn children would be an embarrassment for him, but Robin was a threat. Her son would never be safe, not in England. She would take him to the Colonies or the tropics, anywhere Roderick could not reach. Let Sparrowdale's nephew keep his tarnished title. Her boy did not need an earldom. He needed a mother.

Chapter Eight

"What is wrong, dear?" the Duchess of Mersford asked her son when she heard his sharp intake of breath. "Bad news, like another of your friends stepping into parson's mousetrap?"

Lord Lowell managed to ignore his mother's less than subtle gibes as he studied the letter he held. "No, I believe it is that curricle I had in mind to purchase."

"What, in the post?" Her Grace squinted across the breakfast table where the two of them were opening their correspondence over the coffee cups. "Oh, it is a bank draft."

"A very substantial one at that. As a retainer for my services, to ensure that I will be available when my client arrives in London shortly."

"Lady Sparrow, is it?"

"Yes, but you will forget that instantly, if you please, Mother."

"Hmpf. Of course I will forget that my sapskull of a single second son is corresponding with one of the wealthiest young widows in the kingdom—over a matter of business. You know you can trust me, no matter how I dislike this huggery-muggery occupation of yours."

Lord Lowell reached across the table and patted his mother's hand. "I know I can, Mother. You are invaluable to me in my investigations, without betraying my clients. Sometimes I even think you enjoy dabbling in my inquiries."

Her Grace busied herself spreading jam on another

slice of toast rather than confess any such thing. She
could not, however, resist speculating. "I wonder what
bumblebroth that poor chit has fallen into this time, that
she sends you the price of a curricle as a retainer."

"I am sure I do not know."

"And I am sure you would not tell me if you did,
Lolly. Still, you cannot keep me from hazarding a guess
or two."

"As long as that is all you do. Sometimes these affairs
can grow dangerous." Lord Lowell could have bitten his
tongue for mentioning that his work had an element of
peril. Dealing with fences and felons often did. His
mother had still not forgiven him for stopping the knife
meant for Lord Fortenham—with his shoulder. To dis-
tract her from starting a new lecture about his business
interests and his intelligence in general, he said, "Who
knows? Perhaps the countess wishes to hire me to investigate possible candidates for the position of her next
husband."

"Bosh, I would do that for free, if I could put my own
son's name at the top of her list."

"Find another hobbyhorse, Your Grace. That one will
not trot."

"A mother can dream, can't she?" She pushed aside
the toast and jam, recalling that she had vowed to lose
weight this month. Or was that last month? She decided
to compromise by eating half the slice. "You will talk to
the gel, Lolly, won't you?"

"Of course." He tapped one long finger against the
countess's check. "I am just as curious as you to know
what could trouble a wealthy widow this much. I will call
on your Lady Sparrow as soon as she arrives in Town."

"You and every other eligible young buck in London,"
the duchess muttered, reaching for the second half of
her toast.

Mina arrived in the city a few days after her letter.
She took a suite at the Clarendon. Harkness took control
of organizing the trunks and boxes, and Cousin Dorcas
took to her bed. The trip had been long and tedious,

much too slow for Mina's peace of mind, and not nearly
slow enough for her older cousin's fragile constitution.

Lady Sparrowdale's first stop, accompanied by her butler, was at Mr. Sizemore's office, where she asked him
to search once more through the earl's files for a list of
names, an addendum to a previous will, a personal letter
to his deceased partner. The solicitor found nothing, but
asked to call on Miss Albright, to assure himself that she
was recovered from her harrowing journey.

The only harrowing part was how often Cousin Dorcas
had needed to stop. Mina invited Mr. Sizemore to take
dinner with them at the hotel that evening.

Her second visit was to the bank where the documents
relating to the earldom were now kept. The manager
there did not know her and would have turned her away,
in fact, pending the new earl's approval, despite the evidence of her elegant mourning silks and priceless pearls.
Not even the presence of her distinguished and determined factotum, Harkness at his most formidable, convinced the man to unlock the vault. It was Harkness who
suggested sending 'round to the solicitor's office for a
line of credit, so she might withdraw the considerable
sums of Lady Sparrowdale's personal fortune deposited
at the bank. The implied threats were for naught. There
was no letter or list.

Mina's third call was to a real estate office. Lady Sparrowdale refused to reside in a handful of rooms where
everyone and his uncle could keep track of her comings
and goings through the lobby. Besides, the hotel staff
frowned on her dog.

Fourth, Mina and her escort drove to the office of the
newspaper that held Lord Lowell Merrison's forwarding
address. She did not even need Harkness's dignified presence to sway the clerk there. Bribery did the trick.

Then she waited in the carriage while Harkness delivered her card to his counterpart at Merrison House. The
sprawling building occupied an entire side of Mersford
Square, overlooking a garden behind gates. Her private
investigator lived here, Mina thought to herself, and she
was hiring him? She almost ran after Harkness to re-

trieve her note begging Lord Lowell to call on her on the morrow.

She had no choice, however. If the paper she needed was here in London, at Sparr House, Roderick would have burned it by now. Nor would he permit Mina to inspect the safe there, if she could bear to cross his threshold. She did not even have the excuse of looking for some of her belongings, not that Roderick would believe such a faradiddle. Mina had left nothing behind at the earl's London town house that dreadful Season, nothing except her hopes and dreams.

But now she had to find Perry, and she needed help. A wealthy man, she supposed, might have to do. She could not purchase his loyalty, but neither could anyone else.

He was prompt, she credited him with that, the next afternoon, but nothing else. Lord Lowell was too young, too devastatingly handsome. His blue eyes were too merry, with laugh lines at the corners behind the foolish spectacles he wore. He was too rich, with his finely made clothes and highly polished boots, too much the gentleman in his high neckcloth, tightly fitted coat, and courtly bow when Harkness formally announced him at the door to her suite. Mina shook her head. He would never do, this duke's son turned dilettante detective.

This might be dirty business, for Mina intended to search every inch of Kensington for Perry and his grandmother. She would visit every foundling hospital and magdalene too, if she had to. She needed a bodyguard, not a Town beau—someone to whom working people would speak. Why, Harkness was more intimidating than this pretty fellow.

While Mina was examining Lord Lowell, he was scrutinizing his prospective employer. His mother had called the countess a drab, dowdy little squab of a girl. This was a woman. She was small, yes, but Lady Sparrow was fine-boned and delicate, except where she had lush curves. No, she was not a girl anymore, not at all. She was not the classic English beauty, whose blond hair and blue eyes bordered on insipid. Instead, the countess had soft brown eyes, creamy skin, and silky light brown curls that artfully framed her face beneath a scrap of white lace. Her black silk gown had been designed by a master hand to showcase that alluring figure without revealing more than a respectable widow ought, and the lace adornments kept the widow's weeds from appearing drab. With a strand of pearls that a rajah would have coveted, the woman was anything but drab, anything but dowdy.

Lud, his mother was right. Lady Sparrow would have every single man in London—and half the married ones, too, he'd wager—worshiping at her feet, without even considering her fortune. The last thing he wanted was to get involved with a Society belle and her beaux. But, damn, he'd grown fond of his new curricle.

"I am sorry, my lord, but—"

"I regret, Lady Sparrowdale, that—"

"I shall go fetch tea, my lady," Harkness said. "And wine for the gentleman. And digestive biscuits for Miss Albright." He nodded toward the slightly opened bedroom door, so Lord Lowell would know the countess was not left unchaperoned.

Mina found herself at a loss for words to dismiss the lordling so recently after sending for him. "I was, ah, expecting someone older," she began.

Lowell could not stay he had been expecting someone homelier. He did jump on her words, though, as an out. "I daresay my age will change with time. But I will gladly return your retainer now if you feel I do not suit your needs."

"No, the retainer must be yours to keep, for your trouble."

"Absolutely not. I could not take payment for doing nothing. Do you enjoy curricle rides?"

Mina definitely had to get rid of this man. His attics were to let. "I—"

Then Harkness returned with the refreshments, and Mina could not continue in her butler's hearing. He'd warned her about hiring a blue blood instead of a Bow

Street Runner. He was right; Lord Lowell's smile seemed to say this was all a great game to him, a joke. He did not need her money, and she could not afford to waste her time. She stood, indicating the interview was over.

"You'll come for a ride, then?" Lord Lowell said. "Good. My tiger will be up on back, so you do not have to worry about the properties." This last was directed at the superior servant, who seemed to care more about the conventions than the mistress.

Now Mina understood. She could speak more freely outside, too, and she might as well find some pleasure in this day, since she had not found a new employee.

"It's yours, you see," Lowell told the countess as he handed her into the shiny new vehicle. "That is, you own it, if I am not going to work for you. I spent the retainer on it, but we can always sell it if you don't wish to own the equipage."

What was she going to do with a dashing gentleman's vehicle? She'd never driven anything but a gig, for one thing, and Cousin Dorcas would have palpitations at the height and speed—if she could be convinced to climb aboard. Mina found it exhilarating. The sky was clear, the horses were sleek, the gentleman was attractive— except for his spectacles—and she was not at Sparrows Nest. She looked over at the lordling who played at solving mysteries, and smiled.

Lowell was lost. He saw sweet innocence and a siren's seduction, all at once. He knew he would regret it, but if Lady Sparrow had any dragons that needing slaying, he was ready to polish up his armor and his lance. Especially his lance. He smiled back. "I am a competent investigator, you know."

"But an unusual one, I daresay."

"Quite. My mother despairs of me and my choice of career."

Mina noted that he said career, not hobby. That was something, anyway.

"She remembers you, by the bye," he said.

Mina stiffened on the curricle seat. She waited for the insult, the curled lip or the raised brow she'd received the last time she faced a member of the *ton*. She was Moneybags Malachy's soiled-dove daughter. She did not belong in their hallowed midst, and their actions plainly told her so.

When Lord Lowell showed no overt sign of disrespect, she replied, "I met too many people to recall."

"Then I doubt you were actually introduced. No one could forget Her Grace. She is quite the grand dame, yet a great gun for all that. She would like to make your reacquaintance."

"I am in mourning and do not intend to attend any social functions. In fact, I should not be driving out with you."

"Surely a drive in the park is permitted a recent widow, for her health's sake if nothing else. And a private tea with a duchess cannot be condemned either."

He was correct, and it would be ungracious to refuse. "Thank Her Grace for me," Mina said. "I would be honored to call on her."

"Do you know others in Town? Mother would be happy to introduce you to her friends at quiet, unexceptionable gatherings." Where fortune hunters and philanderers were never admitted. "If my sister were in London, she could introduce you to some of the younger matrons, but she is in the country, awaiting a happy event."

"My best wishes to your sister, but I do not intend to stay in the city long enough to require introductions. I wish to conclude my business here as quickly as possible, then be on my way."

"Back to the earl's country seat?"

"No." Mina thought that sounded too abrupt, so she added, "That is, I am not certain where I shall go."

"But elsewhere. You do not like the city?"

"I have no fond memories, no."

Lowell enjoyed the symphony London played, all the movements and varied tempos. He wanted Lady Sparrow to hear the music too. "You were a green girl then. Your reception would be quite different now."

"Of course. Now my birth will only be whispered

about after my bank account, not before. But I am not here to establish my place in society."

"No, I did not think so. Perhaps we should discuss why you did come, and why you purchased yourself this fine new curricle."

Chapter Nine

Speak of her most private affairs to this perfect stranger, in front of his tiger? Mina could not. She could not trust Lord Lowell, so how could she trust his groom? He was too perfect—the duke's son, not the servant—that was the problem. Lord Lowell was well born, well-to-pass, and well favored. Well, that was enough to make his behavior suspect. Mina thought he should be out sowing wild oats, or whatever it was sons of the nobility did when they were not preening in front of their mirrors. Granted, his lordship had made a fuss over Merlin, bending to pet the barking dog without worrying over hairs on his fawn breeches or scuffs on his Hessians. That was a mark in his favor, but he was still too young. The gentleman had less than thirty years in his dish, Mina estimated, and in no way resembled the reliable, settled old soul she had pictured.

"You know," she said as he expertly tooled the pair of horses around a stopped carrier's cart, "you might as well take those foolish spectacles off. They do not make you appear older or more competent, as you obviously intended."

Lowell took the glasses off with his whip hand and handed them to her. "And here I thought I was impressing you by looking wise."

Mina held the spectacles up and gasped. She could barely see through them. She was mortified at her rudeness—and horrified that he was driving the carriage half blind! "Here. Put them on. Quickly."

He did and then smiled, so Mina did not feel quite as cabbage-headed. He had a very nice smile, she noted. In fact, Lord Lowell seemed a very nice man. And she had no guarantee of finding a better individual to conduct her inquiries. So she asked, "Are you wed?"

The reins almost fell through his fingers. "Good grief, no. Why?"

"I realize it is a personal question, but my investigations might require travel. A married man might not be willing or able to leave Town, in my company. I did not wish to offend anyone, or give rise to unnecessary gossip."

"My mother will be in alt, although she will miss me."

"Why?"

"Why will she be in alt? Because she lives in hopes of seeing me wed. Why will she miss me? Because she is used to having me around to harangue about not providing her with more grandchildren. After my father died and my sister and brother both married, she was so lonely that I moved back into Merrison House to keep her company."

"No, why have you not married?"

Lord Lowell turned the horses into the Hyde Park gate. "Now that *is* a personal question."

Mina's cheeks flooded with color. He truly would think her a country lumpkin with all the polish of a prize pig. "I apologize. It is just that with your obvious advantages, I would have thought . . ."

"My so-called advantages are more pride-worthy than practical. I do not choose to be a hanger-on to my brother and his growing family, and on my own I cannot afford to keep a wife in style. Therefore I have decided to remain single. The dukedom has heirs aplenty, so I am not reneging on any familial obligation." He guided the pair along one of the lesser used paths. "But what of you, since we are discussing private matters of a matrimonial nature. Do you intend to remarry? Perhaps find a new husband while you are here in London?"

"No," Mina answered quickly. "And no." Her negatives were very quick indeed, Lowell noticed, and very definite.

"Then at least we can both be certain we will not be trapped into marriage by a compromising situation," he said, "should we decide to travel together."

Mina left off admiring the scenery, the strollers, the toy boats on the Serpentine, to address Lord Lowell's profile. "I am a widow, my lord, and thus have more leeway in my conduct. I am, however, neither an adventuress nor a schemer. Your bachelorhood is safe. My maid will travel with us, of course, or my butler. My cousin is too infirm and hates being jostled about, or she would come along to satisfy the conventions. No one will claim compromise, I swear it, by our sharing a carriage."

"Are we indeed to share a carriage, then?" They had reached a clearing just off the bridle path, and Lowell got down to hand Lady Sparrowdale out of the carriage for a stroll to where they might have privacy. She was as light as the proverbial feather, he noticed, and graceful. "Am I hired?"

A ball rolled in front of them, and Lowell picked it up and tossed it to the boys playing across the field. He whistled in admiration when one of the boys caught it.

Mina had been all set to say no, that he was not the kind of man she needed, but Lord Lowell was laughing, running to catch another wayward ball. He was fond of his mother, kind to children and dogs—what more could Mina ask, with any reasonable hope of being answered? By now they were far away from the curricle and the tiger. Other strollers were in the distance, out of hearing. Lord Lowell took her arm to lead her over uneven spots in the path. He truly appeared a gentle man.

She nodded. "If you will undertake my investigation."

"That depends on the nature of your problem, of course," Lowell said, having already decided to aid the pretty little widow if he possibly could. He did not like seeing the troubled look in those velvety brown eyes. "It is time to open your budget, my lady. Nothing can be accomplished if you do not trust me, so you have to

choose now. I will understand entirely if you do not wish
to pursue our business relationship.''

He would understand, but he would still be saddened.
Then again, if Lady Sparrow were not his client, Lowell
considered, he might think of pursuing a different sort
of relationship altogether. Neither of them sought marriage, but that did not preclude other courtship rituals.
In fact, he was certain he'd be among the legions calling
at the Clarendon. He would still rather earn the widow's
regard by solving the dilemma that brought her to London and led her to pay him such a substantial retainer.
"I'd ask only that you permit me to accompany you
home before you take over the curricle. I do not fancy
walking the distance across town.''

Mina did not need a new curricle. She needed a confidant. Lord Lowell was smiling, sunlight reflecting off his
blond hair and glasses, making him look like a seraph in
a golden aura. Or a guardian angel, perhaps. She nodded
again and took a deep breath. "It started with the
money.''

"It usually does. Go on.''

Before continuing, Mina asked, "Do you think it improper for a woman to delve into financial matters?
There are those who felt I had no business taking over
the Sparrows Nest ledgers at all when my husband
passed away.''

"How could it be improper for a woman to understand
her own circumstances as a widow? Every female of a
responsible age should have some awareness of her true
situation, so she is neither outrunning the bailiffs constantly, squeezing her every shilling until it squeaks, or
pawning the family heirlooms.''

He peered closely under the rim of Lady Sparrowdale's black bonnet to see if any of his postulations drew
a reaction. No, she did not appear to have a guilty conscience. He was glad.

So was Mina. "I do not think I could continue with a
man who felt women should be content with their needlework and gossip and leave everything of moment to the
masculine gender. I have learned that most gentlemen

believe a woman's smaller stature correspondingly lessens her ability to think."

"I am not most gentlemen."

So Mina was beginning to see, and she felt better about enlisting a stranger—this stranger—to her cause.

"So you inspected the accounts?" he prompted, bringing her back to the matter at hand.

"Yes, and I discovered some discrepancies. At first I was merely curious where the funds were going, since I found no notations of those withdrawals. My recently deceased husband's account books did not tally, it seemed, by fairly large, consistent amounts."

"I certainly would have been curious also, but I have a naturally inquisitive nature, I suppose, drawing me to this line of work. What did you do then?"

"I consulted the estate agent, the bank officer, and the earl's solicitor. None was cooperative."

Lowell paused to wipe his spectacles. When they resumed walking, he said, "They were most likely trying to protect you from unpleasant discoveries, unsuitable for a recent widow's sensitive nature."

"You mean like mistresses and such? I doubt there is a wife alive who does not know of those things, although we are supposed to pretend they do not exist."

They had reached a bench overlooking a pretty scene of water and trees and horses in the distance. "Let us sit awhile," Lowell said. "No one can overhear our conversation, and you do not need to fear offending my tender sensibilities, for I assure you I have none. I take it you suspected your husband had been keeping a *cherie amour* tucked away in a love nest somewhere? Such postmortem revelations are fairly common. I heard of one instance where bequests in a baron's will led to the discovery of an entire separate family, of which his true wife had no prior knowledge."

"I did not know what to suspect, although such possibilities of course occurred to me, to be discarded for various reasons. My husband had more than one vice, I am afraid. Then I was given information by a seemingly trustworthy young man that led me to believe my husband had indeed been conducting illicit liaisons. He was not, however, keeping his birds of paradise in well-feathered nests. He was supporting his children." When her companion did not respond, Mina added, "Many children, that boy Perry included."

Lowell was not surprised. "I believe there were rumors of wagers between Lord Sparrowdale and another old rip over who could father the most sons. The gossip died down at your marriage, I understand, or perhaps the other contestant simply died. I do not recall if the names of the ladybirds were ever mentioned."

"No, nor the fate of those sons, I daresay."

"But you tell me that Lord Sparrowdale did support his progeny? Many men would have walked away from the costly burden, if they acknowledged responsibility at all."

"I suppose my husband had to claim paternity to win his wager. As for maintaining the children in a semblance of comfort, I am not certain he had a choice."

Lord Lowell was polishing his lenses again. He seemed to do that when he was thinking, Mina realized. She did not wait for him to reason it out. "I believe someone was holding a threat over his head. There were grounds, it seems, for at least one valid breech-of-promise suit on behalf of one of the mothers. False marriage certificates and such. Lord Sparrowdale wished to avoid a public trial. So he paid for the children. Now I wish to continue that support." She did not mention that she was planning on gathering the waifs and raising them as a family, her family. Let his lordship find the children first.

"That is a very worthy sentiment indeed," he told her. "You have my admiration, Countess. Only a true lady would act so kindly."

His praise warmed Mina, despite the slight chill from sitting on the bench. They both knew she was no lady born. "Thank you, but I cannot act on my feelings, worthy or not. I cannot find the children, or the boy who brought me the information and knows where they are. That is why I require your services."

"What, no dragons to slay? Finding a lost boy is mere

child's play. Why, I shall barely earn the price of the curricle."

"I told you, the curricle is yours to keep. But I doubt you will find the search as easy as you believe. Finding the children will be more difficult if the new Earl of Sparrowdale does not wish them found." Now Mina was truly chilled, as if a cloud blocked the sun, and drew her black knitted shawl more closely around her shoulders. "My husband's nephew, who had been Roderick Sparr."

"Ah," was all Lowell said, going over in his mind what he knew of the new peer.

Now Mina twisted the fringe on her shawl. "There is more. One of the children might—just might, of course— pose a threat to Roderick's succession."

"A legitimate heir, you mean?" Lowell sat up straighter. "This case grows more interesting by the moment."

"As I said, there is a remote possibility. I . . . I fear the boy is in danger."

"Or you."

"Me?"

"What if Roderick cannot find the boy either? It is easy enough for you to have an accident, or be set upon by thieves. London is a violent place, you know."

Mina found it hard to believe, in this peaceful setting with swans paddling across the water nearby. Then she recalled Roderick's threats. "You think my nephew-by-marriage could be so evil?"

"I think you are the only witness likely to be believed in a hearing of the College of Arms. If there is an actual question of the inheritance, you might stand between an earldom and defeat. Do you have proof?"

She was not ready to give it. "I am not sure."

"Perhaps you ought to visit my mother sooner rather than later, I am thinking."

Chapter Ten

*M*ina could not like the way her retainer's mind rattled around. "What does a visit to your mother have to do with anything?"

"She cannot very well invite you to stay at Merrison House unless she makes your acquaintance first, can she?" When Lady Sparrowdale looked at him as if he were as queer as Dick's hatband, Lowell explained: "If you are seen in my company, an investigator of some repute, if I have to say so myself, although my fame has more to do with my pedigree than my prowess, Roderick will get his wind up. But my mother mentioned knowing the Albrights, your mother's family. What could be more readily accepted than her inviting an old school chum and her young cousin to stay, to relieve the tedium of their mourning period? No one would question my escort of my mother's guest. Most important, you would be a great deal safer at my house, with my trusted servants keeping watch, than among strangers at your hotel."

Mina nervously licked her lips. "Then you do think Roderick is dangerous?"

Lowell had to turn away, lest his thoughts follow Lady Sparrow's tongue instead of her case. She was an appealing little thing, but dragging out a new claimant to a succession was serious business indeed. "To be truthful, I never liked Roderick Sparr when I knew him as a schoolboy. He was a bully, picking on the smaller, younger boys while fawning over the older, titled lads."

"Yes, that is how I have always seen him. He tried to ingratiate himself with Lord Sparrowdale, yet treated the servants abysmally. That is one of the reasons Harkness is in Town with me, because he will not work for the new earl. I cannot imagine what Roderick would have been like as a child if he'd been the heir."

"I'd wager he imagined just such a thing. The question is whether he helped his dreams come true."

"I do not understand. Lord Sparrowdale was not killed. He was ill," Mina said without mentioning the specifics of her husband's ailment. If Lord Lowell was a competent investigator, he would already know. "Everyone understood that Lord Sparrowdale's condition was grave. Furthermore, Roderick was not at Sparrows Nest when his uncle actually passed on. I was there, and nothing untoward hastened the earl's demise."

"No, but Roderick was with young Harmon, Viscount Sparling, when that cloth-head was given notice to quit. Blame my curious nature, but I was never satisfied with the circumstances surrounding Sparling's death."

"What circumstances? He was knifed in a tavern brawl, after being caught cheating. I might have little regard for Roderick myself, but surely you cannot think he stabbed his own cousin."

"I do think that Sparling could have been saved from the dissolute life he was leading. Your husband, forgive my bluntness, was no great example. When he no longer exerted any control over his heir, the cousin still could have. Sparling looked up to his older relation, yet Roderick made no attempt to curb the cub's wilder impulses. There were, in fact, rumors that Sparr made a practice of introducing gullible young men to the seamier segments of the City, bringing green-as-grass gudgeons in to be fleeced by his compatriots in crime. Sparling was another of his gulls."

"I am not surprised, but Roderick still did not wield the knife. He does not like to get his hands dirty."

"The knife may have killed Sparling, but the weighted dice were the actual cause of death."

"Of course, but—"

"I knew Sparling. He was a drunkard and a gambler and a womanizer. He was not a cheat."

Mina, naturally, had not known her stepson in his earlier years. She had never seen him not in his altitudes and not below-hatches, yet neither had she seen him pilfering from the petty-cash drawer or stealing silver from the house. "You think Roderick could have placed those dice in his cousin's pocket? Or switched them at the baize table?"

"What I think is that you will be safer at my house."

Mina felt guilty. She had not told Lord Lowell the half of it, yet here he was inviting her into his home. He did not know that she intended to raise Sparrowdale's children herself, or that the possible heir was her own impossibly alive son.

His mother would set the kindhearted gentleman straight. The duchess would remember, or know someone else who did, that Mina was nothing but a tradesman's daughter with a blotted copybook. Her Grace would not approve her son's association with Lady Sparrow. She certainly would not invite Malachy Caldwell's daughter, the widow of the wastrel, wanton Lord Sparrowdale, into her home.

Mina was wrong. The duchess was elated. Guests in the great house? The more the merrier. A piquet partner? An old friend to reminisce with? Her Grace and Dorcas Albright were not truly friends, but they were both growing old, so they must have been young together. Besides, London was thinning of company these days, and Her Grace was weary of the usual social rounds. She would have traveled to the ducal seat in Somerset, but she was not happy there, with her daughter-in-law in charge. Now she had new faces, new gossip, a bit of intrigue, and a wedding to plan. As for the last, well, a mother could hope, couldn't she?

Her Grace liked the looks of the gel, except that Lady Sparrow still had that birdlike delicacy. She made the duchess appear plump by comparison, when everyone knew the dowager was not fat; she was formidable. No matter, the younger woman's lack of inches was more than amply compensated for by her pounds in the bank. Beyond that, Sparrowdale's widow was passably pretty, neat and dignified, without being coming. She was dressed tastefully instead of being draped in crepe—no one would believe she was grieving for that dirty dish Sparrowdale or her mushroom of a father no matter how much black she wore. The duchess did acknowledge that losing both of them, one on top of the other, had to be unsettling. Now, according to Lowell, she was in London paying Sparrowdale's debts, like the good, sensible woman she seemed. She was not flighty in the least, like those simpering chits he refused to partner at Almack's. In other words, Lady Sparrowdale was a perfect match for her son.

Of course, the chit could be too rich. Lolly just might get on his high horse and balk at living off a wealthy wife. Someone should tell the boy a second son could not afford such scruples—someone other than his mother, who had been repeating that advice for so long, Lolly never listened. Looking on the bright side, perhaps Sparrowdale's debts were so high that they would make inroads into the young widow's inheritance. Not too deep inroads, of course.

All in all, the Duchess of Mersford liked what she saw, and she liked the way her son already appeared to be protective of the lady. She liked how a slight smile played about his lips whenever the countess glanced his way. Her Grace liked, too, how Lady Sparrowdale's eyes followed Lolly's movements. It was a good start. The duchess was happy with her company.

Mina was happy to be at Merrison House until the matter of her husband's by-blows was resolved and she had a home of her own. This way she could make sure Lord Lowell let her participate in the investigation. "For I mean to join you in this inquiry, you understand," she had told him on the way to his family's town house that morning, when they left the park. "If you cannot accept that, having a woman as a partner, tell me now, before we go another block."

"We are not partners, madam, and cannot be, but not because you are a woman. We are employer and employee, which means that when you pay the piper, you get to call the tunes. Since you have not shown me your list of dates and initials, not given me more than the name Peregrine, I would be a fool to refuse your assistance. It is not what I am used to, having someone else along, but I will manage unless things grow dangerous. I do refuse to let you put yourself in peril, however, if for no other reason than that I would have to save you. The curricle could not half cover the cost of rescues. If you cannot accept *that*, tell me before we reach Mersford Square and my mother." Who would likely adopt Lady Sparrowdale, he knew, in her matchmaking glee at having an heiress to hand.

Mina had agreed to his terms, having no choice if she wished Lord Lowell's help. Now she was glad she had. The duchess did remember Mina's mother and was everything kind. Her Grace was an imposing female, with Lord Lowell's fair hair and blue eyes. Her blondness seemed to owe somewhat less to nature than to her coiffeur, and her eyesight appeared to need as much assistance. Still, she was not the least bit disapproving or disdainful of Mina's background. Her invitation to stay seemed sincere.

Of course the duchess did not know of the possible danger or Sparrowdale's indecent number of by-blows. His lordship had merely said that Mina was concluding her husband's unfinished business. With luck, Mina and that business—as many of them as she could find—would soon be on their way.

Cousin Dorcas was thrilled to be at Merrison House. At the Clarendon, no matter that it was the finest hotel in the city, Miss Albright had feared infested sheets, light-fingered maids, spoiled food, and being ogled by strange men in the hallways. She had also feared that Mina would expect chaperonage on her hey-go-mad hunt for Sparrowdale's seedlings. Dirty hired carriages, dirty uncivilized neighborhoods, and more strange men with dirty looks. Oh, dear. No matter how much Dorcas loved her young cousin, and how grateful she was for Mina's generosity, Dorcas was sure to have spasms within the sennight.

Now the escort of their hostess's son ought to placate propriety, although young Merrison was as strange as a two-headed hen. Why, anyone could see how his mother doted on him. Unless the current duke kept both of them punting on Tick, there was no reason for the gentleman to be working for a living, much less in such a nasty way. He did seem a decent sort, though, not at all intimidating in his eyeglasses. As for their hostess, the duchess enjoyed cards, suffered innumerable interesting complaints, and had a vast stock of gossip, ancient or new. Dorcas felt she had landed in clover. Best of all, Merrison House was desperately short of doilies. Miss Albright could be useful without even leaving the premises.

Harkness was pleased to take up residence in a well-run duke's residence, as a guest. The more out of joint the Merrison House butler's nose grew, in fact, the more Harkness enjoyed himself. He was Lady Sparrowdale's man of affairs for the nonce, entrusted with inspecting the various establishments offered for sale or lease by the real estate agents. He was also entrusted with visiting the various public houses where servants gathered, especially the staff of Sparr House. Surely, Lord Lowell and Mina's butler had decided, Sparrowdale's people were more likely to talk about their employers with Harkness than with a swell. Just as surely, someone there, the footmen or the coachmen, would know where the old earl had spent his evenings. Lowell thought he'd like to know where the new earl spent his, too.

Even the dog was happy to be at Merrison House, with its walled garden and tree-lined square just across the street. Merlin did not even need the key to the gate, since he was small enough to squeeze under the rungs. The cook was friendly, too, unlike the stiff-rumped chef at the Clarendon, with his curses and his meat cleaver.

Happiest of all that Lady Sparrowdale was at Merrison House was Lord Lowell Merrison himself. She was safe; he was working. He was never so content as when he was employed on an inquiry, and this one intrigued him. Other men loved to follow the fox. Lowell liked to untangle mysteries. He knew the countess was not telling the entire truth—she was not a good liar, stumbling over the words, studying her shoes—and the additional question of what she was hiding added to his enthusiasm for the chase. Putting Roderick Sparr in his place—or out of his place, as the case might be—was incentive enough for him to track the previous earl's pestilential path. He would pursue the investigation on his own, without remuneration, just to satisfy his curiosity and sense of fair play.

Of course it was always nicer to be paid, especially on the generous terms Lady Sparrowdale offered. The best reward of all, though, he decided, would be removing those worry lines from her brow and the troubled shadows from beneath her doe-brown eyes. Hell, he'd try to find Atlantis for Lady Sparrow, just for one of her sweet smiles. Yes, he was happy to have her under his roof.

Chapter Eleven

They began the search that same afternoon, while Harkness and Ochs, the Merrison House butler, argued over the disposition of Lady Sparrowdale's boxes and belongings. Dorcas and the duchess were busy comparing stitchery and symptoms.

They took the curricle again, with the same boy up behind to hold the horses when they made frequent stops. Often, they walked and he met them a few blocks ahead. They started checking churches in Kensington, then schools. If Peregrine Radway and his granny had lived here any length of time, someone would know them.

Unless, Lowell warned, the lad had given a false name and direction. Mina had the list with *P.R.* written on it, though, and so was hopeful.

None of the curates they spoke to recognized the name, nor did the superintendents of the nearby boys' schools. Mina's description of the boy's dark hair and aquiline nose seemed to strike a familiar chord with one of the instructors, but not even a coin could produce an address.

They could not very well go door to door, asking for a boy and his grandmother. There were too many houses, for one thing, long rows of attached buildings, and Perry had said they merely had rooms there. Scores of places displayed ROOMS TO LET signs outside, and flats were situated over every shop and office. For another thing, they were strangers, and the residents of this neighborhood did not trust anyone asking too many questions. Lowell misdoubted they were getting the honest answers to their inquiries.

He decided to try a new tack. Spotting a respectable-looking linen-draper's, he had Mina purchase a dress length and some ribbons. She refused to buy anything but black, although the clerk tried to show her a new burnt-orange watered silk that would have looked lovely with her hair and eyes. Lowell thought a gold muslin would become her, or peach. Black it was, though. While the clerk was wrapping the package, Lowell handed him an extra coin and quietly asked if he knew of any good seamstresses in the neighborhood, as he did not wish his companion to waste her time cutting and sewing.

The clerk looked at Lady Sparrowdale, winked, and said, "I'll wager you don't." He mentioned two or three names, none of them Radway.

"What was that about?" Mina wanted to know when they were back on the street.

Lowell placed the parcel under one arm and offered her the other. He thought about lying for a moment, but decided against it. The lady had to know what her presence meant in this neighborhood, in his company. "He assumed you were my mistress."

Mina stopped walking. "He what?"

"Well, Kensington is where a great many gentlemen house their *amours*. It is away from the eyes of the *beau monde*, but not too far for visits. The ladies like the bourgeois respectability, with tree-lined streets and children playing nearby, and the men like how the neighbors mind their own business, as we are finding. So when a fellow is seen with a pretty lady at his side, buying gewgaws like ribbons, the merchants suspect an affair."

"But I am a widow! I am not—"

"Bachelor fare. Of course not. I know that, but the clerk did not. What husband goes shopping with his wife? Dashed few. And we do not look like brother and sister, so the clerk's mind found the easiest connection. A man and a woman together are either related, by blood or by marriage, engaged, or engaged in an affair."

Mina could feel the warmth in her cheeks. "How embarrassing for you, that the man could think that you would . . . that I was your . . ."

He had to laugh. "Embarrassing? The fellow was nearly drooling with envy. Don't you know, such a comely conquest raises a fellow's consequence. Why, I'd be bursting with pride," he could not help teasing, just to see the pink tinges come and go in her face, "if the chap's suspicions were real."

Now her cheeks were on fire. "You must not say such things. It is forward."

"It is honest. You are an attractive woman, Lady Sparrowdale. I would be less than a man not to recognize that."

"Are you . . . are you flirting with me?"

"Of course not. I work for you, remember?"

Mina pretended to stare into a shop window so she would not have to look at Lord Lowell until she felt less discomposed. He had to be making fun of her, she thought, this handsome man with his elegant bearing. Gentlemen wanted her for her money, nothing else. Hadn't Sparrowdale told her that often enough, and her father before him? She was plain and skinny. And the window she was staring at contained corsets. Mina quickly moved off down the block, Lord Lowell following.

"I apologize if I gave offense," he said when he caught up with her again. "But it is best if you know what people will think when they see us together. In fact, in this neighborhood, it will serve our purposes better if they do think that, rather than that we are prying into matters better left secret."

"Yes, I can see that." Still, Mina insisted on going alone into the next few dressmaking establishments, asking if they employed a needlewoman she had heard of named Radway, one she could trust with her fine new length of black satin.

No one had heard of Perry's grandmother.

Across the street, his lordship asked a tobacconist if he knew of any seamstresses willing to repair a torn shirt. He asked the apothecary if any neighbor ladies darned

stockings, and he told the barber he fancied his mono-
gram on handkerchiefs, if he could find a willing embroi-
derer. They all looked at the well-built gent with his
Weston-tailored coat and gleaming top boots. They all
suggested he find himself a wife, if his mistress was too
lazy.

At the end of the block of shops, Lowell handed Mina
back into the curricle. It was growing late, and the duchess would be worried if they were not back by dark,
and dinner.

Mina would gladly have missed dinner, to keep going.
She sighed, loudly.

"What, disappointed?" Lowell asked. "We cannot
cover all the avenues in one day, but we can come back
early in the morning. Street vendors are out then, and
they know everyone."

"I suppose I will have to wait. I was hoping we would
have found Perry by now, and could start looking for
the others."

"Well, you will not make much of an investigator if
you become discouraged after one afternoon. Sometimes
these searches take weeks, not one afternoon."

She had been waiting four years. Another hour was
too long.

That evening, dinner was made lively by the duchess's
trying to convince Mina that her attendance at a harp
concert later could in no way be construed as disrespect-
ful to the recently deceased. The younger widow was
adamant, however: She was not in London for socializing. She had not been invited to the musicale. And she
did not like harp music.

"Stubborn chit," Her Grace muttered as she led her
guests from the dining room, but she was not offended.
In fact, she seemed pleased that her guest had backbone,
pleased enough that she decided to stay home too.

"You must not, on my account, Your Grace," Mina
said. "I could not continue to enjoy your hospitality
knowing I was depriving you of your entertainment."

"Bosh, my dear. I despise harp recitals too. I'd much

rather stay in and play at cards. What say you, Dorcas? Are you game?"

Cousin Dorcas was already shuffling the deck.

So was Lowell, at his club. He hoped to gather gossip about old Sparrowdale, but he also wished to spread a bit of information himself. His old friend Aldershaw gave him the perfect opening.

"I say, Lolly, I saw you driving out with a female this morning. Not your regular colorful bird of paradise, either. This one was more like a crow."

Ears perked up, the way Lowell knew they would. He was known to have exquisite taste in women as well as in clothes.

"Actually," he replied into the expectant quiet now surrounding the whist table, "she was more of a sparrow. Old Sparrowdale's widow, in fact. Her cousin was a bosom bow of my mother's, so they are staying in Mersford Square." There, Lowell thought, satisfied. Rumors and mushrooms both sprouted best in the dark. He wanted the lady's identity out in the light, so there would be no whispers and innuendoes. To make sure, he shuffled the deck into an arching cascade of cards, and said, "I had to show her around a bit, was all. My mother's guest, you know. Had to do the pretty."

They all knew his mother. Half of them cringed, remembering rapped knuckles from that indomitable grand dame's lorgnette. The other half, it seemed, remembered the young widow.

"Lady Sparrow is staying with you?" Aldershaw asked. "I'd say that is something to crow about, indeed."

Lord Lowell shrugged and dealt the cards. "She is staying with my mother. It has nothing to do with me, beyond the occasional escort duty. The lady is in mourning, so won't be going out much, thank heaven."

"Lud, with all the pots of gold old Malachy Caldwell left the chit, I'd lock her in my house too," Lord St. Martin said, while Viscount Compton declared Lowell a lucky dog.

Lowell sorted through his hand. "She has a dog too,

a pesky little mongrel that sheds hair on a fellow's inexpressibles, and an old maid cousin who makes lace." He hated to disparage Miss Albright and Merlin, but it was far better that the fellows thought him disinterested in the widow and her entourage. "You will be seeing a great deal more of me at the clubs."

"In that case," St. Martin said, "you'll be seeing less of me. I intend to camp on Merrison's doorstep until the widow is mine, along with her fortune. Is she still a mousy little thing?"

Lowell played a card. And bit his tongue. "She is passable."

"Hell, what heiress ain't?" Compton wanted to know. Then he turned to St. Martin. "And don't go counting your sparrow chicks 'til they hatch. My pockets are as empty as yours, so I'll be making a push for the widow myself."

Aldershaw made a rude noise. "Lady Sparrow is never up to your weight, you great ox. You'd crush the girl on your wedding night."

"As long as she signed the marriage lines first, who cares?"

Before Lord Lowell could object to the vulgarity and the cruelty, the much smaller St. Martin held up his glass in a mock toast. "Well, the little ladybird will fit me perfectly, and her fortune will too. And who said anything about marriage?"

Lowell had had all he could stand. It was one thing for word of Lady Sparrowdale's presence to get around Town. It was quite another for her name to be bandied around the men's clubs. Next these muckworms would be making wagers on who would win her and her wealth, or who would bed her. He threw down his cards. "Forgive me for spoiling your game, gentlemen"—he did not specify which game—"but Lady Sparrowdale is neither a ladybird nor a high flyer. She is a guest of my mother's."

"Does that mean you are staking your own claim, Lowell?" Viscount Compton wanted to know.

"No, it merely means that, as a guest there, Lady Sparrowdale has the protection of Merrison House, the same as, say, my sister would have. Or one of your sisters. I would not see her importuned by down-at-heels hell-rakers, nor her good name sullied. I am afraid I will have to insist on the proper respect due to a lady, and one who is in mourning, besides."

Lord Lowell was not handy with his fives, although he was physically fit. Without his spectacles, he could barely see a fist before it connected with his jaw. Nor was he proficient at swordplay, since his glasses tended to fall off with every lunge or parry. He was, however, a deuced good shot with a pistol. Besides, everyone liked him. Lowell was a good friend, always ready with a loan when the dibs were in tune.

The card players all nodded, understanding about protecting sisters and upholding the honor of one's house.

It was St. Martin who asked, "But we can still bring her bouquets, can't we?"

Chapter Twelve

*C*ousin Dorcas went to bed that evening some twenty pence richer. Mina would have followed, but the duchess asked her to stay behind a moment to share a last cup of tea.

"Old ladies do not need as much sleep, you know," Her Grace said, ignoring the fact that Dorcas had been yawning over the cards for the last hour while the duchess tried to recoup her losses.

"You will have to go out sometime, you know," she said while Mina was pouring out the tea.

Mina suddenly forgot how much sugar the duchess preferred, and had to ask.

"It's plain speaking, I know," Her Grace went on. "Old ladies can be forgiven that, too. But you cannot stay holed up here forever."

"I was out all afternoon, Duchess"—which was how Lord Lowell's mother had announced she wished to be addressed. Her Grace was not going to waste her breath on "Miss Albright" or "Lady Sparrowdale" either. They were Dorcas and Minerva before the first hand of cards that evening.

"Bosh. I do not mean that haring around with my son on whatever quest it is you have. And no, Lolly never discusses his cases with me, so you do not have to worry on that count. I mean showing your face at social gatherings, and I do not refer to balls and Venetian breakfasts, so don't spout that tripe about mourning. If the members of the *ton* do not see you, they will start guessing about you and why you are in hiding. They will likely assume you are afflicted with your husband's condition."

Mina set her teacup down with an audible thunk. "I do not care what any of them think."

"You'll care well enough when you start looking around for a new husband and all the decent men run away. Fortune hunters and basket-scramblers will be all you have to choose from."

"That is no matter. I do not intend to marry again."

"What about children? Dorcas told me how grief-stricken you were at the loss of your son. My sympathies. I lost two infants myself, which made Lolly and his brothers and sister that much more precious to me. You are young now, but you will want others before it is too late."

"I do hope to have children, a houseful." She knew that if Dorcas had mentioned Mina's lost son, she would also have mentioned Sparrowdale's sons. Besides, if Mina found any of the children, she needed a place to bring them until she had a house of her own. The duchess had to know. "In fact, Lol—Lord Lowell is going to help me."

"My son is going to help you start a family? I am delighted. Of course, I would prefer to attend the wedding first. An engagement announcement would do, I suppose, if you were in that much of a hurry."

Mina cursed the blush that flooded her cheeks. She also cursed interfering old ladies, and their spectacled sons, for putting her in such an uncomfortable position. She should have stayed at the hotel and taken her chances with Roderick. "I do not mean children of my own, Duchess."

"Of course you don't, silly chit that you are. I was merely teasing. A mother's dreams, don't you know. Well, you would, if you do not destroy all your chances."

"Your Grace?"

"Dorcas, not Lolly, mind, told me about that debt of your husband's that brought you to London. His bastards, not his vowels, and how you plan to adopt as many as you can. Do not do it, girl."

"Should I leave them in the gutter, then?"

"No one's saying you cannot do right by them. Lud knows you can afford to, if half the rumors are true. But that's not the same as taking them into your home. They will ruin your life."

"They will give it meaning."

The duchess tsk-ed at the idealism of youth. "They will make you a byword. Not even a fortune hunter would have you then, with so many baseborn children to share your bounty."

"Good. I would rather have children who need me, than a man who needs my money."

"Children grow up and go away. What will you do then?"

"What did you do, Duchess?"

"Impertinent chit. Still, I like you. I would not see you dwindle into a lonely old age with naught but letters from the ungrateful brats, and your silly dog."

Merlin had not left the duchess's side, waiting for the tidbits from the tea tray she passed down to him when she thought Mina was not looking. Now Her Grace scratched behind the little dog's ears and stared at the fire in the nearby hearth. "My husband strayed once, you know. Well, of course you do not, but nearly everyone else in London knew at the time, I was that furious. I was outraged when I discovered Mersford had carried on an affair during the months I was away, tending to my dying mother. He broke off the relationship, of course, as soon as I returned, but there was a child. The mother left him on our doorstep. I could have brought him up here, and thought of it, such a sweet little chap he was. Brighter than my own firstborn, I am sorry to admit. But what kind of life would he have led, under the bar sinister? I made sure the boy was well provided for with a respectable family instead. He is a renowned barrister today, a friend and advisor to Merrill, my son who is now duke."

"And what of your husband? Did he have nothing to say?"

"After saying he was sorry? And saying it every time

I invited the boy to Merry's birthday celebrations or vacations to Brighton? What could he say? He never strayed again."

"My husband was not so honorable."

"Your husband was a cad of the first order. Do not let him continue to rule your life. Do what is right for the children—but do what is best for you, too, Minerva. You deserve some happiness."

Mina sat there long after the duchess had sought her bed, thinking. How could she know what was best for Sparrowdale's children? She had to find them first, see if they were situated in pleasant homes. She had never thought much beyond gathering them, if they needed her. She needed them.

And later, when they had gone off to families of their own? She could always take in other orphans, Mina supposed. She could even start a home for unwanted children of the aristocracy. If having Sparrowdale's bastards around put her beyond the pale of polite society, taking in *their* indiscretions ought to see her ostracized once and for all. Good, Mina thought. She did not want anything to do with a world that venerated wastrels and wickedness, yet disdained honest workmen. So what if she was sunk so far beneath contempt that no gentlemen offered her marriage? Then she would not be put to the effort of refusing them.

Mina did not want a husband. An image of a gentle smile intruded into her thoughts, and—no, she did not want a husband. Having children to love would be enough.

She was still in the drawing room, idly turning the cards for Speculation, losing every game for lack of attention, when Lord Lowell returned home.

"Did you learn anything tonight?" she asked after he brought a decanter of wine and two glasses over to the card table.

Lowell had learned that he had an unexpected spark of chivalry where this female was concerned, and an even

more unwelcome streak of jealousy. He'd been furious
when his friends spoke so coarsely of the widow, the way
they spoke of opera dancers and orange-sellers. When
they talked of courting her, though, Lowell had wanted
to strangle St. Martin with his own neckcloth, cut down
Compton, and annihilate Aldershaw.

He was amazed at how angry he got, the man who
prided himself on rational, deductive reason, not raw
emotion. It was not as if he wanted to marry the
woman—or any woman—so why did he care when those
rakes mentioned calling on his Lady Sparrow? Because
they were only interested in her money, that was why.
They had never seen her, to admire those deep brown
eyes and that clear, rosy complexion. They had never
spoken to her, to understand either her intelligence or
her righteous principles. No, they wanted her fortune.
Lady Sparrowdale herself was a minor inconvenience on
the way to the bank.

She deserved better, Lowell thought, especially after
being wed to a bounder like Sparrowdale. She deserved
a man who did not need her money, so she never had
to doubt his affection, and one who would give her children of her own, so she did not need the dead earl's.

Lowell hated that paragon, too, whoever he was.

In the end, of course, he had been forced into granting
his friends permission to call, repeating that the widow
was merely a guest who would choose her own friends,
assemble her own court of admirers. He would not be
among them. He was merely an employee.

"Did you?" she asked again, reminding him of his status after sipping at her wine. "Did you hear anything
about Sparrowdale?"

"Nothing except that no one thought much of him or
his son. Unless you mean Roderick. The word is that he
is desperately trying for Westcott's girl. The odds are
running heavily against that match, though. They say
Westcott has agreed to let the chit have a say in choosing
her fiancée this time, and she has told friends that Roderick is too old."

LADY SPARROW   85

"If she is just now having her come-out, I would say
so too. He is past thirty."

Lowell was eight and twenty. "Thirty is not terribly
old."

"To a miss of seventeen or eighteen, it is, believe me."
She set her glass down and went back to the cards.

Sparrowdale had to have been nearly sixty when they
wed, Lowell calculated. That dastard, he thought, sipping
at his wine and admiring the candlelight glowing on her
smooth skin. And damn her father too.

"Speaking of engagements," Mina said, reshuffling the
deck after yet another loss, "your mother has ambitions,
I fear."

"To see me wed? I know. She always does. With my
sister and older brother married, and my younger brother
in the army, she has to concentrate all her efforts on my
behalf. But I have not let her chivvy me into leg shackles
yet, so I am not worried."

"I meant . . . That is, she thinks that you and I . . ."

"Do not worry about that, either. She may hint, but
she would never force us together. You might have other
concerns, however. Now that you are known to be in
Town, gentlemen will be seeking your company."

"Seeking my purse, more likely. Harkness turned them
away at the door at Sparrows Nest. I can simply instruct
Ochs to do the same. I shall not be at home to gentlemen callers."

Well, that would make Lowell happy, anyway.

The countess continued, "According to your mother,
those so-called suitors will disappear as soon as they
learn I am trying to find Sparrowdale's children." She
raised her chin. "You see, I am meaning to make a home
for them. Cousin Dorcas told the duchess, so you would
learn of my plans sooner or later."

"Sooner. Harkness and I had a comfortable cose before going on our separate fact-finding missions this evening." The talk had been profitable for both of them,
the butler pocketing a gold coin and Lowell learning
more about his employer and her plans.

"He does not approve either." Mina tossed the cards into a pile. "Useless pasteboards that never win. There must be one missing."

"Undoubtedly," he agreed, then said, "they want your happiness, you know."

"I will be happy enough with the children."

"Even if you are ostracized by society and never receive another offer of marriage? That is what Harkness fears, and my mother, I would wager."

"Particularly then. None of those men want to marry me. None could claim the least pretense of affection for the shipbuilder's scrawny daughter, only for his bequest. I want no marriage of convenience. Having my income pay another wastrel's debts, having my fortune handed over to a here-and-thereian, would be most inconvenient to my plans for starting an orphans' home."

"I can see where it would be. But do you not think a decent man might be interested in you? One who would not want your father's money?"

"Hah. I doubt such a pattern card exists. And no. I am still a tradesman's daughter, despite Sparrowdale's title. I am still a drab little female of no particular talent or accomplishment to recommend me."

Perhaps that last glass of wine was one too many, but Lord Lowell muttered an imprecation as he moved to replace the decanter.

"Excuse me, my lord, did you just refer to me as a goose?"

"No, I called you a silly goose. How could you not know what a deucedly attractive woman you are? Slight, yes, but perfectly formed. I am not interested in marriage, and I am not interested in your money, except for my fee, of course, and I find you beautiful. Why, if you were not a guest under my own roof—and if I were not working for you—I would try to get up a flirtation myself."

Mina had not had nearly enough wine for this. She swallowed a large gulp of it. "You . . . you would?"

He stood near her, leaning against the table. "I would. I would tell you that your eyes are like morning choco-

late, hot and sweet and inviting." He reached a hand up
to loosen one of the brown curls near her cheek. "And
I would tell you that your hair feels like a silk waterfall
through my fingers, and that I would trade my new curricle for the chance to spread it across my pillow."

"Oh, dear," Mina said, reaching for her glass again.
"You should not be saying those things."

"I am not. I am just telling you what I would say, were
I flirting with you, to prove that not all men see pound
notes when they look at you. I see a kind, caring woman
of rare determination and honor. And I see an alluring
mix of innocence and mystery that begs a man to discover its secrets." He leaned closer still, close enough
that her breath fogged his glasses. "If I were flirting, of
course, I would beg to taste the wine on your lips."

The glass fell out of Mina's nerveless fingers as her
investigator, her private detective, by all that was holy
and some that were not, leaned closer still. The sound
of the fallen glass brought both of them to their senses.

Lowell stepped back and straightened his waistcoat.
"But I cannot say any of those things, of course. They
would be highly improper in an employee."

They would be highly improper in a bordello! Those
were not words of flirtation. They were words of outright
seduction. Worse, Mina feared, it would have worked, if
Lord Lowell had not recalled that he worked too. For
her.

Chapter Thirteen

They were out early the next morning, as planned. Being from the country, Mina did not mind. She was used to rising with the sun. Lowell was more used to seeing dawn on his way home than on his way out. He was still yawning when he took up the curricle's reins for the drive to Kensington. Not only had his sleep been shortened by a few hours, but it had been disturbed by troubling dreams.

How in the name of Hades had he almost kissed Lady Sparrow? He was her employee, by Jupiter. Surely there were critical principles involved here, although damned if he could recall them so early in the morning. For certain he had never wanted to embrace any of his other clients. He had been absolutely mind-boggled and mortified when Lady Carstair threw herself into his unwilling arms after he returned her diamonds. Of course Lady C was fifty if she was a day, and fifty pounds heavier than he was. Lud, he would have had nightmares, thinking of that woman's kiss. Instead, he'd dreamed of soft, wine-dewed lips, and awoke with a smile on his face and—and nothing that could not be relieved by a cold splash of wash water. For Lady Sparrow, by Jupiter, who was looking her usual neat-as-a-pin, dark-clad self. Obviously their near embrace had not affected the widow one whit, for she was busy reiterating their tactics for the morning.

Mina had to keep her mind busy, or else she was liable to dwell on the man sitting so close to her on the narrow driving bench. His hair as still damp from his morning ablutions, and a bit of sticking plaster was clinging to his chin, from where he had nicked himself shaving. Otherwise he was as elegant as ever, with his intricately tied neckcloth, and Bath blue superfine straining across his broad shoulders. Obviously their near embrace had not affected his lordship one little bit, for he was so bored with her company he was yawning.

When they reached today's destination, they spoke to milkmaids and egg boys and muffin men, to knife sharpeners and coal heavers. If Granny Radway lived in the neighborhood, she did not buy her necessities from these street vendors, or else no one was saying. Lowell thought they would have admitted knowing the woman, for far more coins changed hands than was warranted by their purchases.

The flower-seller thought she might have seen a dark-haired boy with a grandmother who took in sewing, but they never bought her violets or bunches of lavender, so she could not be sure on which street they lived. "Per'aps Cobbler's Court," she suggested after Lowell bought yet another nosegay of violets.

Mina had her lap filled with flowers as they headed in the direction the girl had indicated. She breathed in the sweet country scent and smiled. "I am glad you were so generous. Now that young girl does not have to work as hard today."

"It was nothing to me." Lowell flashed her a quick smile back. "It was your money. You pay my expenses, remember."

No one on Cobbler's Court knew of Perry or his grandmother.

"I do not understand why we cannot find them. Kensington is simply not that big that no one would know of them," Mina complained as they returned to the curricle.

"They might have kept to themselves. Young Peregrine could have been instructed by a retired schoolmaster living next door, and they might attend a church in a neighboring parish. The grandmother might take on sewing from one of the Mayfair modistes, and do her shopping on the way home. Or the boy could have been making the entire story up out of whole cloth. But we have not covered every street. Don't give up. We'll return after breakfast, when more of the shops will be open."

After sampling the sticky buns and the meat pies and the fruit tarts from the street-sellers, Mina was anything but hungry. Lowell, however, declared himself too sharp-set to continue another block. Lady Sparrow might eat like a bird, but he was a full-grown man, he reminded her, with a man's appetites.

She was all too afraid of that.

When they returned home, the dowager duchess was already breaking her fast, the usual stack of invitations next to her well-stocked setting. After filling a plate from the sideboard, Lowell glanced briefly at his correspondence, then raised an eyebrow at the pile of mail next to Lady Sparrowdale's seat.

Mina looked through the letters to see if a note had been forwarded from Sparrows Nest, from Peregrine. There was a message from her solicitor and another from the land agent, but the rest were invitations, all from people she did not know.

Her Grace noticed and frowned. "Yes, we are going to have to do something about that. The gossipmongers will be battering at the door next, to get a glimpse of you, my dear. I will not have the house overrun with snooping scandal-seekers, nor the fortune hunters you are bound to attract like bees to a flower." She leafed through the invitations in her own pile, using her lorgnette to read the inscriptions. "Her Grace and Guest. Amelia, Duchess of Mersford and Minerva, Countess Sparrowdale. Everyone wishes to meet you."

"What, I was not included?" Lowell asked, cutting his beefsteak.

"You have your own invites, you clunch," his fond mother replied. "Besides, these are to quiet affairs, since everyone knows Lady Sparrowdale is in mourning. Hostesses know better than to invite you to a poetry reading or a chorale."

"Thank goodness," he replied, setting his own correspondence aside to scan the newspapers while he ate. It was possible the boy's grandmother advertised for mending.

The duchess tapped his newspaper with her lorgnette. "Pay attention, Lolly. I think we should have a dinner party in Minerva's honor. Get it over with, let them gawk and goggle, then send them on their way. They'll see she is a prettily behaved female, with no airs about her and nothing to hide. They will also see she is not a lamb for the fleecing, not with us as watchdogs." Speaking of dogs, Her Grace slipped a bit of kidney to Merlin, at her side.

"Oh, no. I would not wish you to—" Mina began.

"Nonsense. There is nothing I enjoy more. A select group of friends only, no mushrooms, no mealymouthed misses, and no men on the prowl for a meal ticket. What do you think, Lolly?"

"I think you are going to do what you wish in any case, but it sounds unexceptionable, if Lady Sparrowdale does not object."

They both turned to Mina, who was merely nibbling the edges of a piece of toast. "Perhaps a small"—she stressed the *small*—"gathering would serve to satisfy the curious, and then I could return to obscurity."

Small chance of that, Lowell thought as he helped himself to another serving of kippers. If he were a betting man, he'd not wager a ha'penny against the pretty and wealthy Lady Sparrow becoming a Toast, mourning or not. Tidbits about Sparrowdale's by-blows were an added attraction.

While the duchess planned her party, Lowell decided the best way to keep the countess out of the clutches of her would-be admirers was to keep her out of the house. He pushed his nearly empty plate aside. "If that is all you are going to eat, Countess, we might as well go back to Kensington."

"See that you are returned by luncheon, my dears. Minerva cannot afford to miss any meals, lest people say we have her locked in her chamber on bread and water. What the gel eats could not keep a pigeon alive."

Lowell wrapped two rolls in a napkin to take along, just in case. Mina took the dog. He raised a golden brow. "I am never *that* hungry."

"I thought we might take Merlin. Maybe someone will recognize him. Or else, if we set him down anywhere near his house, perhaps he will lead us there."

"And perhaps I ought to return the curricle after all, if you are going to do all the work. That is brilliant thinking."

The theory was brilliant. The dog was less so.

Set down from the curricle, Merlin raced around, barking at the horses and the pedestrians as if he had never seen street traffic before. Mina attached his leather lead back onto the collar the grooms at Sparrows Nest had fashioned for the small dog.

They walked behind him, the curricle left in the hands of the tiger, but Merlin seemed more interested in the streetlamps than in finding his way home. Then he started wagging his short tail and pulling ahead. Mina let go of the leash, letting it drag behind the dog, and then they had to hurry to keep up as Merlin dashed around a corner.

Into a butcher's shop.

"Blast. I thought we were onto something." Lowell bought the dog a sausage anyway. "I don't suppose you recognize the little beggar, do you?" he asked the butcher.

"Nivver seen 'im afore, an' I keep track o' all th' regulars, like. There's ones you got to keep yer eyes on, ye ken." He tossed the dog another link.

Lowell took his eyes from the view of Lady Sparrowdale bending over the animal to straighten his collar. "While we are here, I might as well ask if you know a lad, a Peregrine Radway? It's his dog, and we are trying to return the mutt."

The butcher shook his head. "I never seen t'only Radway I know with no dog."

"But he is a young boy, about three and ten, with dark hair and a prominent nose?" Mina asked excitedly, stepping closer to Lowell and the butcher. At last, a lead.

Lowell placed another coin on the counter, and the butcher threw a slab of ham to the dog. "Aye, that be our Perry, all right. Welly, m'wife calls 'im, on account a' the general an 'is beak. The nipper makes deliveries for me, or did, afore."

"Afore—that is, before what?" Mina wanted to know, nudging his lordship to offer the man yet another coin.

Lowell was way ahead of her. This time a gold piece found its way into a greasy pocket, and a beefsteak found the floor. "Afore 'is health took a turn."

"He is ill? Oh, no. Has a doctor been called? Does he need special medicines?" Mina would have hired round-the-clock nursing and the king's own physicians.

" 'Twere a sawbones 'e needed, t' set 'is broken jaw back in place, when that bloody bastard—pardon, ma'am—got done w'im."

Lowell put his arm around the countess when he saw her sway. "I knew I should have sent a footman with him," she cried. "It is all my fault, sending him home with a full purse and no guard."

"I don't know about no purse, but t'boy got home all right from wherever 'e took 'isself orf to. It were 'ere in Town some mohunk set on 'im. Near killed t' lad, 'e did, but for someone callin' t' Watch, what scared 'im orf."

"And the boy is all right, except for the broken jaw?" Lowell asked, still keeping one arm on Lady Sparrowdale's shoulder, for comfort. For whose comfort was questionable.

"An' a few cracked ribs, 'sides bruises an' scrapes. 'E looked like one a' my slabs a' beef." The butcher hefted his big meat cleaver. "I'd teach that dirty scum t'pick on men 'is own size, not boys."

Mina gladly accepted Lord Lowell's support. Whatever had befallen the child, she felt responsible. Now she had to find him more than ever, to make sure Perry was cared for, and his grandmother, too, if the purse had been stolen.

The butcher was not quite ready to give up his errand boy's address yet, despite Lord Lowell's coins. He did not trust the gentry, not that he thought they had anything to do with the attack on poor Perry, but just in general. In the end, though, it was the tears in the lady's pretty brown eyes that convinced him.

The boy and his granny lived in rooms out by the gardens, he told them, in a house owned by a retired curate who gave a few local boys lessons. He held services in a tiny chapel there, too, which was why they had found no trace of Perry, as Lowell had suspected.

He gave the butcher the price of a cow, for a sack of sausages for the dog and a street address, and then they left.

Mina was shaken. "Do you think the attack on Perry could be related to my search?" she asked as they drove.

"If it was not a robbery, and young Radway was not involved in other skullduggery, I cannot believe the beating was a mere coincidence. I would guess someone was trying to stop him from speaking, to you or the magistrate. We'll know in a few minutes."

First they had to stop to let the dog be sick.

Chapter Fourteen

Perry was not at the address given. Neither was his grandmother, nor the retired curate. No one answered the front door of the narrow cottage, nor the kitchen entry around back. The place looked abandoned, with one blown flower on the solitary rosebush in the tiny backyard.

Mina felt worse than before. "I only wanted to help, to make his life better." She glanced around at the unkempt dirt path, the missing step. "Now he is hurt, and gone who knows where."

Lowell was looking around, wondering which of the few dwellings in the area might contain someone with knowledge of that very thing. He led her away from the cottage. "Fustian. It is not your fault, none of it. He came to you, if you recall. The boy sought you out, not the other way around. He'd already been to the solicitor and to Roderick, you said. They knew of his existence long before you did. They did not listen to his pleas for help—only you were decent enough to do that—but they knew of the danger, if he is, indeed, a threat to one of them."

"Surely you cannot suspect Mr. Sizemore, my man of affairs."

"No, he is not high on my list. He has nothing to gain, that I can see, and nothing to lose, either. It is your money you would be spending on the children, none of his. I intend to have a conversation with the man this

very afternoon, though, to see what manner of fellow
he is."

"Cousin Dorcas admires him greatly, if that is any rec-
ommendation. She does not, generally, like many
gentlemen."

"She has hardly spoken two words to me, so I must
suppose her approval of Sizemore counts for something.
Does she also esteem Lord Sparrowdale—Roderick,
that is?"

"She will not stay in the room with him."

"Ah. That says a great deal about Miss Albright's acumen." The cottage they had reached was also empty, so
Lowell headed back in the other direction, pacing his
steps to Lady Sparrow's shorter ones.

"Then you agree with me that Roderick might be behind the attack on Perry?"

"If what you say is true, that his title and fortune and
future are in jeopardy, then certainly. Any one of those
is motive enough for mayhem. I doubt if Roderick himself would skulk around street corners to thrash a young
boy—and chance being identified—but he would not be
above hiring a thug to do his bidding. Unfortunately,
one cannot convict a man because his taste in waistcoats
is abominable."

"Or because he pads his calves."

"No, does he? There is something inherently untrust-
worthy about a chap who resorts to sawdust and buckram
wadding, isn't there?" he said with a smile.

Mina could not help glancing at her companion's
nether limbs. She doubted Lord Lowell had to use any
artifice to attain his manly physique. His waistcoat this
morning was a subdued gray, with the narrowest of saf-
fron stripes. If one were to judge a gentleman by his
appearance, her detective was top of the trees. She pulled
her eyes away from her impolite scrutiny and noticed
movement on the top floor of the curate's cottage,
through the small, curtainless window.

They went to investigate. Actually, Lord Lowell went,
telling Mina to stay behind with the curricle and the tiger

and the dog, who was too ill to get down at his own
house. There was no telling what unpleasantness they
might find, Lowell warned, heading up the dark stairwell.
Mina did not stay back, of course. She had nursed Lord
Sparrowdale in his extremities. Nothing could be worse.

As she climbed, the odors of paint and lacquer and
turpentine met her nose, and she could hear Lord Lowell's deep voice in conversation with another man.

"Well, where did they all go, then?" he was asking.

When she reached the final landing, Mina realized she
was in an artist's garret, with canvases stacked from floor
to ceiling. Some were finished and framed, while others
were in various stages of completion. They were all of
women. Naked women. She fixed her eyes on the young
artist himself, rather than on the embarrassing paintings.
He was dark, unshaven, and unwashed, with streaks of
paint on his chest where his shirt was open. No, she
could not look there either. She stared at Lord Lowell
instead. "They must have told you," he said to the artist,
"if they left you here in the house."

"*Non, non.* They do not tell Marcel thees thing. Or I
forgot, *n'est-ce-pas*? The divine inspiration, she comes,
and Marcel paints. He does not bother with the *petit folie*
of the common man who sees no vision of beauty."

He did eat, though. For a half-crown, Marcel recalled
mention of a sister in the country. The curate's sister?
Madame Radway's sister? Perhaps Marcel's sister. He
rubbed his face in thought, leaving a broad new stripe
of carmine on his cheek. "*Non.* I have no more knowledge of thees people. I know a *jeune fille*'s leg, the dimple
on her knee, that fold where her thigh meets a man's
dreams, where—"

Mina choked, and not on the odd smell mixed in with
the turpentine.

Marcel whirled around, paintbrush in hand, and spotted her in the doorway. "*Mon Dieu,* a mirage!"

"No, she is a muttonhead who does not listen to orders," Lowell muttered, trying to shield her from the
artist's view.

Marcel bounded around him. "*Non,* she is my muse, my inspiration! That skin, those eyes, that hair! I must paint her. I will die if I cannot paint her."

Lowell vowed the dauber was going to die anyway, if he came one inch closer to Lady Sparrow. He stepped in front of her again. "Perhaps I would consider commissioning you to do the lady's portrait—"

From behind him, Mina made a sound somewhere between an *eek* and an *eck.*

"Properly clothed, of course," Lowell added. "We can talk about it more when you bring me an address for Mrs. Radway." He handed over one of his cards and dragged the countess down the stairs so fast her half-boots barely touched the worn treads.

"He was quite talented, wasn't he?" Mina ventured when they were in the curricle and Lord Lowell was turning it for home, his jaw set in angry lines.

"The man could have been Michelangelo for all I care. You should have listened to me, dash it. That was no place for a lady!"

"But it was not dangerous, and that was our agreement." Dealing with the dying Lord Sparrowdale had given Mina practice in managing irate gentlemen, if nothing else. She quickly changed the subject. "Do you think Monsieur Marcel will remember the address, or remember to bring it?"

"I am surprised the nodcock can remember his name, with all the fumes in that place. I will send a man around to the other neighbors tonight, when they might be home from their work. And I can have someone check the church registry for the curate's name and next of kin. We will find the boy, do not worry."

Not worrying was easier said than done, which Lowell seemed to understand. "Besides, you gave him enough blunt to get away from any more dangers, so he is safe."

"You do not think Roderick will be looking for him?"

"I think that if we cannot find Perry, neither can the new earl. Why would he try, anyway? If what we suspect is true, the beating was a warning."

"Unless Roderick was trying to find information about

the other children, especially about the one who might usurp his title."

Lowell shook his head. "No, I do not think so. If all he wanted was information, he would have had the boy kidnapped and brought to him for questioning. And if Perry had told what he knew, then he and his grandmother would have had no reason to flee. The others are as safe as they ever were."

Except for the fire at the foundling home.

They did not find out about the fire until after luncheon, during which the duchess planned her dinner party. Mina did not know many of the names Her Grace mentioned, except by repute. When she claimed the company was flying too high for a simple country widow, the duchess raised her lorgnette to an eye the same shade of blue as her son's and announced, "No company is too lofty for the home of the Duke of Mersford, nor for a guest in the house. Some, including our harum-scarum heir to the throne, are not elevated enough. Invitations to Merrison House are highly prized."

"Give over, ma'am," Lowell told Mina from his end of the table. "My mother will not be swayed, so if she says you will enjoy yourself at the dinner, enjoy yourself you will. I have learned it is easier not to argue, for one always loses."

The duchess let her looking glass fall back on its ribbon. "There, do you see what a brilliant son I have, and what a comfortable husband he will make some lucky—"

Lord Lowell's complacency did not extend to discussions of his matrimonial prospects over mutton. "When were you planning on holding this dinner in Lady Sparrowdale's honor, Mother? We might have to travel out of town to pursue the investigation."

"Nonsense. Nothing is more important than establishing Minerva's *bona fides* in the *beau monde*. I thought Tuesday next. You shall have to plan accordingly."

With a wink to the countess, he told his mother, "You might also order a clear night. You would not want the occasion marred by a rainstorm."

The duchess was too busy discussing the menu with Cousin Dorcas to reply to his barb. She did mention that the gardens were lovely this time of year. She would see that lights were strung along the paths, in case any of the company wished to stroll there, anyone with a particle of romance in his soul.

Ignoring her gibe in turn, Lowell turned back to Mina. "I thought you might come with me to visit your solicitor this afternoon while we wait for my men to report back. If he is any kind of decent lawyer, he will not discuss your affairs without your permission." And if Lowell was any decent judge, the house would soon be filled with gentleman callers. The hall was already cluttered with floral tributes—and the caper merchants had not even seen what an angel she looked. They would never see, if he had his druthers, but for now he could keep her away from the hordes, away from the house.

They were about to leave, without the dog this time, when Harkness intercepted them. He ignored Ochs's cluck of disapproval that a jumped-up rustic butler should be using the front door, and followed them back to the privacy of the library, where he told them about the fire.

He had been out looking at properties for sale or rent, without finding anything satisfactory. The ceilings of the house he was inspecting had water spots, not a good sign, so Harkness was ready to move on when the fire brigade went by. Curious as to how the London insurance companies dealt with fires, he had followed along, with a great many other interested spectators.

The building that was ablaze, he had learned from a neighboring onlooker, was a home for orphans, a private establishment, not a government-funded institution. The woman who ran it, Mrs. Ella Strickland, raised up children—for a fee. They were boys and girls no one wanted, but no one wanted to see them thrown into almshouses either. As long as the fee was paid, Ella kept children born when their mothers were "visiting abroad," or when their father's new wives made clean sweeps, or when both parents were dead and the relatives would not take on the chore. One boy, he'd heard, was a cripple, and the parents could not bear to look at him. Conscience money, that's what they all paid, instead of leaving the infants at the door of some church.

When Harkness got there, Mrs. Strickland was being comforted by the captain of the fire brigade—very comforted, indeed, it seemed to the watchers—and the children were in a row, across the street. Harkness could not get a good look at them, through the smoke and the crowds and the horse-drawn water wagons, but someone said they were all rescued. The blaze was quickly extinguished before the house was destroyed, to the onlookers' applause. Harkness thought Lady Sparrowdale and her high-born investigator would be particularly interested in knowing that no one was injured, but all of the home's records had been destroyed. And Ella Strickland had either taken to smoking cigars or entertaining gentlemen callers who did, or else someone had started the fire in her office.

Chapter Fifteen

*T*hey took a carriage this time, at Mina's request. She wanted to be prepared in case they were able to bring a child home with them. She would have no youngster of hers—or her husband's—languish a moment longer than necessary in dire circumstances, if such were the case.

"You will never make a Bow Street investigator, ma'am, leaping to such conclusions," Lowell told her as he handed her up into the coach. "We have no way of knowing yet whether this establishment is one of those filthy rats' nests where infants go barefoot and hungry. Your foundling just might be living a life of ease, healthy and happy. He or she might not wish to leave with you at all."

He told the driver to spring the horses, though, Mina noted, as anxious as she to reach the Strickland Charity Home. She twisted the strings on her reticule, willing traffic to make way for them.

Lowell was content to take the facing seat, his back to the horses, where he might watch the countess, surely a more pleasant view than the scenery he had seen a hundred times. Of course she was in yet another black gown, but he thought her expressive eyes would never grow boring. Trying to lighten the worry lines on her brow, he asked, "Have you given any consideration to what you will do with the child once you have it in your keeping?"

"I did ask your mother," Mina quickly replied, lest he think she was presuming on Her Grace's hospitality.

"She said I might place the child in the old nursery, since your brother seldom visits with his children. It is a temporary arrangement only, of course. Harkness is bound to find something suitable any day. And you must not think that I mean my child—my foster child—to be a burden on your household. Cousin Dorcas and I will take care of him or her until I can hire a nursery maid and a governess or a tutor. Whatever is required. Your people will not be overworked, I swear."

Cousin Dorcas was looking forward to caring for one of Sparrowdale's bastards as much as she was looking forward to old age, but Mina did not mention that.

"Nonsense," Lowell replied, sounding very much like his authoritative mother. "Old Nanny Vann is at her sister's in Hans Town, complaining of too much time on her hands." Vanny was complaining her Lolly ought to settle down and start his own nursery, but Lowell did not mention that. "And we have more than enough servants at Merrison House to look after any number of waifs. No, what I meant was what you will do about the child's future, not tomorrow?"

"I cannot make plans, of course, until I know the child. We do not even know if it is a boy or a girl. For that matter, there might be more than one of Sparrowdale's offspring at this place—or none. Then too, the fire might have been a coincidence. Fires break out all the time, I understand."

"That fire was as coincidental as Perry Radway being set upon by footpads," Lowell stated positively. "There is definitely a connection. We both believe we will find one of the children—a boy, since a girl would be no threat to anyone's inheritance. Would you be doing this lad a favor by taking him into your home? He cannot be educated or trained in the ways of a gentleman, you know, unless you think such traits are born in the blood."

Mina could not imagine that someone like Lord Lowell would not exhibit good breeding, be he acting as blacksmith or boatswain. The man was a gentleman from his knowing blue eyes to his tapered fingers to his kindness to the flower girl. Yet Sparrowdale was born a gentle-

man, as was his makebait son. No, Mina did not think
gentility was inborn. Just look at her, a shipbuilder's
daughter, being treated as a lady, and trying to act like
one. "Then what are you suggesting, that I leave him
where he is, with others of his kind?"

"No, I am merely offering the thought that the boy
might be happier if you found him a position at your
father's shipyards, where he could learn a trade and earn
his living, rather than live among the *ton,* where he will
never be accepted."

"I would never be so selfish as to keep the child where
he would be wretched, just to have him near me."

"I never meant to imply such a thing. You are the
most unselfish female I have ever known."

Mina's heart warming at the praise, she said, "They are
my shipyards now, so I could easily begin an apprentice
program and school. I have been thinking of finding a
place in the country, anyway, and the house in Portsmouth is sitting empty."

"That might do," Lowell agreed. Then he took his
glasses off to inspect them for smudges and pulled out a
clean handkerchief to wipe them. "Unless, of course, this
hypothetical boy is the missing heir to Sparrowdale's
estates."

Mina looked away, busying herself in trying to unknot
the strings of her reticule. "I suppose that is possible."

"Do you not also suppose it is time to tell me why
you think one of these children might be legitimate?"

Mina sighed. She trusted him, her hired investigator,
and yet . . . and yet she wanted to enjoy that look of
approbation she read in his eyes now and then for just
a bit longer. It had been so long since a man had regarded her with appreciation or with admiration, perhaps
never. Men had looked her way with lust and with long-
ing—for her fortune. This gentleman seemed genuinely
pleased with her looks, for he always gave her gentle
smiles when she appeared, and they had already agreed
on a price for his services. He did not have to be kind
to earn it. No, she did not want to have to confess to
him about that foolish elopement. Nor did she want to

hear him say her dreams of getting her own son back were merely that. Not yet.

She told him again of Perry's mother, instead, how Sparrowdale actually married the unsuspecting girl, then admitted he was already wed, invalidating the marriage. "What if he had done the same to other innocent young women, but during the time when he was *not* married? There were five years, I believe, between the death of the first countess and my own marriage. There are two dates, and two sets of initials that fall between that time." She handed him a copy of the list she had made. "He might have been so certain that the young women he chose would not contest his claims, that he did it again."

Lowell studied the list. "Yes, he might have been so arrogant, and so foolish. If he had, in truth, wed one of those girls, you realize, your own marriage, coming later, could be proved invalid."

She nodded. Of course she had thought of that.

"It is lucky you had no children, in that case."

At Mina's sharp intake of breath, he apologized. "I am sorry. That was cruel of me. I know you lost a babe. A son?"

At Mina's second nod, he went on. "He would have been declared illegitimate, in favor of one of these children, then, if someone had evidence."

"Yes, I know. That no longer matters." She stared out the window.

"No, but your widow's jointure does."

"I have ample funds without. Roderick would never be able to deny me the monies, however, unless he produced the heir. That would defeat his own purpose, which has to be keeping the earldom for himself."

"I cannot help wondering just how far old Roderick is willing to go."

To hell, it appeared, from the smoke and soot and ash that wreathed the Strickland Charity Home like a malevolent cloud. Mud marked the path of the fire brigade, and water sat in dirty puddles along the walk.

The moppet who opened the door, rags and bucket in hand, told them that the matron was too agitated for visitors. Mrs. Strickland did agree to meet with the couple, however, after receiving a further message that they wished to make a contribution, after the fire. Understandably shaken, she was slumped in a chair in the parlor with the windows open to clear the smell of smoke. Not quite so understandable to Mina's thinking, the proprietress was attempting to settle her nerves with a bottle of Blue Ruin. She did manage to rise to greet them, and to take the check Mina handed her.

"You cannot know how welcome this is, with us all at sixes and sevens. Not that I could make head nor tails out of the accounts anyway. My Duncan kept the books, you see, all the while he kept coughing. He has been gone half a year, and now so are the ledgers."

Lowell watched Mrs. Strickland's eyes widen at the amount of the bank draft. She did not seem to take any particular notice of the Sparrowdale name, only the total. He expressed sympathy for her losses, thinking that black became Lady Sparrow far better than it did the full-fleshed, florid-faced matron. The touches of lace at the countess's throat gave her an elegance sadly lacking in Ella Strickland. Sparrowdale's widow looked anything but governessy in her dark clothes. Duncan Strickland's widow looked precisely like what she was: an overworked, overwrought, and inebriated old schoolmistress.

"In addition to lending assistance, we have actually come looking for a child," Minerva was saying now. Lowell found himself pleased to be included in her "we."

Mrs. Strickland took her smoke-and-spirit-bleared eyes off the check long enough to note Mina's mourning garb, his lordship's look of concern. She saw a prosperous couple who had lost a child. Likely the quacks had told them she'd never conceive another, likely enough with her all skin and bones. Ella saw a chance to make another windfall. "Ah, then I should be paying you my condolences."

"But you do have children up for adoption?" Lowell asked.

"Some, though others are more in the nature of boarders. Were you looking for an infant? Most young couples are, more's the pity."

Mina did not bother correcting Mrs. Strickland's mistaken assumption that she and Lord Lowell were married. It would have been too complicated, when all she wanted was to find out about the boy. "We are looking for a specific child, one who might have been left in your care. His father would have given his name as Harold Sparr, or Lord Sparrowdale. He is now deceased."

"I'm sorry, to be sure, but I never heard of the nob."

"Well, then, perhaps these initials mean something to you. I have marked the ages I believe the children would now be next to them." Mina handed over her list, then held her breath while the matron held the page at arm's length, squinting down from the names on top, from M.P., who would be older than Mina, so not a primary concern, down through Perry's P.R. midway, and then to her Robert's R.S. second from the bottom.

Mrs. Strickland handed the paper back. "Sorry again. I don't have any young'uns like that. I do have a pretty little gal what has blue eyes like your husband, though."

"He's not my—" Mina began, now that it did not matter how much time was wasted.

Lowell interrupted. "Do you know the name Perry Radway? He might have brought the fees for one of those on the list."

"Dark-haired lad, about three and ten?"

Mina clutched Lowell's arm without thinking. He placed a hand over hers and said, "That's him. Did he come for one of your children?"

Ella took the list back and studied it. "Here it is, this one, G.H. George Hawkins, though we call him Hawk, on account of his nose, which is why I did not recognize his initials." She squinted at the list again. "Yes, the age matches. Hawk is eight, all right. Your Perry brought his quarterlies, and used to take the boy on outings now and again. Called him his brother, now that I recall."

Not four. Not Robin. Mina sank back against the sooty cushions of the couch. What did it matter? She was already wearing black.

Lowell asked about young Hawkins's mother.

"Never seen hide nor hair of her, and the father nei-

ther, only Perry. Hawk says she was a vicar's daughter.
Ain't they all?"

"Was she married to the boy's father?"

Ella snorted and took another swallow from her glass.
"Not by half. The half what makes it all right and tight.
He promised to marry her, but never got around to it
before she died. That's how the boy landed here."

"I do not suppose there is any proof to be had for this
story?" Lowell asked.

"If there was, it's ashes now. Mixed right in there with
my Duncan's ashes. But now that I think on it, I haven't
seen Perry in an age and no one else is paying me to
keep Hawk. If he's the brat you want, you can have him
for the price of the last quarter. If not, it's off to the
mines or the factories with him. They'll pay me what's
owed."

Mina sat up again. "You'd sell him into near slavery?"

"Slavery is illegal. I'd be recouping my losses, is all.
This ain't no charity operation, you know."

Wasn't it called Strickland's Charity Home? Mina did
not bother arguing. "I will pay his debt, if he wishes to
come with me."

The boy's face was so blackened with soot that Mina
could not recognize anything of humankind, much less
of Sparrowdale. He claimed Perry as his half brother,
though, and some rotten nob as their pa. Hawk also
claimed he'd clean Lady Sparrowdale's outhouse rather
than be sent north to the factories.

He went to pack while the transaction was concluded.
Lowell placed the carriage blanket against the velvet
squabs of his coach. Mina asked Mrs. Strickland twice
more if Perry had not visited any of the other children.
Then they were off, with Ella's last words echoing behind
them: "Watch out for that one. He steals."

"Bugger off, you old bat," Hawk shouted back.

He was Sparrowdale's son, all right.

Chapter Sixteen

So Mina had a son. A filthy, foulmouthed, falcon-nosed felon whose pockets were full of Mrs. Strickland's folderols. What was she supposed to do with George Hawkins? He was too old for her to bathe, too big to sit on her lap, too much a Sparrowdale for her to take to her bosom—which the little heathen was staring at.

Luckily, Lord Lowell took charge. After dropping her at the front door of Merrison House, he had the carriage drive him and the boy around to the mews, where there was a water pump, and young grooms with cast-off clothing. First he shook the boy upside down to dislodge any stolen valuables he might have missed the first time, and then he gave young Hawk a warning.

"If one shilling goes missing in this house, one fork or spoon, one candlestick or chicken leg, you will wish you were sold into servitude after all. Lady Sparrowdale has saved your life, not letting you be sent to the factories, so make sure you repay her with respect and honor. If not, they always need boys to haul those trams in the mines. Understand?"

George understood. There were food and toys and horses here. A chap would have to be a regular noddy to queer this deal. So later, when he was clean and combed and in fresh clothes, after old jaw-me-dead Ochs announced him, Hawk was presented to his new step-mother and the duchess. He made a creditable bow, a promise not to cause any difficulties and to study hard at his lessons. Harkness, who had rehearsed the boy, winked from the doorway before Ochs shut the door in his adversary's face.

To show his gratitude, and his new rectitude, Hawk handed Mina a gift, a miniature painting that had been tucked among his few belongings. "It weren't stolen, ma'am," the boy swore. "But I am right fond of it all the same. So I am giving it to you."

"Why, thank you, George. That is very sweet of you. I will treasure it always, because I know it means a lot to you. Is it of your mother?" Mina asked, reaching for the small portrait. Then she looked at it. Good grief, she hoped that was not his mother, posing in so suggestive a manner, in so few draperies.

Her Grace glanced over, then reached for her lorgnette and the picture. "Great Heavens, that is Lady Afton-Glower, and she is not wearing a stitch!"

Cousin Dorcas started fanning herself with her handkerchief.

Lord Lowell put down his newspaper and strolled over, behind Mina. "No, Mother, she is wearing a hat. And if I am not mistaken, this is the work of that artist we met this morning, Marcel."

"He gave it to me, I swear, the time Perry took me to visit. He said the lady didn't like it enough to pay its worth, so I could have it."

Judging from the smile on the viscountess's face, Mad Marcel must have other talents than his painting. Lowell was certain the lady would have paid a great deal indeed to keep the painting out of the hands of grubby schoolboys, or the public eye. At least the young artist could be excused of greed. Marcel's muse did not inspire blackmail, it seemed, nor payment for services rendered. "Perhaps she will have reconsidered by now. I know Marcel can use the money."

The duchess was still peering at the painting. "He is quite good, actually. I wonder if he would consent to do my portrait."

No one wished to see his mother in such a light . . .

in so much light. Lowell snatched the picture out of her
hands and started to return it to Minerva, but he thought
better of that too, and placed it facedown on the table.
"Did Perry take you visiting anywhere else?" he asked
the boy, to redirect the conversation. "To other orphans'
homes, perhaps? Or did he mention other half brothers
you might share?"

Mina was angry that she had not thought to ask the
boy those questions. How silly. And how fortunate she
had such a knowing associate. She smiled at the picture
he made, bending to the boy's level, one hand scratching
the dog's ears. Her smile faded, though, when George
could not remember anything special about the places
where Perry had made his deliveries the few times he'd
taken the younger boy along.

"Well, you keep thinking, lad. Perhaps we'll go riding
out to Perry's house, talk to Marcel again, and see if
anything looks familiar."

"Riding? On a horse?" George grinned, looking more
like the cherub Mina had envisioned. He would need a
pony. Riding lessons. New clothes. A tutor. Lowell would
know how to find them all, thank goodness, for Mina did
not know where to start, raising a boy up to be a gentleman. George Hawkins might not be the child of her body
nor the child of her heart, but he would be Mina's ward
as soon as Mr. Sizemore brought the papers to be signed.
George was hers to love.

Then he put three biscuits in his pocket while he
thought no one was watching. And the sugar tongs. Old
habits died hard.

To get a jump on the other fortune hunters the callers
started coming that afternoon. By four o'clock, the street
in front of Merrison House was filled with gentlemen's
equipages of every sort, from pony carts to racing pha-
etons. The carriage drive was shoulder-to-shoulder
horses, with flower delivery boys darting between gleaming Thoroughbreds and arch-necked Arabians. Hawk es-
caped Harkness's watch to admire the mounts, and

Harkness happily went back to the pubs to ask about Lord Sparrowdale's erstwhile sweethearts. Let Ochs bear-lead the boy until a tutor was hired.

Lowell wished he could escape too, but his mother insisted on his presence, lest the basket-scramblers go beyond the line of what was pleasing in their efforts to fix Minerva's interest.

"Then you need Drew here," he told her, referring to his younger brother Andrew, who was stationed in London with the Horse Guards. "He'll keep order for you."

"And he will bring all of his rackety junior officer friends to throw themselves at Minerva."

Lowell stayed, glaring the gentlemen into no more than their proper twenty-minute calls.

Mina would rather have been anywhere, including outside, making sure that George did not steal any of the gentlemen's horses. She would have fled but for the duchess's insistence that she had to get this over with before she became a challenge to the bored bucks and beaus. So she stayed by Her Grace's side and smiled, and turned down every offer of a drive or a picnic or another visit. Ice could have formed in the room for all the warmth she exhibited toward the callers. She paid more attention to the dog at her side than to the gentlemen throwing their hearts—and their empty pockets—at her feet. They all left disappointed and deeper in debt by a posy or a book or a box of bonbons. That is, until Lord Sparrowdale was announced. After the usual insincere pleasantries, Roderick drew Mina aside, then out through the French doors to the rear gardens.

"Estate matters," he told the fops and fribbles and out-of-funds hopefuls to excuse his stealing away the object of their affections. "Family affairs, don't you know."

In a moment they appeared again, in full view of the house windows, but out of hearing.

Lowell edged nearer the doors. "That little fool," he muttered. Sparrowdale might be an accessory to murder, and Lowell's lady—his employer, that was—was going off alone with the bounder. He decided to take the dog for an outing, in the rear gardens. The gardeners could complain to his mother about the dug-up rosebushes and the brown spots on the lawns. Lowell was not leaving Minerva alone with Roderick the raptor.

Mina had not gone outdoors with Roderick by choice. He had smiled to the company as he took her hand, but no one could see that he was squeezing her fingers so hard that her gold wedding ring was cutting into her knuckle. She did not wish to cause a scene, not in the duchess's parlor, so she went with him. As soon as they were outside, however, she pretended to stumble, stepping on his foot as hard as she could, until he released her.

"I will not be manhandled, Roderick," she said in a low, angry voice, "so say what you have to and begone. Her Grace's gardeners do not permit slugs in the gardens."

"Save your wit for the nodcocks inside, Minerva. Maybe one of them will overlook your shrewish ways in favor of your fortune. I will not. You have made me look the fool by coming to London and staying here instead of at Sparr House."

"Is that what has you in such a taking? Be at ease, then, Roderick. I had no hand in the public's opinion." With his yellow Cossack trousers and spotted neckcloth her husband's nephew resembled nothing so much as a clown to her. Unfortunately, he was not of a comic nature. Wishing to end the conversation as soon as possible, she told him, "With no other females at Sparr House, my visit would have created more talk. The duchess is an old friend of Cousin Dorcas, and so I was pleased to accept her invitation."

"And what of the son?"

"The duke? I have never met him."

Roderick reached for her arm, but Mina had learned to keep her distance. He said, "As you well know, I mean that bug-eyed bobbing block who has been trying to look out the window at us."

"Lord Lowell? He appears quite the gentleman." She did not need to add the "unlike others I could name," but it hung there between them. "He has been every-thing kind."

Roderick sneered. "Of course he has. The flat is a second son. How else is he to feather his nest but with a wealthy wife?"

"I believe Her Grace's son is gainfully employed and has no need to make an advantageous marriage." Again, that "unlike others I could name" stayed silent.

"Hah. He is engaged in nothing but sticking his long nose into other people's business."

Mina considered Lowell's nose nearly perfect, straight, with just the right degree of length to make it dignified. Unlike . . . "I understand he was responsible for the recovery of Lady Carstair's diamonds. But that is beside the point. The duchess assures me her son is not in the Marriage Mart."

"But you are?"

Let him think what he wanted, so long as he did not suspect she had hired Lord Lowell. Mina gave an airy wave toward the still-crowded drawing room.

"Is that what you came to Town for, Minerva? To buy yourself another title?"

"You forget yourself, nephew. But I should think you'd be happy if that were the case. My widow's annuity ceases on my remarriage, of course. Think of the extra pounds in your coffers."

Roderick paced in front of her, his hands clenched into fists. "And that other nonsense? That rot about Sparrow-dale's by-blows? You better have put it from your mind, the way I warned you. For if you've come to Town about those brats, I will not have it, I tell you. I am not going to let you wash the family's dirty linen in public, not while I am close to winning Westcott's daughter."

"I merely wish to make certain the children are cared for. I see nothing wrong in that, and nothing in it to do with you or your courtship. In fact, I should think the lady and her father would appreciate knowing her suitor took his responsibilities seriously."

Roderick's fury did not permit him to listen to anyone else's reasoning, certainly not a plaguesome female's.

"You are making a byword of yourself. Just look at that crowd of puppies in there."

Except the puppy was outside, getting the scent of someone who had once kicked him.

"I would be as far from here as I could get, if I knew those children were safe. You said you knew nothing about them, where I could find them, who was caring for them?"

"Blast it, what would I know about a parcel of brats?" he snarled.

So did Merlin, coming around the corner.

"But you did know of Peregrine Radway, you said," Mina persisted.

"I knew of some snivel-nosed beggar who tried to steal money from me."

Had he already met Hawk? No, Mina decided, he was still speaking of Perry. "And you do not know where he is now, or anything about hired thugs or burned records or fires?"

Roderick looked like he might breathe fire himself any minute. His eyes narrowed to slits. "I have no idea what you are speaking about, you interfering jade. If you—"

"Good," Mina interrupted. "I would hate to have to go to the authorities with my suspicions."

Roderick went for her throat.

Merlin went for his ankle.

Lowell went berserk.

Chapter Seventeen

"*Y*ou threatened him!" Lowell shouted at Mina once the company had been dispersed and gossip averted. They had used the dog's sudden animosity to excuse what looked like a confrontation in the garden. Merrison's ruffled state was explained as his attempt to control the vicious brute—he meant Roderick, but the dunderheads in the doorway took his scowl for the dog. Roderick's slight dishevelment was attributed to Merlin also. The dog was relegated in shame to the kitchens, where he was rewarded with a lamb shank.

The contretemps was smoothed over. Lowell's temper was not. "How could you be such a ninnyhammer as to say you'd go to the authorities?" he yelled.

"I refuse to speak to someone who shouts at me," was all she replied, sipping at her tea, hoping he could not see how her hand was shaking. Her father had been a bellower, shouting orders across his shipyards. Her husband had been another loud, bullish man, even on his sickbed. Mina saw no reason for her to be yelled at any longer, especially not by someone she was paying.

"I am not shouting, by heaven. I am conversing rationally with a peagoose."

"No, Lolly dear," his ever helpful mother put in from the nearby card table. "You were definitely shouting."

Miss Albright had put her cards down and was clutching her vinaigrette, ready to bolt for the door. Lowell supposed he may have been a tad vociferous. "I apologize, ladies. Would you care to step outside with me,

Lady Sparrowdale, where we might continue our discussion?"

Mina might be the fool he took her for, but she was not crazy. One angry gentleman berating her in the bushes was enough for one day. She held up her cup. "I am not finished with my tea."

Lowell took a deep breath. Then he sat down beside her on the couch and tried to regulate his voice. "You practically accused that loose fish of arson, by Jupiter, if not worse. Now our job will be that much harder." He already had men out gathering addresses of orphan asylums, but there must be hundreds of them, thousands if one counted the women who took in a nurseling or two. Finding nameless children, who might not even be in London, was proving an impossible task. Other men were compiling lists of recently retired reverends and who might know their whereabouts. They had to find Perry Radway to find the others—and now they had to do so before Roderick grew more desperate. "Dash it, how do you expect me to do the job you hired me for if you keep meddling in it?"

"Meddling? My stars, this is my investigation, if you recall. I do not see you locating the children." Mina knew that was unfair. She knew all about the men he had hired and the informants he had bribed to find out more. She was upset, though, and worried. For one thing, she could not be happy that Her Grace and Cousin Dorcas were teaching George Hawkins to play whist, which, she considered, was *not* a good idea. Nor was it the best of notions for the boy to earn his betting money by telling Mina's suitors that he could put in a good word with his new guardian. Something had to be done about the boy, and soon, but Harkness had not returned from the employment agencies with a fitting tutor, nor from the real estate offices with a place of their own. In fact, Harkness seemed to be spending most of his time in pubs, when he was not tweaking his counterpart's nose. Something had to be done about her butler, too.

Meanwhile, she was also worried about Perry and the other children. She had seen a look in Roderick's dark

eyes that a badger could have worn, or a rabid rat. He
was dangerous, far more so than she had thought. His
obsession with the title, the family name, his own position, and the duke's daughter, all were bordering on the
brink of insanity, to say nothing of the rage he flew into
at the torn leg of his pantaloons.

And now she had to worry about the Honorable Lord
Lowell Merrison. The dratted man was too honorable.
Why, another moment outside, another word out of Roderick's filthy mouth, and Lowell would have called Sparrowdale out, spectacles and all. Roderick might not be
any Corinthian sportsman, but he could see, for heaven's
sake! Thank goodness the gardener had come to chase
Merlin from the flower beds, recalling the men to their
senses, and reminding them of the interested observers
behind the French doors. Roderick wanted no gossip
about his closet cousins to reach Westcott's ears, but neither did he wish the duke to learn of his tinderbox temper, so he had feigned a polite smile. Mina was reminded
of a picture she'd once seen of a hyena. She shuddered
again, thinking about it.

She had never hired Lord Lowell to indulge in fisti-
cuffs. She had never thought her investigator's well-being
would particularly matter to her, either, but it did. She
looked over at him, where he was frowning, first at her
and then at the few macaroons Hawk had left on the
plate, and she thought again of how lucky she had been
to find his lordship. Without his help . . . Well, she supposed Mr. Sizemore could have found George Hawkins
once they heard about the fire, and she could have
walked every inch of Kensington herself, but she was
certain Lord Lowell was of great assistance.

"I am sorry," she said now, "both for belittling your
efforts and for entangling you with my skirts so you could
not strike Roderick. I also apologize for antagonizing
him further, but my actions were not half so outrageous
as your mother's."

"You are right. I am surrounded by featherbrained
females."

The duchess peered over the top of her cards. "I heard

that, Lolly. And I would not have had to invite the dastard to the dinner in Minerva's honor except for your
looking thunderclouds at him.''

He was still looking stormy, Mina thought, except for
the macaroon crumb at the corner of his mouth. That
was looking—

"How else was I to show there were no ill feelings
between you?" the duchess continued. "Otherwise the
tale of the argle-bargle would have spread through the
clubs by nightfall, what with every jackanapes in Town
there in my drawing room. They would all be wondering
why Minerva was not on terms with her relations, and
why my son and Sparrowdale were arguing over her like
a dog with a bone, to say nothing of the dog and Roderick's ankle bone.''

Mina dragged her eyes away from her investigator.
"Still, Your Grace, I cannot like the thought of sitting
to dinner with such an insect as my husband's nephew.
I do not trust the man.''

"Of course not. Is it not better, though, to keep the
scorpion where you can see him, rather than let him sting
when you least expect it?''

"I agree that a quarrel amid the columbines was unfortunate, Mother," Lowell said, "and you did well to stem
any scandal. But did you have to urge Sparrowdale to
attend, once he claimed he was committed to Westcott
and his daughter for the evening you chose?''

"Urge? Pish-tosh. I merely said I would invite them
also. Westy is an old friend. He'll be sure to accept.''

"So the serpent can fix his interest on the heiress here,
instead of elsewhere?''

His mother shook her head sadly. "How little faith my
own child has in me. What, do you think I would leave
the duke's poor motherless daughter to a serpent like
Sparrowdale? I will invite Andrew to partner the gel.''
She smiled. "You have never seen my youngest son in
his uniform, have you, Minerva?''

How could hiring a tutor be so much of a bother?
Mina wondered. The search for one was keeping her

from the search for her son, and from Lord Lowell, who was pursuing the inquiry while she was interviewing instructors. She missed his company, and the smiles he had given her. She even missed Hawk, who got to ride along with Lowell, to see if he recognized any likely locations. Sitting in the rear parlor Her Grace had set aside for Mina's use, reading recommendations and résumés, was not nearly as interesting or exciting as following leads and bribing informants.

With the long school holidays approaching, most decent, experienced tutors had been snabbled up by all the blue bloods who had no wish to deal with their own children for the summer. Of the others, the ones sent 'round by the agencies, some were too meek to deal with George's idiosyncrasies, for want of a better word. Those quiet young men believed in teaching by example. Others believed in the birch rod. Yet another contingent felt their skills would be wasted on one of such questionable birth, that tutoring a boy from an orphans' home was beneath them. Their references went beneath the cook's canary. Some were so far above Hawk's level of education, in fact, that he would have been at sea, instead of at Lowell's side, learning to tool a curricle. Some were so ignorant, Mina wondered how they managed to read her advertisement.

Hawk was magnanimous. He volunteered to go without a tutor. Lowell wrote letters to his college. The dowager wrote letters to her wealthy friends with sons who might have outgrown their tutors, and to her poor friends with sons who might need a position. Mina wrote advertisements for the newspapers. Harkness asked at the pubs. No one had yet answered.

Mina did not want to send the boy away to school, if she could find one to take him. She doubted a boarding school would keep him, for one thing, and she wanted to get to know him better, for another. What kind of family lived apart? Most of the aristocracy and half of the merchant class, Mina knew. She had been away at an academy for young ladies much of her own life, and she thought George Hawkins deserved a more caring upbringing. She cared. Now she had to find a teacher who would care too.

Two frustrating days later, the perfect candidate walked into the parlor behind Ochs. The Merrison House butler was, as usual, displeased at being called to the door so often for such unillustrious young persons as this threadbare scholar. Ochs showed his disdain by sniffing the air, as though the dog had been indiscreet. The dog got to go to the park with Hawk while Mina stayed in. She was none too pleased either.

"Are you coming down with a chill, Ochs?" Mina asked. "My cousin is certain to have a potion to ward off an ague."

"Mr. Homer Gilpin," he announced without answering her. "Here for the advertisement."

Mr. Gilpin was a soberly dressed young man of about nineteen years. He wore spectacles like Lord Lowell, but any similarity ended there. Gilpin was dark and slight and wore his thin hair parted in the middle and smoothed down on either side. He wore his glasses low on his nose so he could peer over them when not reading, which gave him a perpetually startled look, with his eyebrows raised. He reminded Mina of an owl, and a bit of her dead husband, because of his unfortunately pocked complexion. She could not hold that against him, she told herself, nor his obvious shyness. He was standing across from her desk, twisting the hat Ochs had not bothered to take.

The butler was right. Mr. Gilpin would not be staying long, Mina reluctantly decided. George needed a stronger hand on the reins than this diffident scholar. Then she read his references from the dons and her own eyebrows raised. "Brilliant, a natural student, gifted" were some of the encomiums heaped upon Gilpin's head. And "a capital cricketer, superb oarsman," which surprised her even more.

"It seems the university is your natural milieu, Mr. Gilpin, not drumming Latin declensions into recalcitrant schoolboys."

"I, um, like children."

He had not met George Hawkins yet. "And what of your own studies? I see you hope to become a dean at Oxford yourself someday."

"I, ah, hope to go back in the autumn, with the funds I earn. My, um, patron recently succumbed to a fatal illness, so I need to raise the fees myself. The scholarships were already bestowed when he, ah, passed on. I can tutor some of the less advanced students next term, when they return from holidays."

"I see. So this would be a temporary position only?"

"Oh, dear. I, um, never thought you wanted a permanent tutor. I could stay on, I suppose. Or you could decide to send your, um, ward to school. He will be ready after the summer. I swear."

What school would be ready for Hawk, who had already won Cousin Dorcas's pin money at cards, likely by marking the deck? Mina did not dare loose him on the shipyard either, else he might rob the ships of their rudders. She sighed and turned back to the young man who needed the position so badly he looked ready to weep.

"I am sorry," she said, wondering how she could offer to pay his tuition, "but you have no background in teaching. I fear my ward needs an older, more experienced tutor, despite your erudition in six ancient languages and"—she referred back to the references—"five modern ones."

"But—but I could love him."

Mina almost tossed the inkwell at him, starving scholar or not, but then Homer took his spectacles off a prominent proboscis and said, "I could love him like a brother. Or a half brother."

Chapter Eighteen

*H*omer Gilpin. H.G., whose entry date on the list was nineteen years ago, right below M.P., who would be twenty and five, wherever he was. Another of the late earl's sons was here. Mina could not believe it.

Neither could Lowell. "Sparrowdale's son, a scholar?"

Mina laughed, that enchanting sound Lowell was coming to know and to savor. She should laugh all the time, and smile so brightly. No, then the carriages would be lined up outside his house three deep, instead of single file.

"I know," she was saying, "but Homer's mother was a schoolteacher. Her father, Homer's grandfather, was an Edinburgh don. I cannot imagine how such an intelligent man came to let his daughter near Sparrowdale, although I suppose the earl was not so ill favored twenty years ago."

"And most of those scholars have their heads in their research, not their surroundings, in my experience. Did Sparrowdale offer to marry this one?"

"He did better, actually going through the ceremony. In Scotland, where he was supposedly off shooting. He was already wed, of course, but he used a different name, to be sure the marriage was invalid."

"Why the deuce did he go through such roundaboutation? He could have visited a whor—a house of convenience, like all the other married men."

Mina's cheeks were awash with color, but she gamely answered, "My late husband did not care for, ah, women of that profession. He blamed them for his condition. Soiled doves did not suit him."

"Very well, he tricked a gently raised female into a false marriage. What I cannot understand is why, after he purposely ruined a young lady, he would show enough scruples to keep supporting her son?"

"Homer believes his grandfather brought him as an infant to England, threatening to go to Sparrows Nest unless the earl made provision. He did, finding a family near Oxford to take in the baby. Homer never knew his mother, or his grandfather."

"And Sparrowdale kept paying the boy's way through school?"

"I know it sounds unreasonable, since no one was blackmailing Sparrowdale over this child. The mother moved to the Colonies, and the grandfather simply did not want him. I have often wondered about it, why the earl kept up his records and his withdrawals. Aside from not wanting his wife or his father-in-law to know, I think he actually liked his sons. When Viscount Sparling was killed, he cried for weeks. And Homer says Sparrowdale visited a few times and was good to him, taking him for dinner, watching his cricket matches."

"I suppose even Beelzebub had one redeeming trait."

"And Homer is a fine young man, despite his father's blood. He has taken George under his wing, impressing him with his hurling if not his scholarship."

Both boys were installed in the Merrison nursery now, but they were seldom at home, the owlish scholar taking his brother—and his grateful self—to see the sights of London Town. Mina was going to pay for the rest of Homer's education, since she would never approach Roderick about the matter. She saw no reason, with his facility with languages and the dowager duchess's connections, that Homer could not attain a government post someday, an ambassadorship perhaps. Meanwhile, she was already giving him an allowance for watching over George and preparing the younger boy to enter school next term. Homer refused to accept a salary to tutor his own brother, the family he had never had, but the allowance was necessary to get the two boys entry to the Menagerie and the Steam Engine and the Elgin Exhibit. And meals along the way, of course.

Unknown to Mina, Lowell had also slipped Homer some coins, to keep Hawk away from the house, and away from chousing the stable lads out of their quarterly wages. "I hope Homer has his pockets sewn shut," he said now. "By the way, I asked our resident linguist if he had ever spoken to Peregrine Radway."

So had Mina. Homer had been delighted to learn of yet another brother, and the possibility of more, but he had never heard of Perry. His funds had come through the solicitor's office, Mr. Sizemore's partner who had had a heart attack, or directly from Sparrowdale, who had thought it a great joke that he had sired such a somber, sober chap. It was the university bursar who had informed Homer of his father's death when the obituary was published, and asked his intentions. He intended to apply for a scholarship, or a position as tutor once the tuition fees ran out. He would never have approached Roderick, either, being worldly enough to know the welcome an out-of-wedlock cousin would receive. He was much too embarrassed to come to his father's lawful widow. Then he'd seen the advertisement for a tutor from Lady Sparrowdale. Now he thanked the Lord, in nine languages.

"I still find it hard to believe that he simply walked in here," Lowell said, "when we are searching high and low for Sparrowdale's relicts."

"But Homer is a sign. He has to be. We are getting closer. I know it!"

"Closer to finding the one who is the heir?"

Mina pulled out the much-studied list. "Closer to finding the little ones, the ones who might need me the most." She pointed to the three sets of initials that came after George's G.H.: M.B., R.S., and W.S. "They would be six, four, and three, if we are interpreting this list correctly. Which we have to be, now that we know three of the boys match their entries."

Lowell knew the list by heart. He'd been to scores of

foundling homes, asking for those same initials, or a friend of Perry Radway's, or a connection to Sparrow-dale, or a dark-haired, large-nosed brat of the appropriate age. He'd seen hundreds of moppets and sprites who needed the love Lady Sparrow was so obviously eager to give—but none of them were the ones she wanted. He'd left money, and a bit of his own heart, behind, cursing once more that he did not have the funds to help them all. Lowell vowed to enlist his mother and his brother in bettering those infants' lives. What good was having a duke and a duchess in the family if one could not count on their charity?

And what good had he been to Lady Sparrow? "With Homer rescuing himself, I have hardly done a thing to earn my keep—or that curricle," he said now. "The least I can do is get you out of the house on this lovely day."

The sky looked as gray as a dove's back, and the trees were bending in the breeze, but Mina said, "Yes, I would enjoy a drive." And she would, with him.

They stopped first at the solicitor's office to sign documents making Mina's guardianship of both boys official. Not that Roderick was apt to claim either as his ward, but she was not leaving anything to chance or challenge. With Homer not of legal age, he could not be George's trustee. For that matter, being a woman, neither could Mina, on her own. Mr. Sizemore looked from her to Lord Lowell and cleared his throat.

She could ask the solicitor to sign his name beside hers, or she could ask the man who had taken the boys for ices and punting on the river. It would not mean giving up any authority for the children, she told herself; it was merely a way of providing for their future if something untoward happened to her. They would be wealthy, then, for she had nowhere else to leave her father's fortune except to charity and Cousin Dorcas. In that dire case, she had no doubts, Roderick would be quick to claim them as kin. Lord Lowell could be trusted to look after the accounts without feathering his own nest. Mina looked at Lowell, the question in her eyes.

What a huge responsibility, Lowell thought. Did he

want to help Minerva guide her orphans through adolescence into manhood? Yes. Did he want an excuse to visit with her, communicate with her, after this case was closed? Yes.

Furthermore, so long as he lacked the funds to support a wife, he was not likely to have children of his own. Just as his mother felt she could never have enough grandchildren, Lowell concluded that he could never have enough nieces and nephews with whom to play and upon whom to dote. And what did Lady Sparrow know about raising boys, anyway? He had to assist her, didn't he? Yes.

So yes it was, and Minerva and Lowell found themselves guardians of a scholar and a scamp. They went to a nearby tea shop to celebrate, since Lowell was, as usual, hungry and Lady Sparrowdale still looked too thin to him. She did not finish her tarts, as usual, so they wrapped the extras in a cloth to feed to the birds, and drove to the park.

Rather than stopping every few yards to greet Minerva's suitors, Lowell set his horses to a trot. He ignored the other drivers and riders and pedestrians who waved and nodded and called out greetings. Devil take them all, he thought. He wanted to enjoy the afternoon in private with his . . . employer. Damn. How was it that ten minutes in the female's company made him forget? He had no business driving out with her, and no business pulling the curricle off the path so they could get down and walk. He definitely had no business taking her hand to lead her to the water, where a flock of ducks waited for crumbs. He must have forgotten again.

They spoke about books at first, which ones she ought to purchase for Hawk. Literature had been one of her few companions for the past five lonely years, but she was not certain what would appeal to a young boy. Pirates, Lowell suggested, and ghost stories, the gorier the better. He was impressed at the range of Minerva's reading, and her understanding.

Then the conversation turned to his career in solving mysteries. He told her about Lady Carstair's diamonds,

since the lady herself had broadcast the news to all and
sundry, in her joy at recovering her missing baubles.
Then, without naming names, he described his most interesting investigation, which was recovering both an ab-
ducted heiress and the ransom money. The kidnapper
had named him as intermediary because Lowell Merrison
was known as an honest chap, one not given to physical
force. The gallows' bird had made Lowell remove his
spectacles for added insurance. He never suspected the
special lens fixed atop the small pistol in Lowell's
waistband.

Mina was impressed with his ingenuity and bravery.

He admired the way she spoke softly to the birds, ad-
monishing the larger ones to be fair, and how the water
cast silvery reflections on her creamy skin.

She admired his aim in throwing the crumbs, and the
way his coat stretched across his broad, muscular
shoulders.

He was happy she looked so carefree for a change.
She was happy she'd tucked a bouquet of violets beneath
the brim of her black bonnet, for a change. The dowager
duchess would have been happiest of all—ecstatic, in
fact—if she'd seen how close the pair stood, how they
ignored the ducks altogether, how their hands were
clasped again, and how they stared into each other's eyes.

Lowell had forgotten what it was he was supposed to
remember. Mina had forgotten that she did not really
like men or physical intimacy.

Their lips were drawing together as inexorably as the
tide, it felt to both of them, a movement that was guided
by the stars. Then the brim of her bonnet hit the frame
of his spectacles, dislodging them, and shattering the moment. He was chagrined, she was mortified, and the
duchess would have been gnashing her teeth. The glasses
fell to the ground, and both of them bent down to retrieve them.

Something else shattered. Not the glasses, but the tree
behind them. The ducks took wing in a great *whoosh*,
and the horses, standing with the groom at some distance
away, reared in their traces.

In a flash, Lowell had his spectacles in one hand and Mina's hand in the other, racing for the cover of the trees. There he threw her to the ground, his body over hers, and pulled that same sighted pistol out of his boot. Nothing moved.

The groom called out, and some children came running, hoping to see fireworks. Their nursemaids followed, one pushing a pram.

"It is over." Lowell rolled off Mina and stood up, then offered her a hand, while he kept scanning the surrounding area, still holding the pistol at the ready. "Are you all right?"

All right? A gentleman had almost kissed her, then almost crushed her into the dirt. Mina did not know if she was angry or frightened or embarrassed. Most likely all three, she decided.

She twitched at her skirts, then tried to smooth her disordered hair, only to find too many hairpins missing to do the job properly. She brushed at her flattened hat— the violets were strewn at her feet—not meeting his eyes. Heavens, they had been about to kiss! She might never be able to meet his eyes again. "I did not know they permitted duck hunting in Hyde Park," she said.

"They don't," he said.

Chapter Nineteen

"*I* am going to kill that bastard!"

"Hawk?"

Lowell looked at Mina as if a draft had just blown through her cockloft. "No, that rat-breathed Roderick."

"You think it was Roderick who shot at us?"

"No, I think it was Roderick who shot at you. You are the one who is determined to find the boy who can destroy Roderick's life. He obviously does not know where the possible heir is any more than you do or he'd go after the child. This way Roderick makes certain you do not find him first."

"But outright murder? Roderick?" Mina was finding it easier to believe with every unpleasant conversation she had with her husband's nephew. Still, cold-blooded murder, in the park?

Lowell was leading her back toward the restive horses. "Either Roderick or one of his minions. He has friends in places where human lives are valued by the gold in their teeth. Someone scared Perry Radway out of town, and someone set the Strickland place on fire, and now someone has shot at you. I do not think it takes any great deductive reasoning to assume the connection, nor the perpetrator. One was a warning, one was an attempt to hide something, and the last was a permanent solution. I'll give that cur a permanent solution as soon as I get my hands on him."

Mina gave a nervous laugh. "You'll throw off your mother's dinner arrangements. And you have no proof."

Lowell's curse set the horses to stomping again. "Until I get it, I'll hire guards and additional watchmen. You are not to go anywhere on your own. In fact, I do not want you to leave the house unless I am with you."

Mina forbore commenting that his presence had not kept her from being someone's target this afternoon. Granted, his near kiss had caused her to duck suddenly, but she did not suppose that counted as protection. Still, Lord Lowell was upset on her behalf, not, she had to believe, because a dead employer could not pay his fee. Her first thought was that he liked her enough to care. Her second thought was that someone else disliked her enough to want her dead. Mina much preferred the first thought.

Lowell had reached many of the same conclusions. He cared about Lady Sparrow, the money be damned, and he could not protect her from an assassin's bullet or a thrown knife. A runaway horse he might be able to stop, if he had his spectacles on and could see the blasted thing coming. "Perhaps it would be better if you did not leave the house at all until this is over."

"How can it be over if I never leave the house? I have to keep looking."

"That is my job. You gave your word not to interfere if it grew dangerous. You will stay at Merrison House and I will keep searching for Perry Radway."

That might be best, Mina thought. Not that she would stop looking, but that they would have less opportunity to be alone, to share confidences . . . and kisses. A plain shipbuilder's daughter had no business kissing a duke's handsome son. A tiny voice inside her head whispered that Lowell was only a second son, the "lord" in front of his name being a mere courtesy title. He was not impossibly far above her, now that she seemed to have a modicum of social acceptance, if she were looking for a husband.

She was not, Mina shouted back to that small voice of temptation. She did not need a husband. She had the children now, and begetting them was the only reason she could imagine for a woman to willingly give her free-

dom and fortune into a man's keeping. She would keep
her distance.

Zeus, Lowell thought, the investigation could proceed
a lot quicker if he was not distracted by her lilac scent
or those soft curls fallen out of her coiled braid. He
would keep his distance—right after he wiped a smudge
of dirt from Minerva's chin. His gloved fingers reached
out to cup her jaw. He leaned closer to see. She turned
her face up. Deuce take it, what could be more natural
than that he complete their disastrous attempt at a first
kiss?

A loose thread could not have fallen between them.
So much for keeping their distance.

Her lips were warm and a bit trembly, uncertain beneath his. His were firm, and sure. His hand moved from
her jaw to her neck, to her shoulder, to her back. Her
hand raised to his chin, his cheek, his hair.

Her eyes were closed. His glasses were fogged, so it
did not matter.

They ran out of breath, so they shared each other's,
then they ran out of strength, so they clung to each other.
Then some laughing children ran out of the bushes. So
they went home.

They did not have to search for Roderick, Lord Sparrowdale. He was sitting in the parlor having tea with the
duchess, a handful of Mina's would-be wooers, and two
of the Almack's patronesses. He appeared neither surprised nor disappointed to see them. Cousin Dorcas was
gone, and so was any suspicion that Roderick had pulled
the trigger himself. His teacup was nearly empty; he had
been here too long.

As far as Lowell was concerned, the blighter had been
alive too long. This was not the appropriate time for a
confrontation, however, not if Minerva ever had hopes
of being accepted in the first circles.

She hurriedly excused herself to freshen her appearance, citing a minor mishap in the park.

The duchess looked to her son, who shook his head.
He was fine. Minerva was unhurt.

"A bit of cow-handed driving, Merrison?" Roderick asked. "Perhaps you should consider a driver, with your poor eyesight."

Lowell set aside the teacup his mother handed him and stepped toward the tray of decanters on a side table. "My tooling was not at fault. It was a bird."

"What, a bird flew up and caused your horses to bolt?"

"My cattle are too well trained for that, Sparrowdale," Lowell said. "It was a vulture."

"Do we have vultures here in England, Lolly, dear?" his mother asked.

"You'd be surprised what foul carrion eaters we have right in Hyde Park." He poured himself a glass of wine, without offering any to Roderick. "I would like a word, Sparrowdale, before you leave."

"Oh, I was not leaving, not quite yet. I am sorry, but I need a few moments of Lady Sparrowdale's time. A matter of family business, you understand."

Lowell understood that pigs would fly before he let this swine near Minerva. "The lady might be a while. I can relate your message."

Or he could pick the fop up and toss him out of the room. The Almack's matrons had their ears perked like cats at a fishpond. The fortune-hunting fribbles were on the scent of scandal. His mother was frowning.

Then Lady Sparrowdale returned. She looked lovely, in Lowell's mind, elegant in the black silk that clung to her body, made demure instead of deucedly intoxicating by the touches of white lace, and the lace cap on her brown curls. She assured everyone of her well-being, accepted a cup of tea and fulsome compliments from the empty-pockets, then stood next to Lowell, so the other gentlemen, perforce, also had to stay on their feet after rising at her entry. As an invitation to take one's leave, the maneuver was masterful. Lowell thought she had the countess role memorized perfectly. Now if she did not ruin her performance by glaring at her nephew-by-marriage. Lowell tried to shield her from the old biddies' view, as they bade his mother farewell. Then he glared at Roderick, for daring to approach her.

"A word, Minerva, if you please," Sparrowdale said, smiling and bowing to Lady Cowper, who was on her way out.

"I doubt you have anything to say that I wish to hear, Roderick. You may be assured, however, that I have a thing or two to say to you about your efforts to keep me from finding your uncle's children."

First Roderick looked around to see if her words about Sparrowdale's leavings had been overheard by any of the hostesses he wished to impress. Then he raised his quizzing glass to Lord Lowell, who obviously knew all about Minerva's hare-brained hunt.

"What, your eyesight failing, Sparrowdale?" Lowell asked, belittling the other man's affectation. "Perhaps I should ask Her Grace to lend you her spare pince-nez."

Roderick turned his back on the younger gentleman, an equally purposeful insult. "Shall we step outside, Minerva?"

"After last time? I think not," she replied, her chin raised in determination. "Say what you wish, Roderick. It is bound to be tiresome in any event."

"Quite the contrary, ma'am. I think you will be eager to hear that I have brought you a gift. Something of Uncle's that I recently chanced upon. Something for which you have been searching, I believe."

That was all he could say in front of the departing guests. It was enough. Mina had to hear him out. She was not, however, foolish enough to go off with him alone.

Lowell feared she might be, so he said, "I shall join your conversation, if I might, Countess." Then he told Roderick, "I have been assisting Lady Sparrowdale with her inquiry."

"I thought you might be," Roderick said, curling his lip. "You won't win the widow's favors with your phiz marred by those ugly lenses, so you might as well lead her fortune on a wild goose chase. Anything for money, eh?"

"No, I don't stoop to murder, arson, or kidnapping. Can you say the same?"

Mina stepped between the men before she expired of

embarrassment or a challenge could be issued. "What is this gift, Roderick? Have you found a ledger or a memorandum of Sparrowdale's with the children's addresses?"

"Better. I have brought you one of the brats itself. The butler put him in the library down the hall."

"Perry Radway?" she asked.

"That guttersnipe? He'd steal the books off the shelves, most likely. The whoreson can fend for himself, anyway, as I told him. This one's younger."

Mina clutched Lord Lowell's sleeve without being aware of her action. "How young?"

"About six, the director of the boys' home said."

Roderick did not seem to hear Mina's moan-like sigh, but Lowell did, and looked at her quizzically. She shook her head, knowing that she was going to have to explain to Lowell about her son, but not now. She told Roderick to go on.

"The home had him for four years, after his mother died. Oh, yes, Uncle married her, but there's no chance the boy is legitimate."

Mina did not think so, or Roderick would not have brought him. In fact, she had her doubts the boy would live to see seven if he were a lawful heir. She went over the list in her mind. M.B. would be six, born during the interval between Sparrowdale's legal marriages. "How are you so certain the child was born on the wrong side of the blanket?" she asked.

"Because the brat's records say so. The vicar who performed the marriage was a hired actor. The wedding was a sham, another of Uncle's little pranks."

Pranks? Mina would not have termed them such. They were cruel hoaxes, the product of a depraved, deranged mind. An innocent babe in a foundling home was no joke. "What is his name?"

"Martin something. Browne or Boone or Bowen. Something like that. No matter. When the money stopped coming, the board of directors decided to drop the brat on my doorstep. I cannot afford to send him back, nor pay for his upkeep at Sparr House."

Mina knew almost to the shilling how much Sparrow Nest brought in. If Roderick returned there, husbanded the estate to keep it profitable, and did not spend all his blunt on his London wardrobe and impressing dukes— or on hiring bullies—he could afford any number of boys' tuitions and expenses.

Mina was glad Roderick was such a squeezecrab, though, for now she could claim another boy. "I will take him, and gladly."

"You will have to sign over legal guardianship of the child first," Lowell told Roderick, not mentioning that he would also be named as trustee. He had no doubt that, without a court decree, sometime in the future when Sparrowdale was short of funds, he would demand the return of Martin Whomever, unless he were paid. Softhearted Minerva would pay anything, Lowell knew, rather than part with the child she already thought of as hers.

Roderick took out his quizzing glass again and inspected Lord Lowell's somewhat imperfectly tied neckcloth, which he had not had opportunity to retie since the disastrous trip to the park. Roderick might have surveyed a dead moth that floated in his water glass with the same look. "I cannot see that this is any of your affair, Merrison. But I shall sign whatever papers your man draws up, Minerva, if this sees an end to your airing the family's dirty linen. That goes for you too, sirrah. Stay out of my affairs."

Roderick meant Martin as a trade, Mina understood. She could have the boy, without fearing he'd be stolen away from her later, if she stopped trying to find any of the others. How could she promise any such thing, while one of them was her own son? She looked toward Lowell for an answer.

"I think—" He thought the ceiling-high bookcases must have toppled to the ground, from the noise coming from the library, his favorite room in the house. He started to run down the hall, Mina following.

"That is one of the reasons I could not afford to keep the brat at Sparr House," Roderick called after them. "The bastard is blind."

Chapter Twenty

*M*ina did not care that Martin could not see. Love was blind, too. She could see him, a thin, frightened little boy, cowering amid a pile of books, and that was enough.

"I . . . I was trying to find the door." Martin spoke in their direction when he heard them come in, a quaver in his voice. "I thought everyone forgot me."

Lowell cursed to see his favorite books, which had once been arranged in a freestanding case, all in a heap. Martin cowered amid the splintered shelves.

Mina glared at Lowell, then walked closer to the child, telling him that hardly any books had fallen, and none of them were harmed. He couldn't see the dismay on Lord Lowell's face, thank goodness. She told him that no one was angry and that she was sorry he'd been left alone, with no refreshments and no company. She glared at Ochs, too, who came to see what the commotion was. "It will never happen again, will it, Mr. Ochs?" she asked in her most lady-of-the-manor tone, although this was not her home. "Harkness would never have forgotten his duties to a guest in the house this way."

Since she put it that way, Ochs apologized—to a six-year-old with two missing teeth. He glared at Mina behind her back.

Lowell glared at the butler.

Neither Mina nor Martin noticed the dark looks. She had knelt down in front of the little boy—doing more damage to the leather-bound volumes—and reached for his hand. "I am Lady Sparrowdale, dearest, and I will make certain you never feel abandoned again. We will fix the nursery so nothing can topple over on you, and you will know where everything is in no time at all, I am sure." She could feel his cold hand trembling, so she rubbed it between hers. "Your brothers will help."

Martin's head tilted to the side in disbelief, but he left his hand in hers. "I have brothers?"

"Half brothers, but they are your family nonetheless, and mine now. George is eight and Homer is nineteen. Perry is thirteen, but he lives with his grandmother."

"I know a Perry, but he never said he was my brother."

"He is, dear. You look just like him." Poor child.

Martin's dark brows were furrowed. "Will they steal my food like the big boys at the home do?"

"No one will ever steal your food again," Mina promised, although she was not sure about George Hawkins, or the dog, for that matter. Merlin was sniffing at the newcomer, who was closer to his size. The boy took his hand from Mina's and reached out tentatively to stroke the shaggy mutt, getting his fingers licked in return.

"That's Merlin, Perry's dog."

Martin put his face down for another lick, and smiled at last. "They did not let dogs in the school. I never touched one before."

"Merlin is the best of dogs, and will let you pet him endlessly. He might even sleep on your bed at night." Currently, the dog was sleeping in her room, to Mina's dissatisfaction. He snored.

"Then I am to stay here?" Martin asked.

"Until we find a place of our own, perhaps in the country, where we can have any number of dogs or cats or rabbits as pets. We'll find someone to teach you to ride, too. Would you like that, Martin?"

He brought his hand—damp from the mongrel's affections—up to touch her face, her lips, her hair. "You smell nice, ma'am. And you have a dog."

Mina took that as a yes, and hugged the slender boy to her, lifting him out of the pile of Plato and Plutarch.

She set him down near the desk, but he started when
Roderick called out from the doorway. "So is it a deal,
Minerva?"

When Martin jumped back, his hand struck the inkwell, which Mina managed to right before it spilled onto
the Aubusson carpet.

"No harm done," Mina declared, but Martin was
afraid of being punished. This time the punishment
would see him sent back to the boys' home. He spun
around in dismay and bumped into a delicate cherrywood
tiered table. Lowell dove for the vase, the Ming Dynasty
one, on the middle shelf, and the fern on the top. As he
lunged, his spectacles fell to the floor, along with himself,
and the box containing his brother's prized butterfly collection that was on the bottom level. Merlin came to
investigate the inanimate insects—and Martin tripped
over him, falling flat on top of Lord Lowell's glasses.

The dog cried. The boy cried. Lowell cursed. Roderick laughed.

Mina pointed at the door. "Get out. My solicitor will
contact you." Then she knelt on the floor and asked,
"Are you all right, dearest?"

Martin crawled into her arms, shivering. Merlin
climbed onto her lap, trembling. Lowell clambered to his
feet, cursing. He brushed dead butterflies out of his hair.
He could barely see Minerva's expression—but he knew
she did not mean him.

"Don't you think it is time we talked, Minerva?" Lowell asked later. Martin was settled in the nursery, all small
objects moved out of his path, and at lessons. Hawk was
reading aloud from a storybook, while Homer corrected
his pronunciation and helped with unknown words. Both
of his brothers would learn that way, Homer felt. Hawk
felt his new little brother would rather learn how to swim
or ride or row. A fellow did not need to see to pull the
oars, as long as he had a good coxswain. They would
have a capital time, Hawk assured the younger boy,
switching his lemon tart for Martin's raspberry one.

Lord Lowell's old nanny would arrive in the morning.

She was nearly deaf, so Lowell had already promoted one of the maids to attend the nursery. Lucy said she had two younger brothers at home and made Hawk return the tart. She would do for now. His lordship was not so sure about Ochs, who was spending more time in the wine cellars than seemed strictly necessary. Lowell did not know what to do about Roderick, either. He was having the muckworm watched, to see if he met with his hireling. If Lowell could identify the thug, he could threaten him or bribe him into confessing, naming Roderick Sparr, Lord Sparrowdale, as his employer. Meanwhile, Lowell could not very well call Sparrowdale out, blast his poor eyesight, for the bounder was bound to choose swords. Besides, then Minerva's name would be bandied about. Botheration.

Lowell could not go to the magistrate or to Bow Street with his suspicions until he had proof, or a better understanding of the situation, so he had to ask the questions Lady Sparrow never wanted to answer. He was an investigator, after all.

"Martin is obviously not the possible heir," he began. "Roderick could have him declared incompetent to assume the earldom in a flash, anyway, by reason of his blindness. At the least, he would have had himself named guardian, and heaven help Martin then. If not Martin, or Hawk or Homer or Perry, we are running out of possibilities. I doubt the one listed first, the M.P. on the list, is the heir. He would be five and twenty, and would have come forth long ago to make his claim."

"If he knew of the connection," Mina pointed out.

"All of the others knew. Sparrowdale never tried to hide his paternity, it seems." The countess was studying the tea leaves left in the bottom of her cup. She was not seeking answers there, Lowell knew. She already had them. What she was doing was avoiding his eyes, getting set to lie to him. Not this time. "Now," he said, polishing his new spectacles, "now I have to know about the other boys on the list, and why you think one might be the true earl. No one is safe until I do, not you, not the

missing children. That is, unless, of course, you still do
not trust me."

Mina set aside her empty teacup and went back to
helping restore the fallen books to the library shelf. The
maids and footmen did not know their letters well
enough to get the volumes in the correct order, and
Homer's time was better spent tutoring his brothers.
Martin might never go to school, and he would obviously
not learn to read, but there was no reason he could not
learn from books, especially when Homer was so eager
to teach him. So Mina had insisted on donning an apron
and dusting the books before handing them to Lowell to
place back on the repaired shelves.

She carefully smoothed out a bent corner of a well-
read *Aeneid*. The boys would like that, she thought.
George ought to know his Latin. But what was she thinking? That they would be here forever? They would not
be staying. There was no reason to, if she was going to
honor Roderick's terms: Martin in exchange for the end
of her search. She had three boys now, and they should
have been enough, especially with Martin needing extra
care, extra affection They were not. She would acquiesce
to Roderick's demands—once the paper was in her hand,
guaranteeing her guardianship of Martin. Until then, she
intended to leave no stone unturned and no orphanage
uninspected. After, when Martin could never be taken
away again, she could have Lord Lowell pursue the inquiry while she was somewhere far away from London,
where Roderick could not harm her or the children. A
man who hired paid gunmen did not deserve honesty in
return, she told herself. And she had to find her son.
Only Roderick could think a mother would give up; he
had never loved anything that much.

If she was leaving, Mina thought, it did not matter
what her paid investigator thought of her. That's what
she tried to convince herself of, at any rate. If he thought
her no better than she ought to be . . . or foolish beyond
permission, so be it. She did trust him. How could she
not? He had never raised his voice to Martin, despite

the disaster and its expense. He had never shouted at
Merlin, who had left a damp spot on the rug in his dis-
tress at being stepped on. He had never even lifted a
finger to George, except to turn him upside down occa-
sionally to retrieve a snuffbox or an oyster fork. Lowell
had accepted all of them into his home, turning it upside
down, too. Of course she trusted him. She had let him
kiss her, hadn't she?

She put down her dustcloth and spread her skirts
around her on the floor. She looked up at him in his
shirtsleeves, a book in his hand, and thought she did far
more than trust him, and had more to lose than the
chance of finding her son. She licked her dry lips and
began. "I had a child once, a son."

Lowell sat beside her, taking her hand in his. "Yes, I
know. He was premature and stillborn."

"No. He was not."

"Not premature? He was born seven months after
your marriage to Sparrowdale. Everyone knew that."

"He was not born early," she repeated. "Nor was he
stillborn. I heard him cry."

Lowell chose to ignore the first statement for now. The
thought of Lady Sparrow anticipating her vows to that
old reprobate was enough to turn his stomach. "Very
well, what happened to him?"

"I think—no, I believe—that they took him away, my
husband, my father, Viscount Sparling, perhaps Roderick. He was there. They told me my baby died. They
held a funeral. They put a marker on his grave."

She drew the ever-present list out of her pocket. She'd
looked at it so often, she'd had to make a fresh copy.
"He would have been four," she said, holding the page
out to Lowell. "R.S., Robert Sparr. My Robin. I think
he is still alive."

He whistled. "Those are grave charges indeed. But
why—"

Mina interrupted. "Sparrowdale acknowledged him.
He had them carve his own family name on the head-
stone."

"What he did was acknowledge a dead baby, not a live heir. Yet if your child is indeed alive, he would be earl."

"Yes, and Roderick knows it."

Lowell had to think about that a moment, idly stroking her hand while he did so. He would have to consult a barrister, the College of Arms, his mother, who knew that kind of thing.

Minerva interrupted his thoughts. "I do not mean to claim the earldom in Robin's name. Roderick would challenge me with a long, sordid court case to prove him illegitimate. I would not subject my son to that."

"He is most likely subjected to the taint of bastardy right now, wherever he is. You would be denying him what is rightfully his."

"Not rightfully." Mina swallowed around the dryness in her mouth. "He is not Sparrowdale's son."

"Ah," was all Lowell said.

Chapter Twenty-one

So that was Lady Sparrow's secret. Lowell had de-
duced as much. He was a detective, after all. Surpris-
ingly, he thought none the less of Minerva, only that the
poor girl must have led a wretched life, finding herself
shackled to Sparrowdale, then having her own infant
wrenched from her. It was no wonder she wore a somber
mien along with her blacks, for he doubted if the countess had known much joy in her childhood or in her marriage. It was also no wonder that she was so eager to
find the other children, too, to replace the one she had
lost. Most of all, it was no wonder that Roderick sought
to stop her. Lowell shoved a stack of books aside so he
could move closer to her, as if his nearness could keep
her safe. It was a comfort to him, anyway. So was the
idea that he had to get Roderick to call off his dogs: "If
you can convince Roderick that you do not covet his title
for your son, perhaps he will tell us what became of
the boy."

"How could he, without admitting he had helped kidnap my baby and that he gave false witness for the funeral? He was right there in the house. He had to have
heard the baby's cry. He knew Robin was alive." Mina
deplored the catch she heard in her voice, but Lowell
did not seem to mind, merely handing over his mono-
grammed handkerchief, in case she needed it.

"We cannot be so certain he knew where the child
was taken, though," he argued. "If he saw your baby as
a menace to his ambitions, Roderick would have re-

moved the danger years ago, or as soon as Viscount
Sparling died—or was murdered—and Roderick was in
line for the succession. Then he would not have you to
plague him now. No, I do not think Sparrowdale trusted
him with that information. Perhaps the late earl even
used the child's existence to keep Roderick dancing to
his tune."

"That sounds like Sparrowdale. Roderick swears he
knows of no other children, but I doubt he would tell
me if he did know, out of sheer cruelty."

Lowell could see that. He had seen the maggot kick
at a little mongrel, make a blind child cringe at the sound
of his voice, and manhandle Minerva. No, Roderick
would not prove cooperative. His glass of the milk of
human kindness had obviously gone sour through lack
of use. On the other hand, things were not altogether
bleak. "Your son was a newborn, so maybe Sparrowdale
found a kind family to adopt the infant."

"I pray that is so. Since the earl's payments continued
until recently, I doubt he placed him in some filthy orphanage or charity home, where infants die so frequently.
Now that Sparrowdale is not paying his way, I pray even
harder that my Robin is with loving parents who will not
abandon him for lack of funds."

"What will you do if he has been adopted into a family
as their beloved son? Would you take him from them?"

Mina shook her head no. "I could not claim him, not
to be another bastard here, or wherever I settle with the
other boys. It might kill me to leave him, but I would,
if he is happy."

"Even if the foster parents are farmers or shop-
keepers? What then?"

"You forget I am a merchant's daughter. I would not
hold a man's trade against him if it is honest labor and
feeds his family. I have to know, though. I have to know
that Robin is well, and well cared for. Then I can walk
away, I hope. Can you understand that?"

He could understand the gut-wrenching sacrifice she
was willing to make for the boy's happiness. "Of course,"
he said. "He is your son." Lowell let his fingers trace

the gold ring she still wore. "And he is his father's son, too. Is that man waiting for your mourning period to end, to marry you and claim his child?"

Mina laughed, but without humor. "Mr. Rourke knows nothing of the boy. Before I left Sparrows Nest, I sent a man to search for him, to see if he is even alive."

"And to bring him back if he is?" Lowell held his breath.

"No, to find out if we were actually married."

"Married?" Lowell exhaled. He was relieved in a way, not liking to think of Minerva as a light skirt. He had been excusing her in his mind, imagining the young, innocent miss she would have been, manipulated by the rakish Rourke. If she were married to the mawworm, however, she needed no defense. She had done nothing wrong . . . except marry Sparrowdale too. "But you wed the earl. I refuse to believe you were as bad as that loose screw, committing bigamy without a conscience."

"I had a conscience, but no choice. My first marriage took place at night. We were exhausted, having just arrived across the border, and did not wish to roust out the local vicar so late. So we performed a Scottish handfast ceremony, a simple declaration in front of witnesses that we thought would be binding, binding enough to share a bedroom, for we were running out of funds. We intended to have a proper kirk wedding in the morning, to register the marriage and get written lines to show. We never had time. My father and Lord Sparrowdale arrived in the middle of the night, along with Viscount Sparling, and declared the marriage void. Father had it annulled, or perhaps he bought a divorce, or he paid the witnesses to lie. He would never say. I had nothing to prove otherwise."

"You had a blasted husband! That ought to be proof enough of a marriage." He let go of her hand to pound his fist on a book, sending up a cloud of dust.

Mina started pleating the fabric of the borrowed handkerchief. "No. My father paid Ninian to recant. He took the money and left. I never saw him again."

Now Lowell slammed one book on top of another,

rather than putting them in any order. "The cad! How could he leave the woman he loved—and his child—to the likes of Sparrowdale?"

"'We . . . we had not been intimate until our wedding night." If Mina had known what an uncomfortable, embarrassing ordeal it would be, she would never have gone through with the elopement. "Ninian did not know about the babe then, of course. Neither did I, but it would not have mattered. Mr. Rourke did not love me, it turned out. He only wanted my father's money, the same as Sparrowdale. In fact, I believe Ninian must be dead, or else he'd be here now, thinking he could charm another fortune out of Malachy Caldwell's coffers."

"Poor puss. Did you love him very much?" Lowell had to ask. If the dastard was alive, he'd track him down and drag him back to marry Lady Sparrow again, with no way to weasel out of it this time, if that was what it took to make her happy.

Had she loved Ninian? Mina asked herself. She thought now that she did not understand love then. She had not watched for his smile, or tingled at his touch, or marveled at the gilt flecks in his blue eyes, reflected off his glass lenses.

Ninian Rourke had not worn spectacles.

"I do not know if I loved him," she finally replied. "I was a girl, horrified at the man my father chose for me. I had never been in love, so I told myself the infatuation I felt for Mr. Rourke was enough. He swore to adore me past redemption. His ardor did not last past the first jingle of my father's coins. My affection died at the same instant he accepted that purse, with no tender, lasting emotions." Mina recalled now that she had not even felt any attraction for Ninian. Consummating the marriage before any kind of public wedding had been Ninian's idea, not hers.

Lowell was doubly relieved. Not only was Lady Sparrow not a whore, giving her favors freely, but she had never loved the craven Ninian Rourke, and certainly not the crude Lord Sparrowdale. For a woman married twice, just long enough the first time to beget a son, her kiss was unpracticed. Minerva was pure in heart, where it mattered, if not in body. Speaking of bodies, his was reacting predictably—if problematically—to Minerva's nearness.

"So you want your son, but not the earldom," he said, getting back to the case, not the sad case he was in. "You cannot acknowledge him, you know." She would be permanently ostracized from the *haute monde*. One of their own could succeed in foisting a baseborn child on them, but a shipbuilder's daughter could not.

"I do know that admitting the birth of a child out of wedlock would undo your mother's efforts at seeing me established among the *ton*." She snapped her fingers. "That is how much I care for society's acceptance. But having a mother labeled a light skirt will do Robin no good, either. I cannot decide what is best to do until I see him." She leaned over to pick up the book nearest to her. Caesar. The boys did not need to learn how to conduct a war. She swiped at it with the dustcloth—except she was still holding Lowell's handkerchief—and added it to the pile to be reshelved. "There are other complications, too."

Lowell did not think he could take much more, smelling the lilac scent she wore, watching that apron's bib pull across her breasts when she reached for a book, knowing she was not pining for a lost love.

He reached out, intending to lift the pile of books. Somehow his arms reached Minerva instead, and closed tightly around her as he brought their mouths together. The stack of books beside her fell over again. Herodotus hit the floor.

Mina did not notice. She went willingly into his embrace, elated that Lowell did not seem to mind about Robin. He did not think any worse of her or find her less attractive—unless he was kissing her because he thought she was fast. She was no wanton, willing widow. She pushed him away with a copy of Catullus. "I do not make a habit of kissing gentlemen on library floors," she announced, straightening the lace cap on her head.

"Thank heavens. It is devilishly hard on the books."
Lowell smiled and pressed a quick kiss on her nose. He
stood and began putting the books away again. "Now
tell me the rest of the complications."

Mina found the list on the floor. She pointed to the
last set of initials, W. S. "Perry said there were other
instances of bigamy, other possible breach-of-promise
cases. This last child would be three years of age, conceived after my marriage to Sparrowdale. But what if I
were still wed to Ninian Rourke at the time? Then I
really was a bigamist, and my marriage to Sparrowdale
could be overturned in favor of my earlier union."

"Which declares your son a cuckoobird in Sparrowdale's nest."

"Yes, but a legitimate Rourke. That is not the point."

"W.S. is. And he is the heir."

"Exactly, if Sparrowdale actually wed this child's
mother, thinking his prior marriage to me was his excuse
to leave her."

Lowell forgot to look at the titles of the books he held,
shoving them into shelves willy-nilly in his excitement of
having a fine and worthy mystery to solve. "Then that
marriage, W.S.'s mother to the earl, was actually legal,
and the child W.S. is Sparrowdale's lawful son. If he is
a boy. If an unacknowledged child, bearing another's
name, can be a legal heir. If Sparrowdale did not use
another of his ploys to trick the mother, like his false
names or his fake clerics. If we can find the tot. There
are so many if's, it is a good thing you have an excellent
investigator at your service."

He smiled at her, and Mina felt her insides flutter. She
wished either Lowell had a less appealing smile or she
had fewer scruples. Lively kisses among dead Romans
were altogether too tempting for her piece of mind. *Alea
jacta est,* indeed, she feared. The die is cast.

"The first thing," Lowell said, "is to send a man to
Scotland to see if your marriage was registered or
annulled. Do you recall the town or the names of any
witnesses?"

"No, but the inn was the Tartan Rooster, which should not be hard to find, right at the border, just off the Great North Road."

"Good. I will send one of my most trusted men immediately. Meanwhile, you and I, my dear, shall go have your portrait painted."

"Why in the world would we do such a goosish thing? I should like to commission a painting of the boys eventually, but there is time for that later, when we find the rest of them."

"Ah, but we need to go visit Marcel now. While he spends time capturing his Vision, he just might recall Perry's direction."

That was if Mad Marcel remembered them, or Perry. "I am not posing without my clothes on, like those paintings he has everywhere!"

"I should hope not! Not for Marcel, anyway." Lowell winked and grinned, in a decidedly wicked fashion.

Could a rake wear glasses?

Chapter Twenty-two

*T*hey traveled by closed carriage late the next morning, with a guard next to the driver, a groom up behind, and a ladies' maid. The maid was there less for propriety's sake than for propinquity's. Lowell knew that if he sat near Minerva, he would have to kiss her. It was that simple. Instead he faced her and the maid across the coach, marveling again at the perfection of Lady Sparrow's skin, the dainty grace of her fine-boned posture, the fullness of her pink lips.

Marcel was equally entranced with the countess's appearance. Roused from his slumber, although the day—and the daylight he required for painting—was half gone, he was in raptures at their arrival. "*La belle étoile!* My beautiful star! My Vision, she has returned to me."

They waited in the empty parlor below, unwarmed by any fire or refreshment, while he dressed. Granny Radway and the curate had not returned, obviously. Lowell sent the footman off to find a pastry shop or a hot-bun vendor and sent the maid to the kitchen to see if she could put water on for tea.

When Marcel came down, unwashed and uncombed, with paint smears still dried on his unshaven cheeks and in his dark hair, to bring them up to his attic studio, he was *au anges*. He was soaring with something, at any rate. Lowell went around opening the atelier windows before they all started to see visions.

Mina thought the artist looked thinner than last time, so she had the servants set up an informal tea on the only empty surface, which happened to be the model's couch. She hoped Mrs. Radway could forgive their trespassing, but thought any woman would rather return to a messy kitchen than an emaciated lodger.

Marcel wolfed down the pastries and the tea. Either he was in a hurry to get to his easel or he was starving. "Haven't you eaten since the curate left?" Mina asked, signaling the maid to bring more.

"What is food, when one has Art?" he replied.

"Necessary," Lowell said, and then returned the miniature portrait of Lady Afton-Glover. "I was impressed by your, ah, style and thought to commission a portrait of the countess. I also thought we might chat about Perry Radway while you painted."

"*Non.* No spectators while Marcel paints. No talk. The concentration, you know, it cannot be broken."

Neither could the dauber's ugly nose, to Lowell's regret, not if they wanted to get any information out of him. Lord Lowell knew the artist only wished to get Lady Sparrowdale out of her clothes. One of his nudes would hang in Westminster Cathedral sooner. "No, I could not leave the lady unattended." He took Minerva's arm and headed for the stairs.

"*Non, non!* Wait. For the chance to paint the prefect face, the perfect form, Marcel can make the exception, *non?*"

"The perfect form?" Mina gasped.

"No, it is to be a facial portrait only," Lowell said.

"Never! Mon Dieu, a sacrilege to leave such beauty unrecorded for posterity! She is to be my masterpiece, my grand opus, yes? Is that how you say it? My naked Madonna."

"No!" they both shouted.

"The portrait will hang in public view, you see," Mina explained, thinking they had been too harsh with the artist.

"But of course. Where else would a painting by Marcel Palombe hang?"

A cannon would not be too harsh.

"No nude. No body. No Madonna," Lowell ordered.

"We thought a small portrait, the kind that could sit on a desk or a mantel, to be admired."

A crafty look came over Marcel's face, between the streaks of paint. "What you are asking, interruptions while I paint, a new style, this is above my usual fee, *n'est-ce-pas*?"

"But of course," Lowell agreed, then turned to Mina. "No price is too high for such beauty, do you not agree, my dear?"

Mina thought he was being altogether too free with her money. After all, what did she want with a portrait of herself? Who was going to see it except the servants and the children? "I am not so sure . . ."

"No matter, Countess. This is my painting, for my library. I say cost is no object."

"Ah, a man of great taste." Marcel kissed his fingers. "A connoisseur, *mais oui*. I should have known by your choice of companion."

So Mina was posed on the couch, and Marcel took up his charcoal crayon for a preliminary sketch. Lowell started pacing, until Marcel frowned him into stillness.

"Such bones! Such eyes! Such lace—we remove some of the lace, no? To show the column of the neck."

Mina pulled at the loose stitches that held the white lace to the high neckline of her black gown. She held it in her hands, for something to do while Marcel kept drawing. It was disconcerting to be stared at so intently. Marcel at least made lines on the canvas. Lord Lowell did not.

Marcel rubbed out the sketched lace with his fingers, then wiped his brow before returning to his canvas. He began to look like a coal heaver, and started cursing like one too. "*Non!* This is all wrong. Black, pah!"

He draped a turpentine-smelling yellow cloth over her shoulders, then a red velvet cape, then the brown blanket from his bed in the corner. Mina screwed her eyes shut and tried not to think of what might be crawling out of it. When she opened her eyes, the blanket was gone, and her gown's tapes were loosened so the neckline fell well below her collarbone.

"Ah, that is better," Marcel said, going back to his work.

Lowell sighed. That was much worse. "About Perry," he began.

Marcel put his charcoal down and came out from behind his easel, a scowl drawing his eyebrows together. Mina thought he would banish Lowell from the room after all, but he merely tugged at the sleeves of her dress, baring her shoulders except for the charcoal streak his fingers left there.

"I do not think this is such a good idea," she started to complain.

"What is it you wish to know about our Perry?" Marcel asked, stifling her protest.

"Where he is, of course." If Lowell sounded a bit breathless, it was because of the paint smell, he told himself. "Where did Perry and his grandmother and the curate go when they left here?"

Marcel switched from the charcoal to a brush and a sienna wash, dabbing at the painting with the brush or a rag or his hand until it looked like one big reddish-brown smear to Lord Lowell, but what did he know? He would rather look at Minerva anyway.

"The hair!"

"Yes, they went there, but where?"

Marcel tossed the brush and the rag to the floor. "No, the hair, it is all wrong. Madame looks like the curate's sister."

"So the curate does have a sister?" Mina asked. "You mentioned a lot of sisters when we spoke last, but you were vague." Which was the understatement of the day. Marcel's mind was like a dandelion puffball in a breeze. "Is that where he went?"

Marcel had pulled the white lace cap from her head, staining it beyond repair in the process, Mina was sure, sorry for the waste of Cousin Dorcas's work. Then he started pulling the hairpins out of her hair. "No, wait!"

"*Monsieur*'s sister?" Marcel hinted.

Mina nodded, and let him proceed. Soon the pins were out and her hair was spread in waves down her back and

across one shoulder, which had somehow become further
bared under his long, darting fingers. Another few inches
and her nipples would be showing. They tautened at the
idea that Lord Lowell would see. Color stained her
cheeks. "Please . . ."

"*Oui.* The curate's sister. She lives in Kent. A dried-
up prune, yet where else would he go so no one could
ask him questions? The curate, he cannot lie, *cer-
tainement.*"

Lowell hoped Minerva was making note of the cleric's
direction. The man could be in hell, for all Lowell cared
at this moment. Devil take it, he was burning up himself
at the houri she was becoming. He forced open a window
that had not worked in years, so he could take a breath
of cooler air.

"Did the boy and his grandmother go with them?"
Mina asked, since her investigator seemed to have lost
his tongue. "Are they all in Kent?"

Marcel twitched at her loosened gown again, and her
curling hair. Mina moaned. So did Lowell.

"Why would Granmere go to Kent? Her sister lives
in Bath."

Lowell needed a bath, all right. A cold one.

Mina shivered. She was half naked, the windows were
open, and her discreet inquirer was being anything but
discreet in his ogling. A gentleman would turn his back,
but then she would miss the gleam of naked hunger she
saw in his eyes. That wanting brought a smile to her lips.

"*Oui!* That is it! That is the look I must capture! The
allure, the power to make men grovel. The angel and
the—*qu'est-ce que c'est?*—flirt."

Flirt? Mina had never flirted a day in her life! Was
that what she was doing? She thought she was posing
for her portrait. And getting closer to finding the key
to the whole mystery of Sparrowdale's succession. That
reminded her of her mission. "So Mrs. Radway is in
Bath, with Peregrine?"

"*Non,* do not wrinkle the forehead!" Marcel blotted
the canvas with his sleeve in exasperation. Still aggra-
vated, he almost shouted, "My sister! I told you Perry is

with my sister! Now sit still, *madame,* unless you wish to
look like a cross-eyed toad."

She smiled at that, and Marcel was content. He started
to mix colors on his palette, muttering to himself.

Lowell had managed to get his baser instincts under
control by the simple remedy of removing his spectacles.
Now his interest in the case took precedence to his interest in a blur of skin and hair and—who was he fooling?
He put his glasses back on, the better to think, and the
better to lust after the woman who was paying him to
find young Radway. Damn. "The boy is with your sister,
you say, but where?"

Marcel stepped back, holding his brush up to match
skin tones.

"We mean him no harm," Lowell said. "In fact, the
lady wishes to help with his schooling and such. He will
benefit from her generosity, I assure you."

The artist tilted his head, squinting.

Mina lowered her neckline another fraction of an inch.

"My sister, she lives in London. Me, I do not pay
attention to your English street names. I walk, I find my
so-beautiful sister, I walk home. Granmere Radway, she
knows those things."

"Mrs. Radway is in Bath," Lowell almost shouted.
Then he lowered his voice, recalling he was supposed to
be the cool-headed detective. "Perhaps if we drove you
in my carriage, you could direct us."

Marcel nodded. "But of course. Next week, when my
masterpiece, she is completed."

Mina started to tuck her lace collar back.

Marcel slammed his palette down on the worktable
next to his easel. Two brushes, a cigarillo, and a shriveled
sausage rolled onto the floor. "I knew this was the bad
idea. How can I think with all this stupid noise?" He
stomped over to a stack of leaning paintings, some
framed, some not quite completed, and pulled one out.
He took Mina's portrait off the easel and replaced it with
the larger canvas. "Here. Here is my sister. Now go,
monsieur. Even an *imbécile* could find her in London."

Mina got up to look at the painting. She saw a beauti-

ful auburn-haired woman who held herself gracefully, in
a dancer's pose. She held her feathered fan . . . strategi-
cally. Marcel's sister wore nothing but another feather,
this one in her hair. Mina's cheeks turned scarlet and
she gaped. All she could think to say was: "You do not
look much like her, do you?"

Marcel shrugged. "Belle is my half sister only. She
looks like our sainted mother. I take after my father."

Lowell was staring at the painting. "My word," he ex-
claimed, "that's La Paloma, the Dove. She's the highest-
paid—"

"Dancer," Marcel supplied. "In all of London. Belle
Palombe. Our mother was the premier ballerina in all of
Europe. Belle dances in her footsteps. My genius leads
me in other directions, no?"

Mina could not believe his genius led him to paint his
own sister that way. Even if she was his half sister and
a ballet dancer. Some of her shock must have shown on
her face, for Marcel shrugged again and said, "She brings
her wealthy lovers here to commission her portrait. We
both make the profit, no?"

"Her wealthy lovers? You mean she is a—?" Mina
turned to Lowell. "And you know her?"

The tips of his ears turned red. "Ah, by reputation
only."

"Hah! That is not what Belle says."

The world was soon to be short one genius. "I have
met the young lady," Lowell admitted, "at parties and
such."

"But you do know her address?" the iceberg that used
to be Lady Sparrowdale asked him.

It was Marcel who told her, "*Cherie,* you would not
want a man who did *not* know my sister's direction."

Chapter Twenty-three

"*I* am too going."

"No, you are not."

"I am."

"It is no place for a lady."

"It is no place for a little boy. I shall not leave Peregrine one minute longer with a courtesan."

"Do you remember discreet inquiries? How discreet do you think it will be when the scandal sheets broadcast Lady Sparrowdale's visit to the Dove's love nest? You hired me to transact such business for you."

"Then I am dismissing you."

"I'll go anyway."

"So shall I, if you will not take me."

"You do not know where."

"Half the gentlemen in your mother's parlor must know where, it seems. I shall ask one of them."

"And bid farewell to your reputation as a lady."

"When are you going to understand that I am no lady? I was born a cit, and I remain one, thanks to the shipyard that pays your salary. Paid."

"You are a countess, dash it!"

"I might be nothing more than wife to a man who once was an assistant foreman at that shipworks. Heaven knows what Ninian Rourke does now, since he lost his position when we eloped."

"You are a lady. If you married a miner or a mercer or . . . or Marcel, heaven forfend, you would still be a lady. Where it matters."

And if she wed a private investigator?
"I am going."
"No, you are not."

Neither of them was going, not that day. Marcel had
insisted that the countess remain in the studio as long as
there was light, and now they had to get ready for Her
Grace's dinner party. Mina would need at least an hour
to scrub away the paint and the charcoal and the smell
of turpentine, before donning her best black evening
gown, her pearls, and . . . one feather in her hair.

Lord Lowell needed that hour to buy her flowers, to
change his mother's seating arrangements, and to find
out the name of La Paloma's current protector. A chap
with glasses learned to be cautious about calling on a
stranger's mistress. Half the gentlemen at White's were
more jealous over their ladybirds than they were over
their wives.

Harkness would know who currently paid the rent on
the Dove's Garson Street house, or he could find out in
an instant. Unfortunately, both butlers were enlisted tonight to serve the company.

Lowell intended to go to Marcel's sister's house this
evening, nevertheless, after his mother's dinner party,
while Lady Sparrow was snug in her bed. He could have
the boy back here before she came down to breakfast,
all rosy from sleep and grateful to him for fetching Perry
without jeopardizing her reputation. It was about time
he earned his fee—and Minerva's respect. He might be
a mere second son and a professional man besides, but
he swore to prove to the countess that he was not absolutely worthless.

So he tossed out four neckcloths before getting one
right.

Almost everyone was pleased with the duchess's dinner. The food was superb, the service was meticulous,
the conversation was sparkling.

Except at one end of the long table.

Roderick had come with the Duke of Westcott's party,

and had fully intended on impressing the duke and his daughter, Lady Millicent. To that end, his shirt points reached his ears, his neckcloth reached his chin, and his waistcoat reached new heights of fashion, covered as it was with fire-breathing dragons embroidered in silk. His carnelian coat had matching flame-colored lining, and he wore a red rose in his buttonhole, and red-heeled shoes. He did sport a black armband, in memory of his uncle. And a black look, in memory of Minerva's machinations.

As second-highest-ranking gentleman, Roderick should have escorted Lady Millicent into the dining room, while her father led in their hostess. Roderick should have sat beside the heiress, filling her ear with sweet pleasantries during the long, many-coursed meal. Instead, Duchess Mersford, with Minerva's contrivance, Roderick was certain, had unearthed a widowed marchioness who took precedence over the duke's daughter, and who took his arm. Lady Pomfrey was seventy if she was a day, used an ear trumpet, and smelled of camphor.

When he had tried to protest, Her Grace had rapped him with her fan—doing heaven knew what damage to the padded shoulders of his tailed coat. "Lady Pomfrey knows everyone, Sparrowdale. She will be good for your career."

"My career?" Roderick was a gentleman. Unlike others he could name, but would not, for fear of insulting his hostess, he did not work.

"Why, your career as a toadeater, of course." The duchess was obviously not afraid of insulting anyone. Why should she be, with a silver-haired duke at her right hand? At Roderick's right hand was a deaf old lady who kept poking him with her knife to get his attention. Across the table, out of the bounds of polite conversation, sat Lady Millicent, giggling and blushing and batting her golden eyelashes at the youngest Mersford male, Lieutenant Andrew Merrison. The officer's scarlet regimentals and gold braid put Roderick's ensemble in the shade, and those shoulders needed no buckram wadding either, Roderick supposed, almost choking on his turbot in oyster sauce. They were old childhood friends, the

duchess had announced as she paired them off for dinner, with a great deal of catching up to do. What was
the lieutenant going to do, Roderick wondered—show
Lady Millicent his tin soldiers?

The paper-skulled soldier seemed to be showing her
his cursed dimple and white teeth a lot. Of course. Why
wouldn't he be trying to reestablish himself in the young
lady's affections? Dash it, Roderick's chosen wife was a
frothy soufflé in white lace and ruffles, with gold curls, a
rosebud mouth, and thirty thousand pounds. No man
worth his salt could ignore the opportunity.

"What's that? Salt on the asparagus? Never." Lady
Pomfrey stabbed him with her fork this time.

Further down the table, after a number of society's
leading lights and lions, sat Minerva's dunderheaded
Cousin Dorcas, an addlepate if Roderick ever saw one,
but an Albright for all that. Her partner was the solicitor,
Sizemore. He no more belonged in such elevated company than . . . than Minerva herself, a merchant mogul's
gel who'd climbed her way into Her Grace's good graces.
The shrew likely had more blunt than anyone else at the
table, too. There was no way he could get his hands on
the widow's wealth, and he seemed to be losing his
chance at the duke's daughter's dowry. Damnation. Roderick's veal vol-au-vents tasted vile.

He did not trust his uncle's widow, nor that stuffed-
shirt solicitor of hers, who was always nattering on about
duties and responsibilities. If the man was so responsible,
why was he not in his office drawing up those guardianship papers? Roderick wanted the matter settled, that
blind brat in Minerva's hands, and her out of his hair.
For that matter, why was Roderick's own butler waiting
on table at Merrison House? Harkness ought to be at
Sparrows Nest, making certain the other servants were
not making inroads on Roderick's inheritance while
Lieutenant Merrison was inveigling his intended.

His stomach protested the braised partridges. At least
Lady Pomfrey was too deaf to hear.

Confound it, nothing had gone right since Minerva had
come to Town. Now his tailor was dunning him for funds

he did not have, the cents-per-centers were calling in his
vouchers, and he could not return to his old haunts and
habits. He could not keep preying on those green-as-
grass fools who came to London with their heads full of
dreams and their pockets full of gold, not if he wanted
to make an advantageous match. Want to? Hell, he
needed to, or having an earldom was worth tuppence.
He would never have the power that went with the title
if he did not have influential connections.

What he had was a cabbagehead who could not shoot
straight, a thief who decided it was easier to light a fire
than steal a folder from an orphanage. The dolt had not
bothered to tell Roderick he could not read! Now Harry
the Hammer wanted his money, his payment, his share
of—nothing. Roderick did not have the blunt. He had
dyspepsia.

Swallowing bile, he studied his nemesis, his aunt-by-
marriage. Too bad an alliance between them was illegal.
He'd take her away and marry her—a man had ways to
convince a feather-weighted woman to do his bidding—
and then he'd never have to worry about her testifying
against him in court, dragging those bastards out of the
woodwork, or bankrupting the shipyard. He'd have
enough brass to buy himself a place by Prinny's side,
by Jupiter.

Instead, by Minerva's side, at the foot of the table, sat
their host, Lord Lowell. By the looks of things, the meddling Merrison would likely get all of Malachy Caldwell's
gold before he was dead a year. Mousy little Minerva was
looking better these days, too, so the lucky dog would be
getting a real bargain for his efforts. Too bad he couldn't
see half the advantages through those bottle-bottom
spectacles.

Too bad the syllabub tasted like sawdust. It was Roderick's favorite dessert.

By the time dinner was over and the ladies had with-
drawn, Roderick had drunk his indigestion into submis-
sion. He nursed his port, and his resentment.

"I say, Lolly, are you working on any interesting cases now?" Andrew asked his brother.

Lowell smiled. "A good detective never tells."

"No? I thought the widow might have hired you. You and Lady Sparrow seemed thick as inkle weavers during the meal."

He'd been dismissed. Lowell smiled wider. "That would be pleasure, not work."

"Not much pleasure, according to my uncle," Roderick said, slurring his words. "But I don't s'pose it matters if the bride's as cold as a witch's backside, when you're hanging out for a rich wife."

The other gentlemen set their glasses down and conversation ceased until Westcott cleared his throat. "I do not suggest you speak that way about my daughter, sirrah, or any female, when you hang out for *another* rich man's daughter."

Andrew looked uncertainly between his brother and the man who had so crudely described Lolly's lady friend. Lady Sparrow seemed a good sort, and she was his mother's houseguest besides. The lieutenant was ready to call the cad out, in his brother's name.

Lowell was too far away to toss his wine in the dastard's face, but he was going to toss him out of his house, by George.

Harkness took care of the matter with a pitcher of water. "Oh, I am sorry, Lord Sparrowdale. I thought your waistcoat was on fire. All those fire-breathing dragons, you know." The butler was so upset about mistakenly dousing the earl that he dropped the heavy pitcher, too.

On his way out, half-carried between Harkness and a strong footman, Roderick spotted Mina. She had gone to fetch Cousin Dorcas's lacework and was crossing the hall to the music room where Lady Millicent was going to entertain them.

"I hold you responsible for this, dash it," Roderick yelled. "And do not think you can get away with it. I'll have that blind cub put in an asylum, see if I don't."

"Actually, Roderick, I do not think you can. Mr. Sizemore sent a messenger to Mersford, and the duke has agreed to become Martin's guardian."

Lowell had suggested bringing out the heavy artillery in light of Roderick's threats, and Mina had agreed. What good were rank, power, and prestige if they could not protect a little boy?

Unfortunately, with Roderick in a frenzy, it was even more imperative now to protect the others. Mina would go to La Paloma's house this evening, as soon as the rest of the company left. Harkness had told her the address.

"I am going."
"No, you are not!"
"Yes, I am."

Chapter Twenty-four

*L*adies did not acknowledge the existence of high flyers such as Belle Palombe, La Paloma. They certainly did not visit them, not even after midnight when protective darkness shielded them from the curious eyes of society.

Ladies, single, married, or widowed, did not ride alone in closed carriages with gentlemen, especially after midnight, when seductive shadows bred temptation. They took their chaperones or their mothers or their maids.

Mina took her butler. A maidservant might have spoken to her friends. Harkness never would. Besides, no abigail was going to make this visit acceptable. They kept the curtains drawn, and Mina wore a veiled black bonnet.

Harkness sat across from Mina and Lord Lowell, more referee than duenna. When they finally reached Garson Street, he settled the argument almost as expeditiously as he'd stifled Roderick. He simply got out of the coach before either of them.

"I have no reputation to protect," he said, "and will not be challenged for, ahem, hunting on another gentleman's preserves. Therefore, I shall be the one to inquire after young Radway and bring him out to the carriage. This is not what we are accustomed to, but what is one more urchin, after all?"

He shut the door before they could follow.

While they were waiting, the carriage seemed to grow smaller and darker, a private world that was already breaking a hundred rules. What was one more, after all? So Lowell said he was sorry, pulled the countess into his arms, and kissed her. He would have stopped on the instant, had she protested. The fact that she did not, that she came so sweetly and so willingly into his embrace, meant he could never stop, or he'd expire on the spot. Instead, he felt more alive than he had ever been, burning hotter than Roderick's fire-dragons. "I am sorry," he whispered again, tasting her lips with his tongue until they opened.

Mina did not know if he was sorry they'd argued, or sorry he could not help kissing her. She did not care. She was only sorry when he moved away.

All Lowell was doing was removing his spectacles. And her bonnet. And a few hairpins. He had to run his fingers through those long brown tresses the way Marcel had. He had to touch the flesh the artist had uncovered. He had to—open the door when Harkness rapped on the covered window.

Heavens, Mina thought, how could she have forgotten about Perry? Lowell stole her senses, that was how. He was a man, with his masculine urges, so he could be forgiven his dereliction of duty—or was he still fired?—but she should have known better. Thank goodness the carriage lanterns cast so little light on the interior. And thank goodness Harkness was talking to the driver before getting inside. She stuffed her bonnet back on her head and tucked her hair under its brim.

Harkness did not have good news. According to the housekeeper, the Dove had flown the coop. She and her current gentleman had left last week for his cottage in Richmond. She had, moreover, taken along her new young page, although the lad was still feeling poorly.

"Richmond is not far away," Lowell told her. "We can make a day of it, bring a picnic luncheon."

Mina tried to sound pleased instead of despondent. "We could bring the children, I suppose, and the dog. I would wager that Martin has never been to the countryside."

Harkness harumphed something that sounded very

much like "A handful of orphans will not be chaperon enough."

"What was that, Harkness?"

"I said, madam, I will speak to Cook about a hamper."

They did not set out for Richmond the next morning as planned, for Harkness found another of Sparrowdale's children, J.D. All of the butler's time at the pubs paid off when one of his old comrades at Sparr House let slip something about Sparrowdale's butter stamp. The boy was six and ten, a sturdy groom right in the earl's London stables. His name was Jack Dawes.

When the butler reported his find, Mina almost threw her arms around him. "What would I do without you, Harkness?"

He looked past her, and past Lowell, and said, "Most likely, madam, you would hire a private investigator."

Jack did not want to go to school, live in a duchess's house, or wear a gentleman's clothes. He was glad enough to know he had half brothers, without needing to spend his days with them.

"Me mum was nobbut a maid his lordship fancied. He had his way w'her, and that was that. I reckon I'm luckier'n most, 'cause he gave me a place to live 'stead of the streets, and a position 'stead of the poorhouse. Beggin' your pardon, ma'am, but bein' a groom is good enough fer the likes of me."

The brawny lad was so obviously uncomfortable in the spotless elegance of Merrison House, standing in front of them with his hat in his hand, that Lowell had to feel sorry for him, and for Minerva, who wanted so badly to make up for her husband's sins. The probable rape of a young maid in his employ was another black mark against the late, unlamented earl, but some debts simply could not be repaid.

Lowell could only wonder at the life Minerva must have endured as the knave's countess. It was a marvel she was neither bitter nor browbeaten. Instead of shutting out the world, she was trying her best to embrace it. Unfortunately, poor Jack had been raised to keep his distance from the Quality. "Is the new Lord Sparrowdale a good employer?" Lowell asked now, thinking of bridging that gap.

If Jack were in the stable, he would have spit. "Himself? He treats his cattle worse'n dogs"—Merlin was sleeping in front of the fire, a bone between his feet—"and his staff worse still. He'd as lief box a groom's ears as look at him, and the way he looks at the maids . . ."

He did not finish. He did not need too.

"Then perhaps you would not mind working here?" Lowell offered, knowing his brother would never mind the added expense. "I have just bought a new curricle and pair, so we are shorthanded."

Jack bobbed his dark head. "I've seen your cattle, sir. Sweet-goers, they look. I'd be proud to work for such a bang-up judge of horseflesh, I would. An' I can teach the nippers to ride proper, too, even the one what Mr. Harkness says is blind. Lead lines and a good-natured pony's all it would take."

Mina put her foot down. Hard. Merlin jumped. "No. No ward of mine is going to muck out stalls his whole life long, and that is final."

"But, ma'am, I am too old for schoolin', and horses is all I know."

"Then I have another suggestion," Lowell said, still smarting under Harkness's sarcasm. Deuce take it if he'd let the butler unravel this snag too. "Perhaps young Mr. Dawes would consider traveling to Ireland, at my brother's expense, of course. Mersford maintains a racing stud there, and his manager is always looking for strong, likely lads to help with the training. A smart chap could learn a lot from old McGinnis—enough, maybe, to run a stable of his own someday. Would you like that?"

Would Jack like to manage a racing stable? That was like asking the dog if he'd like a steak wrapped around that old bone.

Before Mina could object, Lord Lowell went on.

"Then, once you knew the business, perhaps we could go into partnership in a horse farm in the Colonies. I have always fancied raising Thoroughbreds, and I hear they have the perfect climate and terrain. Of course, Lady Sparrowdale might have to lend us both the ready to get started, but it would be a good investment, don't you think? People might have enough ships, but they can never have enough horses."

Lowell was sending Jack to Ireland, when she'd just found him? Then America? Here she'd thought he was top of the trees. He was a toad.

"Naturally," he was telling Jack, "you'd have to get more proficient with your letters and numbers, lest some horse trader try to swindle us. I should think spending the summer here with Homer should do the trick. Your half brother could teach the dog to count, I swear. Then, when he goes back to university and the others go off to school, you can go to Ireland ready to help McGinnis with the bookkeeping and the bloodlines. What do you think, Countess?"

She thought he was a genius, besides being inordinately handsome, undeniably appealing, and a superlative kisser. "It might do," she said, then smiled. "Unless I decide to raise horses on the Plymouth property, of course."

"Of course," Lowell agreed, smiling back. "Meantime, just for the next few days or so, Jack, do you think you could be a spy?"

"What, sell army secrets to the Frenchies? I ain't no—"

"No, that's a traitor to the country. I mean more of a scout, keeping an eye on the enemy lines."

Jack scratched his chin. Maybe the nob was touched in the upper stories after all, which meant the trip to Ireland was nothing but a pretty dream. "I s'pose," he said, resigned to returning to his straw bed in whichever stall wasn't occupied.

"The current Lord Sparrowdale is the enemy."

Then Jack Dawes was the man—or the boy—for the job. "What do you want me to do, my lord?"

"Right now, the earl is trying to keep the former Lord Sparrowdale's other children from us. From Lady Sparrowdale, that is, who wishes to ensure their well-being. He has his reasons, but his methods are cruel, and criminal: arson at orphanages, shots in the park. I need someone there on the scene, someone who will not be suspected of snooping, who can watch and listen to see if Roderick meets with any shady characters who are doing the actual foul deeds."

"You mean like Harry the Hammer?"

Lowell drew out a breath. "That ogre is who Sparrowdale hired to do his dirty work?"

Mina was astounded. "You actually know someone named Harry the Hammer?" Belle Palombe was bad enough.

"Strictly in the line of business, I swear."

Which meant La Paloma was not.

"I know his reputation, too," he said. "He is an ugly customer, for certain. I'll get men to watch his every move so he does not surprise us again. But I need you, Jack, to warn us if Sparrowdale finds a new thug. Can you go back before you are missed, and keep your eyes and ears open?"

Jack was almost out the door before Lord Lowell finished his instructions about sending word to them here, or to Harkness at the pub.

Mina watched him go, feeling a lump in her throat. Jack Dawes was sixteen, not ten years younger than she, as tall as Lord Lowell. He was not her son and was never going to be. She could not kiss him good-bye, only wish him godspeed. Homer was too old too, and George Hawkins was too quicksilver for hugs. Peregrine had his granny. Martin had sat beside her for a story last night, not touching, but he'd rather sit next to Merlin, she knew.

Her arms were empty still.

Mina could not fill them with the solid comfort of Lord Lowell. He had not offered it, for one thing, and Harkness came into the room, for another. The butler was eager to hear the outcome of their meeting with

Jack—and to annoy Ochs by rearranging the drinks tray.

So Mina picked up the dog. The mongrel, who thought she was stealing his bone, growled.

Chapter Twenty-five

The trip to Richmond to find Perry was postponed for a day because of rain. Then it was postponed because Lady Millicent had an appointment with her dressmaker.

"Lady Millicent?" Lowell glared at his mother over his morning coffee. Instead of having breakfast with them, Minerva had decided to join the nursery party upstairs, and Lowell's day was off to a poor start. "What has Westcott's daughter got to do with the trip to Richmond?"

"You need a group to hold a picnic, you know. Otherwise people will talk of you and dear Minerva going off by yourselves, out of Town at that. Roderick will be certain to hear, of course. No, this will make him think you are on nothing but a pleasure jaunt. Children, dogs, an alfresco meal, innocent young maidens. What could be less suspicious? And Westy and I will be along to lend countenance, naturally."

"Westy?" he echoed.

The dowager raised her lorgnette, and an eyebrow, to peer at her second son. "Do you find anything wrong with the duke and I renewing our friendship?"

Lowell took a swallow of his coffee, wishing it were something stronger. His mother and Westcott, smelling of April and May? More like September and October. "Nothing, Mother."

She went back to her correspondence. "Good. Neither do I. He is not about to let the gal out of his sight anyway, not after almost promising her to Sparrowdale. He'll see what a fine young man your brother is."

"I take it Andrew is coming along also?"

"Do not be more of a ninny than you need. Of course Andrew is joining us. How else can he fix his interests with dear Millicent?"

So Westcott's daughter was already dear Millicent, Lowell noted. Knowing his mother, the pretty little miss would no doubt be Andrew's wife before the cat could lick its ear. If Andrew did not mind having a china doll for a bride—and he gave every evidence of being bowled over by the beribboned beauty—the match was vastly advantageous. Lord Lowell raised his cup to his mother in silent salute.

Lowell had no wish to hear his mother's plans for himself, which, naturally, did not stop the duchess from telling him.

"If you cannot manage to get dear Minerva aside from the gathering for a moment or two, you are more of a clunch than I thought."

Uh-oh. Lady Sparrow was dear Minerva. Well, she was a dear. Still, "This is not a mere day's outing to see the scenery, Mother," he insisted. "We are going to visit—"

"I know whom you are going to visit, Lolly. And why. Minerva explained it to me. That makes it more imperative to give the appearance of a holiday. Where one is expected to make merry," she added, in case he truly was too stupid to grasp the opportunity. "Nanny Vann is coming along so Minerva does not have to worry about the younger boys, and Dorcas and that nice Mr. Sizemore are joining us, so Westy and I can play whist after luncheon. I have great expectations in that direction, also."

Lowell did not for an instant think she was hoping to win a fortune. He was not disappointed.

"Miss Albright's nerves are not strong enough for a battery of boys," his mother was explaining. "She will be much more content as the solicitor's spouse. I daresay all of his chairs require new arm covers."

"I daresay." He pitied the poor lawyer, who had made it to staunch middle age as a satisfied bachelor. His days

were marked. Lowell decided he'd better go tell Ochs to
add a bottle or two of wine to the picnic hamper. No,
he'd ask Harkness, who would know better how many
and which of his brother's best bottles to bring. On his
way out, he could not resist teasing: "Is Prinny coming
too?"

Without so much as looking up from the letter she was
reading, the duchess said, "No, he was busy that day."

They were three carriages, two wagons, and Lowell's
curricle. This was not a picnic, Mina thought, it was a
caravan. Armies traveled with less baggage. She doubted
if Wellesley brought his own tables and chairs, dishes
and glassware, footmen and maids along on a day's foray.
She thought a picnic meant sitting on a cloth on the
ground, guarding one's cold chicken and Scotch eggs
from insects. To the duchess it meant moving her mansion under a tree.

After the meal, the younger people decided to visit
the famous maze while the duke, the duchess, Cousin
Dorcas, and the solicitor played at cards, and Nanny
Vann napped. Andrew promised Lady Millicent he
would not let her get lost. In fact, he insisted on holding
her hand to make sure they did not get separated in the
twists and turns.

Homer pointed out the names of every bird, bush, and
butterfly, in Latin, while George tested the statuary to
see if any was light enough to carry away. Martin decided
he wanted to try the path through the hedges himself,
one hand on the high shrubbery, his face turned to catch
the sunlight. With Merlin at his side, barking, there was
no danger of him getting any more lost than the others.
Harkness had purchased a map of the maze, anyway.
Of course.

Mina and Lowell slipped away to where his curricle
was standing.

"What are we going to tell them?" she asked as he
handed her up.

"We won't tell them anything. No one will miss us. If

they do, they'll just think we are lost in the maze, or strolling the gardens."

"No, I meant Lord Penworth, when we two strangers knock on his door in the middle of the day."

"Penny's no stranger. I went to school with him. I have even been to a party or two out here." He was not going to mention what kind of gatherings his lordship threw at his country place, of course.

Penworth was not actually a stranger to Mina, either. The baron had sent her a bouquet of flowers, although for the life of her she could not recall his appearance. He was most likely another of the wantwits who wanted her fortune to finance their loose way of life. Ladybirds and bachelor parties, she had no doubt, the Dove and who knew what other debauchery. She sniffed her disapproval. Then, warm in her blacks out in the sun, she opened her parasol.

Lowell thought she did not approve of popping up on Penworth's doorstep, as if on a social call. "I'll merely say we were out driving and the wheel felt loose, that I knew he would not mind us stopping in while his grooms looked it over. Or else I will blame my eyesight, say I misread a signpost and we got lost."

He did get lost, for practice, and only for a moment. Long enough for her parasol to jab him in the ear before he tossed the ruffled thing under the seat so he could kiss the countess. Now she was warmer than ever, and the sun had nothing to do with it.

Amazingly enough, Lowell found his way immediately after.

All of their excuses for calling at Lord Penworth's rendezvous cottage were wasted when Peregrine himself answered the door. The boy looked neat and efficient in silver and black livery, and he appeared fit, except for a discoloration on his jaw. Mina was so happy to see Perry, she would have hugged him—except he was running too fast.

As the lad flew past them and out the door, Lowell

caught him by the collar. "Hold, my boy. Lady Sparrow-dale and I mean you no harm."

"It don't matter what you mean. The bloke said he'd kill me, was I to talk to her. Me or granny, leastways. He said he didn't care which. And I can't give your money back on account of I gave it to her to get out of town."

"I do not want the money, Perry. And no one is going to hurt you," Mina promised, "or your grandmother. We'll all be safe at the duke's house."

Perry looked at Lord Lowell, with his good-natured good looks and his thick glasses. "He don't look like no duke to me."

"I am not," Lowell told him, "but my brother is. He would be pleased if you came to stay at Merrison House."

"Why? He need a footman? Belle says I'm a quick learner."

Mina said, "No. I need you to help take care of George and Martin."

A smile lit Perry's bruised face. "You got Hawk out of that stinking place! I never believed you really meant it about taking care of us, and you even took the blind nipper. No one ever looked his way, to adopt the poor little bloke. They wouldn't let me take him out, neither, saying he was always causing damage."

He turned to Lord Lowell. "If you've got Hawk, does your brother have any silverware left, gov?"

"My man empties his pockets every night. We are working on the problem."

Perry grinned. "I'll wager you are."

Mina told him about Jack Dawes, another half brother, who would be joining them soon. "He's a goodly sized lad, so you won't have to worry about anyone threatening you while he is around. And he knows all there is to know about horses, or will soon. Homer knows everything else, it seems."

Perry was not thrilled at having a scholar for a relative. "I don't need no schooling."

"You do not need any schooling," Mina said, correcting his grammar.

"That's right."

"No, that's wrong. What, do you want to be a footman for the rest of your life? Waiting on—" She almost said "light skirts," but corrected herself. Belle had been good to take Perry in, to nurse him and keep him safe. "Waiting on others?"

"Belle says I can get to be butler someday."

"And if that is what you want to do, I know precisely the man to teach you what you will need to know. But there is a world of opportunities out there for a boy who is willing to learn. There's an entire shipyard looking for clerks and engineers and master builders, besides sailors and navigators and sea captains. You can become whatever you wish, not dependent on the whims of an employer."

"Truly?" He looked from Mina to Lowell for confirmation.

Lowell raised his hand. "Word of a gentleman."

Mina raised hers too. "Word of a shipyard owner. And a countess. So come home with us, Perry. Your dog misses you."

"Dog? I don't have no dog. Granny would never allow one in the house."

Mina was confused. "The dog you brought to Sparrows Nest with you. The one you left with me to guarantee you'd be back after delivering the money for the children's upkeep. I named him Merlin."

"Oh, that dog. I found him on the road."

Lowell was smiling at her. "It seems George is not the only Sparrowdale nestling with a villainous bent. I guess that means Merlin is your dog now, my lady. So what say you, Perry? Time flies and the others are waiting. Will you come with us back to London?"

Perry was torn, they could tell. He looked from one to the other, then back down the hall of Lord Penworth's house, where he was warm and fed but the most junior servant for all that, with no brother or friend. And Gran-

ny'd have his hide, knowing he was working for Belle
and the paying gentleman. "What's the catch?" he
wanted to know. "There's always a price, Granny says."

"No, you have already paid the price," Mina said.

"But we could use your help," Lowell added, "to find
the rest of the children Lady Sparrowdale seeks, especially the youngest two. Did you make any deliveries for
the earl for two infants?"

Perry studied the tops of his shoes. Fancy ones, they
were, that one of Belle's callers had left behind once.
They only pinched a little. "That's just what he told me
not to tell you."

"Who told you, Harry the Hammer?"

"That's him. A regular giant, with fists as big as anvils,
and twice as hard."

"He won't bother you again. In fact, he won't be bothering anyone, from Botany Bay. But you can tell us
about the children later. We need to leave soon to reach
London by nightfall."

"I'd better tell Belle. She took me in and all." He
glanced up at the stairs again. "But she's busy right
now."

"We'll go help the others pack up and return in half
an hour, all right?"

Perry grinned. "It's Belle. Better make it an hour."

The day was growing overcast when they went back
to wait outside Lord Penworth's cottage. Lowell spread
the lap robe around Mina's legs. "I thought you would
be happier once we found Perry, so he could lead us to
the others, but you seem disappointed."

"I am disappointed. I wanted to see La Paloma, to see
if she could possibly be as beautiful as her brother
painted her to be."

"She is," Lowell said, making the day darker, drearier,
and colder still. Then he added, "But you are far more
beautiful."

And the sun came out.

Chapter Twenty-six

*H*e did not look much like an earl. He did not look like much of a boy, either, the W.S. on the bottom of the list. Perry led them right to Wendell Sparr, though, a tiny three-year-old, the youngest of Sparrowdale's side-slips.

He was a little scrap of a thing, with huge brown eyes and a nose that was bigger than his fist. The two were easy to compare, for Wren, as he was called, constantly held his hand to his mouth, sucking on his thumb. He would grow out of the habit, Mina told herself, and into his nose. And he would talk, eventually. For now, he did not smile or laugh or chatter or run around. He just sat, staring and sucking.

For all that he looked like the runt of an unfortunate litter, Wendell might very well be the heir to the earldom, if Mina's first marriage proved binding, negating her second one, to Sparrowdale. She had not heard from the man sent to find Ninian Rourke, tracing him through his family and friends. Nor had Lowell heard from the investigator he'd sent to Scotland, to look for witnesses to her marriage or records of an annulment. But Perry swore Wren's mother had been rightfully married to Sparrowdale—his grandmother had the papers hidden away somewhere safe—and so did Wren's aunt Mary, who'd had the raising of the little boy since his mother took her own life.

Mary Tilbey was a thin, tired woman, whose eyes were as faded as the gray gown she wore, except for the purplish bruise under one of them. She had nine children of her own to feed and a loutish husband who drank. He used to be a coachman, one of the elite mail drivers, handy with his whip and his fists, until Sparrowdale came into the shop where Wren's mother was working. Then Tilbey decided he did not have to work anymore. Now the money was all gone, and the quarterly support, and no one would hire Fred Tilbey to drive an oxcart. The house was dilapidated, damp and dank from the wash Mary took in to make ends meet. Sheets hung everywhere, but those ends never quite connected.

Tilbey blamed Mina. "If it wasn't for you, our Eve would be alive, married all right and tight, instead of getting passed over by a blasted bigamist. I could of had my own posting inn."

"But . . . but could you not see what Sparrowdale was like? He was already sickly three years ago. How could you let your sister-in-law wed him?"

Tilbey waved a hand around the pawky room, the crying infants, the squabbling children. "We had Evie living here too, lady, and two other sisters. Can you see what *this* was like? She married the old crimp in order to make a better life for herself, and for all of us. How was we to know he was a blooming earl with an heir and a new young wife? We thought he was just an old codger who wanted a pretty young thing to look after him in his dotage—and that he'd leave her better off after a few years. The fewer the better. We didn't figure he could get a babe on her." He made a rude noise. " 'Stead, she killed herself out of shame, and the dastard wouldn't even pay for her burial. We made sure his name went on the stone anyways, and on the brat, 'cause she married him in good faith."

"Why the devil did you not take him to court?" Lowell asked. "Bigamy is illegal, for heaven's sake."

Tilbey cast a cold look at his lordship, in his shiny boots and his expensive buckskin breeches. "Lawyers cost money, that's why. And who's going to take the word of a poor man 'stead of an earl? He paid us to forget there ever was a wedding, then he forgot all about

LADY SPARROW   181

Evie. If old Granny Radway hadn't got wind of it, Sparrowdale wouldn't of given us a shilling for the boy's keep."

"My sister was a good girl, ma'am," Mary told Mina.
"A seamstress, she was, and she gave us all her pay. She
wouldn't of married your man if she knew he was wed.
She wouldn't of married such an old stick anyway, but
he offered to pay our mortgage. Now Fred's saying our
oldest has to go north to the factories, and young Wren
has to go on the parish." She patted her stomach. "Lud
knows where we'll get the money to feed this new 'un."

Mina already had Perry and one of the girls out buying
foodstuffs. She would arrange for credit at the markets,
she decided, and decent apprenticeships for the children
as they grew older. What she would not do was give Fred
Tilbey a farthing. The sot was lucky she did not have
him castrated.

Lowell was going to ask his own half brother the barrister to pay a visit to Granny Radway in Bath, to look
at the papers she had stashed away. Then he was going
to explain to Fred Tilbey how French letters worked.
Something in this house ought to.

When they took the boy away, he did not have one
belonging to pack, not one shirt or gown. Mary did not
even kiss him good-bye. The other children were too
busy fighting over the bread and cheese to notice. Fred
Tilbey spit on the half-dead bush outside his front door.
"And good riddance," he said, which was more than the
little boy said.

They took him back to the duchess's house, the silent,
skinny, potential peer. If Mina's first marriage would
hold up in court, and if Wren's mother's would too, then
Wendell Sparr was the new earl—if Roderick did not kill
him first. Mina could only pray that Roderick knew less
than they did and that Lowell could keep Wren safe.

The Mersford Square town house was like a fortress.
Guards patrolled the grounds day and night, and armed
footmen were stationed outside the nursery. Andrew
moved back from the barracks with a few of his fellow
officers. Ochs was dismayed, but the other boys were in
it. Now Martin had heroes to tell him tales, Homer had

warriors to discuss the general's tactics, Perry had young men to slip him a sip of brandy, and George had real soldiers to help deploy the lead ones he found in the nursery while searching for more valuable items.

Everyone fought over Wren—except Ochs, of course. They carried him around, tossed him in the air, sang him lullabies and drinking songs. Even blind Martin liked to have the baby sit in his lap when someone read to them, once he was tidied up. The dog took care of face-washing after all the treats the officers brought.

Homer took it as a personal affront that his baby brother was lagging far behind his age in speaking and was positive that the child's understanding was not at fault. He was likely cuffed for speaking out in Fred Tilbey's household, Homer reasoned, and had learned to be still. The young scholar was determined that his half brother would speak— if not spell his name—before the end of the summer, and spent hours coaxing Wren to talk.

Mina had to act like a countess, just to get to hold her newest ward. She tried not to feel jealous, for the boys were thriving, and reveling in being a family. When Jack rejoined them they would be complete except for the oldest child.

And her own son. Perry had no idea where another tot might be. As soon as the messengers returned, she intended to take her family—how sweet that sounded— to the Portsmouth property to go through her father's papers. Somewhere there had to be a record, more than a pair of initials on a list. There simply had to be.

She would have an excuse to invite Lowell along, too, to help her go through Malachy Caldwell's effects. Lord Lowell's reinstatement as her detective might be unspoken, but she knew he would help her pursue any avenue of search. He was already going far beyond the capacity of hired investigator, finding nursemaids and ponies and toys. Once the search was over, though, for good or for ill, he would return to his fashionable London life. Mina decided she would stay on in Portsmouth.

The countryside was healthier for the children, and safer from Roderick's venom. Her fortune would guaran-

tee that the boys were readily accepted as her wards,
distant connections of her late husband's, without as
much societal prejudice as they would find here in London. And Mina would not have to worry about meeting
Lowell on the street there, or have to pretend he was
just another acquaintance. She told Harkness to stop
looking at London properties. Harkness already had.

Dismal thoughts for a dreary day, Mina told herself,
climbing the grand staircase of Merrison House up to the
nursery floor that rainy afternoon while the older boys
were visiting the army barracks with Andrew and his
friends. Today she should rejoice in what she had, not
regret what she had not. How better to celebrate than
to look on the face of a sleeping child?

Nanny Vann was napping. Wren was not. He was sitting in Lord Lowell's lap, staring up at the top-of-the-
trees gentleman, sucking on his thumb and drooling on
Lowell's satin-striped waistcoat.

Mina stayed in the doorway, unseen and unheard, admiring the picture they made, ignoring the wrench on
her heartstrings.

"Come now, my lad," Lowell was saying. "We know
you can speak if you wish. If you do, you can have anything you want, I swear. Just name it and it is yours. A
pony? Can you say pony, Wren? A biscuit? The moon?
No?" He gave a great sigh, but the child simply stared,
and sucked.

"I know," Lowell said. "I am not a detective for nothing." He shifted the boy's slight weight and removed his
watch from his fob pocket, dangling it on the chain. Wren
reached for the timepiece. "No, no, my friend. You cannot put it in your mouth. Here, let me show you." He
held it to Wren's ear, then turned the stem to make the
hands go around. Wren took it from him to study, with
his free hand.

"Well, that's a start," Lowell told him, reaching into
his other pocket to see what he could find to amuse the
boy. A key, a pencil, no—a coin. Wren took his fist away
from his mouth to reach for the golden guinea.

"Ah, I can see you are Hawk's brother, anyway. But

now, my boy, with both hands full, you can use your mouth for something else. Can you say my name, bantling? I am called Lord Lowell, you know, but my special friends call me Lolly. Would you like to try? Lolly, Wren. Just say Lolly. La, as if you were singing. La-la-la."

Mina had to put her hands over her mouth to keep from laughing aloud. She doubted Lowell would appreciate her overhearing this conversation. But then she gasped when his nonsense worked. Wren spoke! He did not say "La," not "Lolly," not even "Lowell." He said "Papa."

Lowell looked up and blushed like a schoolboy when he noted it was Minerva in the doorway. "At least he did not call me Fred," he said.

Mina beamed at him, tears in her eyes. "I do not care what he calls you. You got him to speak. What else can you say, my precious boy? Can you say Wendell? Mina? Lady Sparrowdale?" She knelt beside their chair and patted her own chest, hoping for "mama," but getting "clock," and "pretty," instead.

"Yes, she is," Lowell quickly agreed, lest Wren mean the guinea. "Very pretty."

Now Mina blushed. "Gammon. Don't go teaching him Spanish coin his first words out. Come, Wren," she said, taking him from Lowell's arms, "let us go find Mr. Harkness and show him what a smart boy you are."

Wren called the butler papa too. But not Ochs.

That afternoon and evening Wren spoke himself hoarse for his brothers and the dowager, until George told him to put a sock in it. Later, when the children were all snug in their chambers with Nanny and the nursemaid and a footman and Merlin keeping watch, Mina found herself alone in the library with Lowell. They had both come to find a book to read, to make sleep come easier.

She tried to thank him again for what he had done, but Lowell was having none of it.

"It was you, taking Wren from that house and showing him your love, that let him talk. He would have spoke to the next one to pay him attention, even if it were the dog. He was ready."

"Is understanding children part of your investigative skill? Or do you simply like them?"

"I never realized how much I miss my brother's pair, although they are usually just trotted past me in their lace gowns and blankets. But, yes, I do like children, more than I thought. I never knew they could be so much fun."

"Most men never discover that, leaving their progeny to the womenfolk to raise. Thank you for spending time with my wards. I am glad they have a man's influence."

Lowell set aside the book he'd been skimming and smiled. "They have a score of men here playing at soldiers with them, and menservants everywhere you look."

"No, I mean a real man." She could not explain it better, but Lowell seemed to understand and take it for the great compliment it was.

"Why, thank you. And you are a magnificent example of what a lady should be, except you really had not ought to let George see where you keep your diamonds."

The library was quiet around them, cushioning them in candleglow and the scent of old leather books. Mina had the courage to ask, "Have you never wanted children of your own?"

Lowell poured them each a glass of sherry from the decanter on the desk. He handed one to her, admiring the way gold flecks danced in her soft brown eyes. "I never thought a family was in my reach," he said, sipping at his wine. "I merely have a small competence, you know, and the investigation business has not proved lucrative."

Mina looked at him over her glass's rim, noting how a lock of pale hair had fallen to his forehead. "I think any woman, rich or poor, would be proud to call you father to her children. Or papa."

"Any woman?"

When Mina simply stared at her toes, rosy color in her cheeks, he set his empty glass back down, and took

Mina's from her. "You know, I do not go around kissing just any pretty young woman who chances into my library."

She replied, "If I thought you did, I would not have come here now."

No amount of books, not even a library full, was going to make sleep come easier that night.

Chapter Twenty-seven

Some questions had answers. Some did not. Some answers were too uncertain or too dreadful, so the questions were left unasked, and some questions had to wait until other riddles were solved.

Mina finally had one issue decided. Twice.

The man Lowell had posted to Scotland sent his findings back by special messenger. That same day Ninian Rourke showed up on the duchess's doorstop.

Throwing convention to the wind, Mina met him, alone, in the library. There was too much between them for politeness or public view. If Lowell's feelings were hurt to be left out of the conversation, Mina regretted it, but Ninian was her past and her problem. She had to know more than the facts in the matter of her marriage; she had to understand her feelings, too, to see if there was the slightest ember of affection.

There was not. She barely recognized the gone-to-fat man with the florid complexion. He looked as out of place in this room of learning and refinement as scruffy Merlin would look at a fox hunt. Ninian looked more like a farmer than a shipyard foreman. Well, he was a farmer, it seemed. The smell of manure was still in his clothes, despite days of travel. His hands were rough, his language coarse, his manners rude. The thought that she had ever lain with this man mortified her, and the very idea of ever doing so again made her wish for one of Cousin Dorcas's restoratives. Could she truly have been so young, so innocent, so utterly stupid? Yes, unfortunately.

Ninian, however, did not want to claim her and her fortune as his wife, as Mina had feared when Ochs announced the caller, with a supercilious sniff. Ninian did not want to claim their son, either. He still did not know about the boy, and Mina, still not knowing Robin's whereabouts, had no intention of telling Ninian of the boy's parentage. He had turned his back on them once.

He was intending to do so again. What Ninian wanted, the reason he had taken the journey to London, was to protect his own three sons. If Minerva kept sending men with questions, Ninian's wife and father-in-law would start asking a few of their own. He and his boys would inherit a profitable farm when the old squeezecrab finally stuck his spoon in the wall, Ninian angrily told her—unless her blasted investigation had the boys declared bastards. If that happened, the moralistic old fool and his puritanical daughter would toss all of them out on their collective ears.

"The deuced elopement was supposed to be annulled, Minerva," he said, stamping his big feet in worn boots, sending up clouds of sheep dung, for all she knew.

"It seems it was not, not that anyone could find."

He cursed. "Your damned father told me that's what you wanted."

"I? You took his money and left! How was I supposed to stay married to a bridegroom who abandoned me?"

"Bloody hell, what was I supposed to do, with Sparrowdale and his son there too? They would of killed me unless I agreed to go."

"Greed it was, not agreed. You took that purse so fast the coins did not have time to jingle. You could have come back for me, before they made me marry that horrible old man. I was a mere girl, with nowhere to turn except you. And you left."

"What would I stay for? Your father said he'd cut you off without a shilling. I'd already lost my position. What were we going to live on, dash it? A silly schoolgirl's dreams?"

"We could have found something. You did."

"That's right. I found a sheep farmer with a homely daughter. Now I've got a piece of land, instead of taking orders from Moneybags Caldwell and getting nothing back but more orders. My boys have a chance to better themselves, unless you queer their pitch, claiming to be my rightful wife. And why would you?" He gestured at the lavishly decorated room with a hand that had dirt under the fingernails. "You landed on your feet, didn't you? Rich widow, hobnobbing with dukes and the like. Damn, woman, I don't see what you've got to complain of."

Four years with Sparrowdale? Having her son stolen? "No. I do not suppose you would see, Mr. Rourke." On the other hand, she might still be married to this lumpkin, who looked healthy enough to live forever, not that Mina actually wished him ill.

Ninian looked relieved, as if he had thought *she* was going to claim her marriage rights. "Then it's done, over, and you're not going digging in the past?"

"It is done." She reached for a letter from the desk, the one that had just arrived from Lowell's agent. "And you do not have to worry anymore. Our marriage was never annulled, because there was no need. Do you recall that inn we stayed at that first night, where we made our wedding vows before the innkeeper and his wife? That one on the Scottish border?"

"Yeah?"

"It was on the English side of the border. We had not crossed into Scotland yet."

Ninian slapped his fleshy thigh. "If that don't beat all. What a good joke. Too bad I can't share it with the fellows at the local."

"Yes," she murmured. "Too bad." She put the letter back on the desk, straightening the blotter and the penknife. Then she asked the question that she'd been asking herself all these years of living through what he thought of as a jest. "Tell me something, Mr. Rourke, for old times' sake. Did you ever love me the least little bit?"

Ninian wiped his greasy forehead with his sleeve. "A man's got to do what a man's got to do," was all he said.

So Mina did not tell him about his son. He would never take the boy in, not with those others. His religious wife would not accept an illegitimate child, so Robin would end in the poorhouse or worse. On the reverse, Ninian would bedevil Mina forever, and Robin longer, about exposing the nature of the child's birth. After Roderick's machinations, she could trust almost no one. No, she saw no reason to mention the fruit of their one unpleasant coupling.

A mother had to do what a mother had to do.

So little Wendell Sparr was not in line for a peerage. Her Robert was, rightfully or wrongfully. Her legal husband had not sired him, but he had acknowledged her child as his own. Mina did not want the earldom for Robin. She did not need the money or the property or the high-flown title. She wanted her son.

Let Roderick keep the title and the estates, with her blessings, she told Lowell, as long as he left her and hers alone. Let him find a wife of his own—not Lady Millicent, of course, whose betrothal to Andrew would be announced at the end of her first Season—and beget a dozen little Sparrs to follow in his high-heeled footsteps.

She was glad Robin had no Sparr blood in him—although she was truly fond of the other boys, and Ninian Rourke's blood flowed no more honorably. If—no, *when*—they found her son, she swore to Lowell, she would not press Robin's claim. All they had to do was convince Roderick of that.

Her leaving for Portsmouth ought to show the new earl that the succession and all of its secrets were secure, but she found she did not wish to leave Merrison House, with its safety, its comfort, its second son, her confidant. A few days more, she told herself. She would give a few days more to see if they could find a hint or a whisper of her baby's whereabouts. Then she would go.

* * *

In those next days the *ton* grew accustomed to seeing the peculiar Lady Sparrow out and about with a flock of dark-haired boys—and fair-haired men, men in army uniforms, men in livery, one man in spectacles. She was never alone, and was frequently accompanied by ducal connections, Her Grace of Mersford and two of her sons, His Grace of Westcott and his daughter. In those circles, no one was going to accuse the countess of impropriety, or impiety to her husband's passing, not with her keeping his memory alive and playing ball in the park. She was considered an eccentric, perhaps, or, more kindly, an Original. There was gossip—how could there not be with Lord Lowell hovering at her side?—but not a hint of scandal. Even the recently priggish Roderick would be happy at the respect the Sparrowdale name was earning. Well, he would be happy if he were not afraid to leave his house.

With Westcott's door shut to him, the cents-per-centers' doors were shut, too. He had no collateral, and no promise of future riches to ensure yet another loan. Roderick could not pay his bills, or his bullies. Tailors might wait, but toughs-to-hire would not. He could not go courting another heiress or haunt the gaming hells. He could not even sell off the few valuables left at the London town house, for they were entailed, as was the place itself and Sparrows Nest. He could not afford a solicitor to petition to break the entail, either, although no other legitimate Sparr male existed anywhere to inherit—he had made certain of that, at least. Besides, how could he hope to live as a gentleman without a proper address and a country seat?

No, Roderick's only hope of coming about lay with the family diamonds, and the diamonds lay in the vault at Sparrows Nest. They were entailed also, but a thief would not care, especially not a thief who now had the combination to Roderick's uncle's safe and a key to the side door. The stones had merely to be pried out of the old settings and sold. With that money, Roderick could pay off his most pressing debt-holders, the ones who were talking of pressing knives to his throat, and begin again. He might have to lower himself to a cit's daughter, but, hell, Minerva had not turned out so badly.

Unfortunately, Roderick could not be seen in the vicinity of Sparrows Nest. It would not take any Bow Street Runner—no, nor any nosy gentleman playing at detective either—to connect Lord Sparrowdale's sudden appearance in the country with the diamonds' disappearance.

Harry the Hammer would travel to Sparrows Nest, on the promise of finally getting paid. The hulking henwit was just as liable to double-cross Roderick as he was to get the combination of the safe wrong, so Roderick would have to dispose of him before he got back to London to fence the diamonds. That would be killing two birds with one stone, three if Roderick could blame Minerva for stealing the heirlooms. A fine plan. One of his best.

He sent a message.

"You are sure about that, Jack?" Lord Lowell asked the groom from Roderick's stables. "He sent a message to Harry the Hammer to meet him at the Spotted Dog tonight?" He knew the thieves' den in the Rookery.

"Of course, I am sure," Jack Dawes told him. "I brung it myself."

"And you got to read it?" Lowell prodded, not believing their luck. Roderick and the paid assassin, together, and with advance notice.

Jack scratched his head. For such a downy cove as this one was supposed to be, the swell in specs wasn't using his upper works. "There weren't no written message. Harry can't read. But I told the bartender there, and he'll get a message to Harry all right. Hammer'll be looking for the blunt his lordship owes, so he'll be at the Spotted Dog on time."

"So will we," Lowell vowed. "But not you, lad. You've done your job. Go fetch your things from Sparrowdale's place, for you will not be going back. It will be far too dangerous if Roderick hears that you cried rope on him, and Lady Sparrow would have my hide if something happened to you."

Jack nodded knowingly. "I thought that's the way the wind blew."

"It does not blow, my boy. It howls. Now go. I have plans to make. When you return, Harkness will show you where to go."

The nursery with the other boys? Jack was too old. The stables? He was the countess's new ward. A guest chamber? The young groom would be horrified, and most were filled with Lieutenant Merrison's friends anyway. In the end Harkness consulted with the dowager duchess, but she was too involved in her card game with the duke to worry about one more of dear Minerva's foundlings.

"You figure it out, Harkness," she told him. "Whatever you decide will be fine. Tell Ochs I said so."

So Harkness found Jack Dawes a nice suite belowstairs, where his half brothers could visit him at will, but not so full of priceless furnishings the boy would be afraid to turn around.

He gave Jack Ochs's apartment.

Chapter Twenty-eight

*L*owell kept Minerva from going to the Spotted Dog by the simple expedient of not telling her.

He had let her handle that country clodpole Rourke on her own, against every one of his screaming instincts. She'd come out of the library white-faced and trembling, but with her spine stiff and her eyes dry. Best of all, she'd gone straight into Lowell's arms, without a backward glance for her departing lover.

This meeting with Roderick, however, was Lowell's right. This was the job he was paid to do, and the onus he carried as a gentleman, to protect those weaker than himself. More so, it was the primitive rite of stag and stallion—no one threatened his mate with impunity. Lowell felt his blood pounding and his heart racing. Tonight was his. This would not be a mere part of the investigation; it would be the end of it. If he could not get Harry the Hammer to peach on Sparrowdale so they could put him away forever, he'd have to challenge the cur himself. Actually, he had to make Roderick challenge him, so he could choose pistols. Feckless Roderick was likely no dab hand at swords, either, but the glasses rendered Lowell hopeless at fencing. Either way, Roderick would be out of Minerva's hair by daybreak, dead or delivered to a ship bound for New Zealand. She could not get on with her life, not with Roderick in it.

Lowell's best plan was to have a representative of the law overhear a conversation with criminal intent, which his lordship had no doubt was the focus of the evening's meeting. Barring that, he and his men would follow Harry the Hammer and threaten him with hanging unless he confessed to Roderick's part in the attempt on Lady Sparrow's life. A challenge was the least appealing choice, not that Lowell was afraid for himself, or cared that duels were outlawed. Affairs of honor were for gentlemen. Roderick did not fit the bill.

There was honor among thieves, it appeared. The owner of the Spotted Dog, one Charlie Lake, would not permit Lowell or his men to take his usual barkeep's place. There was also avarice among thieves. For a hefty price, Charlie let them take booths in the tavern's back room, occupy strategic positions in the taproom, and rent two of the three upstairs chambers.

By nightfall, when Lady Sparrow was reading bedtime stories, Lowell had assembled six minions of the law, dressed in various shabby outfits that matched the low surroundings. The magistrate's aide, a sheriff's assistant, and four Bow Street Runners, minus their red vests, were all in position long before the appointed hour. While Minerva played at loo with the duchess and her cousin, Lowell spread his own cadre of informants and agents, who needed no disguises since they patronized just such establishments, throughout the smoky, sour-smelling bar. About the time she found her big, empty bed, he had a group of loud, inebriated soldiers seated at a table, out for a night of gaming, drinking, and wenching, singing lewd lyrics at the top of their lungs. He had a big-bosomed, redheaded bawd and her slick-haired pimp playing cards at another table, two doxies and their customers in the upstairs rooms. Just as Mina blew out her candle, a bearded old man with green-tinted spectacles slumped over his mug of ale at the table nearest the door. Drury Lane could not have put on a better-directed production.

The regulars of the Spotted Dog found their haunt more crowded than usual, but more convivial, too, with the soldiers buying rounds of Blue Ruin for everyone and making outrageous bets at darts and dice. There would be easy pickings here tonight, the cardsharps, cutpurses, and whores decided. Of course, they had not read the script.

The metaphorical curtains rose.

Harry the Hammer filled the door and blocked the light from the oil lamp hanging there. Beef-size fists hung low at his sides, his mouth just hung open. The hulking man-of-all-dirty-work looked around, then jerked his head at Charlie, indicating the back room. Behind the sticky, scarred bar, Charlie hunched his shoulders. "Got a batch o' redcoats 'ere t'night."

Harry grunted and kicked Light-fingered Louie out of his seat at the corner table, next to the card-playing couple. He grunted again when the barmaid brought him an ale. A man of few words—and few teeth, fewer thoughts, and fewest scruples—he was going to be a hard one to wring a confession out of.

Then Roderick, the star of the drama, entered the scene. He was wearing a dark frieze coat over his fashionable ensemble, tall boots instead of his mincing heeled pumps, and a dark hat pulled low over his eyes. No disguise or makeup was going to hide the Sparrowdale nose.

Right now that aquiline appendage was wrinkled in disgust. Since he had become earl, his senses had also been elevated. Now the stench of unwashed bodies, stale ale, and cigar smoke assailed Roderick's fastidious nostrils, so he withdrew a rosewater-scented handkerchief from his pocket and held it to his nose. So much for trying to look like a denizen of the Rookery.

The regular patrons of the thieves' den would have marked him down as a gull, a flat, an easy target, except they knew Roderick, knew he used to be one of them, nearly, before he rose up in the world. They also knew how vicious he could be when crossed. If Roderick Sparr was hiring the likes of Harry the Hammer, someone ought to be saying his prayers. A few of the lesser crooks decided to take their evening revels elsewhere. No sense borrowing trouble.

Roderick threaded his way through the occupied tables, snarling at the serving girl who stood in his way with her heavy tray. He took a seat opposite Harry the Hammer. The soldiers raised their voices louder.

"Devil take it, why didn't you go to the back room, as we arranged?" Roderick shouted over the din, keeping his hat low and his coat on, his hands in the pockets.

"S'full," Harry said, almost losing the mug of ale between his huge hands. "Where's my blunt?"

"You'll get it. In time."

"Now. Or else."

"I don't have it now, by Zeus. I do have a pistol aimed at your privates under the table, though, so shut your trap and listen."

That got Harry's attention. His brow lowered and his jaw jutted out, but he listened. "It better be good." He did not have to add the "or else" this time. They both knew what happened to coves what reneged on their deals, or held weapons on their one-time business partners.

"I've got a proposition."

"A what?"

"A plan, damn it," Roderick yelled to be heard over the raucous soldiers. He looked around to make sure the oily pimp and his improbably red-haired woman were concentrating on their cards, then leaned forward. "A plan where we'll both profit."

" 'At's what you said when you told me to pop the gentry mort," Harry said, after a loud belch that almost matched the soldiers for loudness. "I ain't seen sixpence, an' I don't move 'til I does."

The barmaid came by then to see if Roderick wanted anything. After she brought his glass, he grabbed her arm and shoved her into the next table. "Now get away. We've got business."

"Nah. I don't do no business with pikers." Harry made to rise, but the barrel of the pistol rose too, aimed at his gut where it hung over the table.

Roderick said, "This is a sure bet. All you have to do is lift some sparklers from a safe. I'll give you the combination."

"I ain't no cracksman."

"There are three numbers to the combination, damn it. Even you can remember them." Roderick tossed back a swig of Blue Ruin with his left hand, putting his right hand, with the gun, back under the table. "Hell, I'll write them down so you can match them to the numbers on the lock."

"I want my blunt first."

The singing stopped when an argument broke out among the soldiers. Some of the other patrons fled; the others started making book on the fight. The noise in the taproom grew louder yet.

"Deuce take it." Roderick did not hesitate to shout to be heard, since now everyone but the passed-out old relic near the door was concentrating on the scuffling officers. "It's not as if you earned the money. You didn't kill the woman, and you didn't get me those records from the orphanage."

"But I tried, an' that's what you paid me for," Harry bellowed back, slamming his fist on the table, shaking the empty glasses, mugs, and bottles there. "Only you din't pay up, did you, you scurvy bastid?"

"Enough!" Roderick yelled.

At the same time the pomaded man at the nearby table threw down his cards and shouted, "Enough!"

The brawl ended suddenly, the cheering and the wagering coming to a halt as all eyes swung to the pimp and his painted woman. The erstwhile prostitute pulled off her red wig and pulled a gun out of her padded bosom. The man was standing now, a pistol in one hand, a warrant in the other. "I have heard enough. I arrest you both in the name of the crown!"

Ten more bar patrons dove for the door. Six fled out the back. The barkeep ducked behind his counter.

Roderick headed for the front door, but the way was blocked with red-coated soldiers, stone sober, sabers and pistols in hand. Harry let out a roar and ran for the stairs, which was not as dumb a move as it looked. From the upper story he could reach the connecting buildings and escape over the rooftops. The only problem was, he had not counted on Lord Lowell's men pouring out of the bedrooms there, weapons drawn. The Hammer never could count. He stopped halfway up the bare wooden stairs.

"I ain't gonna hang for that whoreson," he shouted. "He were the one what hired me to kill the widow."

"What about the arson, and the loaded dice?" the Bow Street Runner at the top of the stairs called down. "The uphills found on his cousin that got Viscount Sparling stabbed? You tell us about that and maybe you won't go dancing with Jack Ketch."

"He—" Harry started to say when a shot rang out. Harry clutched his shoulder. He spun around, off balance, careening first into the wall, then into the rickety stair rail. The Runner tried to grab him, but the old wood gave way beneath the big man's weight. Harry kept going, down and down.

Straight to hell, the onlookers supposed, with his neck broken. Now they shifted their focus to Roderick, who had tossed away his empty, smoking gun and pulled a long, thin knife out of his boot. He saw his way out blocked, and he saw a weapon in the hand of every blasted man in the room, except one. Every man was looking at him with loathing and bloodlust, except one, whose eyes he could not read behind the thick lenses. He grabbed that one, the old graybeard, by his musty coat, and held the knife to his throat.

"You're going to get me out of here, Grandpa." He called to the Runners and the soldiers, "One move and he's a dead man. He might not have many years left anyway, but they'll be on your conscience, not mine."

"You don't have a conscience, Sparrowdale," the ancient told him, "and you don't have a chance."

Roderick looked own at the still seated man. He finally realized the shoulder he'd grabbed was too muscular for a dodderer. The man was too weighty under that shapeless cloak, too tall when he finally stood to his full, unbowed height. He was all too familiar, way too late.

"You!" Roderick spit out.

Lowell pulled off the beard. "Deuced thing itches."

"Minerva's bloody hired man."

"Not your first mistake, Sparrowdale, but definitely your last."

Roderick knew he was finished, but he was not taking his final exit by himself. "You've been a thorn in my side from the first, you interfering fool. Now you'll pay!"

He pressed the knife closer to Lowell's throat, but with a shout that was almost a battle cry, Lowell brought his arm up, and his booted foot. The knife went flying and Roderick's wrist hung limply. He dropped to the floor, crawling for the door. Military boots blocked his way. He looked up, into a face almost identical to that of his nemesis, only in a scarlet coat.

"You're not going anywhere but to the devil," Lieutenant Andrew Merrison told Roderick. "I don't take kindly to anyone threatening my family, you know. But you wouldn't understand that, would you, you swine?"

The villain had one ace left up his double-dealing sleeve. A small ivory-handled pistol materialized in his hand. He swung it up—and shots rang out from nearly every corner of the room.

Curtain.

Applause.

No bows.

Chapter Twenty-nine

There was no heir to the Sparrowdale succession. No brother, no son, no far-flung cousin from any cadet branch, no legitimate male heir anywhere.

That was not Mina's problem. Finding her son was.

Now that Roderick could never tell what he knew, if he had known anything, she had to go to Portsmouth. Somewhere in her father's papers might be a mention of a child. She had to look.

With Roderick gone, they might never know the truth about Viscount Sparling's death, either, but the gossip was racing around London like a pig at the mention of bacon. They had not been able to keep Roderick's manner of death—or manner of life, for that matter—quiet, not with all the young soldiers at the Spotted Dog as witnesses. So Mina had another reason for getting the boys out of London, to shield them from the worst of the talk. The boys were safe now. Robin would be, too.

She told Harkness to start making arrangements, hiring coaches, sending riders ahead to reserve all the rooms they would need along the way. Lowell did not try to stop her. That was her other problem.

If he had mentioned coming along, she would have leaped at the chance to have him nearby. If he had begged her to stay, she might have, for a while, at least, telling herself he was a good influence on the boys, and he was their guardian, too. He had not done either, and she could not be so brazen as to invite him to come with her, now that his work was done. He was a polished creature of the city, a light of the social world. How could she ask him to share the lackluster life of a ship-builder in dreary Portsmouth? They shared trusteeship of some of the boys, and they had shared magical kisses, but they truly did not share a way of life. Lowell had his fee, and her gratitude. He had his bachelor freedom, too, along with the shattered shards of her heart.

Confound it, Lowell thought, he was a failure. Minerva was safe from that dirty dish Roderick, but she was as unhappy as when she'd first come to Town. The Sparrow-dale sprats were not enough to bring light to her eyes. His own love was not enough to warm the frozen re-cesses of her soul that ached for her missing son—the son he could not find for her. Now she wanted to leave Town, take the boys and start a new life, without him, dash it. She had not even mentioned him going along. He told Harkness to stop packing. He needed more time.

"I still think the child is here in London," he told her. "Why else would Roderick have been so angry that you came to Town?"

"London is a big place," she said. "You said yourself there might be thousands of orphans here."

"Yes, but with the news of Roderick's death, someone might come forward with information. I think you should wait a few weeks before leaving, so they know where to find you."

"Why would anyone say anything now, when they have not for four years?"

"Because now your son could be earl."

"No. He was not Sparrowdale's son. You know that."

"But the world does not. The law cannot question his parentage."

"Society can," Mina insisted. "They will remember the gossip about my elopement, and they will say that Spar-rowdale would never have tossed away his own son, if he believed for an instant that the infant was his."

"And we would answer that it was Roderick who kid-napped the babe. No one would believe anything to be beneath that lizard, now. Most likely it was his idea, anyway."

Harkness came into the library to see if he was to hire carriages or not. He could not tell, listening at the door, but if Lord Lowell needed more time, Harkness would add his mite to keeping the countess from going to Portsmouth. No proper butler ever butled a shipyard.

He set down the tea tray no one had requested and said, "Pardon, my lady, but if I may be so bold, you have not considered Sparrows Nest."

Lack of boldness had never stopped the butler before, nor from listening at keyholes, Mina knew. "I cannot imagine why I should consider Sparrows Nest," she answered, irritated that everyone was discussing the situation as if finding an earl was more important than finding a little boy. "And why are you not seeing to the packing?"

Harkness moved the biscuits closer to Lord Lowell, further from Merlin, who was sitting on the chaise beside the countess. "I mention Sparrows Nest because of its servants and tenants and villagers, the scores of families dependent on the estate. Without an heir, the title and the property revert to the crown. What happens to everyone then, or in the interval between owners? You know no one will care for them or for the land itself, like family."

"My son is *not* family." Harkness had to have known the whole story by now. He always did.

He bowed, acknowledging her confiding in him. "The dark-haired, large-nosed gremlins upstairs are, however, and they should learn their heritage. They cannot, without an heir. In every way that matters, Master Robert is the new earl, in absentia." On his way out, Harkness added, "Sparrows Nest needs him, and you."

"There, you see? Even Harkness agrees with me." Lowell fed a macaroon to the dog, who wagged his tail. "Merlin agrees with me. If we say Roderick stole the boy, we can place advertisements. Someone will know of the child."

"Someone? They will be bringing me every four-year-old boy in the empire! No, I will not claim the earldom. It would be dishonest."

"Not the way I see it. Sparrowdale owes you. And it
is not as if you would be stealing something from a distant cousin. There are none. My mother and Westcott
both checked their Debrett's. Besides, Lud knows the
Sparrs could use some new blood."

He tossed a biscuit to the floor so Merlin would get
down, then sat beside Minerva on the chaise, taking her
hand. "And think of the boy."

"I am! That is all I am thinking of! Where he is today,
not whether he will be wearing ermine tomorrow!"

When Lowell brought Mina's ungloved hand to his
lips, she did not pull it away, so he kissed every finger
in turn. "When you find your son, what will you tell him
of his father?"

Mina was trying to pay attention to the conversation,
not the shivers racing from her fingers to her toes. "I . . .
I will tell him he died."

"But Robert Sparr's mother is a countess. You are no
obscure widow who can claim a dead soldier as husband.
Everyone will know you, in Portsmouth or in Patagonia.
How can you keep the fact that his father was an earl
from the boy, when he hears the man's name? Will you
label your son a bastard for the world to despise?"

His kisses were traveling up her bare arm now, and
Mina could barely think, much less reason coherently. "I
can . . . I can change his name, say he is just another
orphan I have taken in. He is too little to—"

"That's it!" Lowell yelled, soundly kissing Mina's
cheek and jumping up. "That's it! They've changed his
name, of course. They could not let it be known that a
legitimate Sparr was sent to a foundling home."

Mina regretted the loss of his closeness. Now she regretted his new idea. "Then we will never find him."

"No, my love. Now we know precisely where to look!
Where Roderick burned the records!"

My love? That is, "The Stricklands'?" she asked. "But
we inquired there."

"We asked for R.S. Remember, Mrs. Strickland's dead
husband was the one who kept the records. She did not

know what was owed, nor for which boy. How could she know who brought the child, or what name they gave?"

"George did not know of it, and neither did Perry." Mina sounded doubtful, but she wanted to believe him.

"Of course not. Who would trust children with such a secret? Thank goodness no one did, or Roderick might have felt he had to get rid of them, too. He could not have known which boy it was either, or he'd have acted long ago. He must have thought Robert was well enough hidden. But recall when you told me of the ledgers, we thought the exorbitant sum for George's upkeep was to pay for what he'd stolen. It wasn't. Half was for Robert, your Robin!"

Now Mina threw her arms around Lowell and kissed him, before running to the door and telling Harkness to stop the packing, which he had, of course, not begun.

Mrs. Strickland was still assuaging her grief in a glass. The children were shouting in the halls, and she could barely recall her dead husband's name, much less any of the four-year-olds'. Half the children came without birth dates or baptismal records, so she was not even certain of their ages. She did not think she had any Roberts or Robins, and Sparr did not sound at all familiar. Still, for the coin Mina handed her, and Lowell's promise to find a bookkeeper and a schoolmaster, she agreed to send for the boys she thought were the right age.

The boys were like a pack of imps, darting around, pushing each other, pummeling the smallest one with a chair cushion, shouting. Mrs. Strickland clapped her hands—to her ears. She sank down onto a chair, not the one missing its pillow. "Take any of them you want."

A harried-looking young woman rushed into the room with two more tots, curtsied to Lowell and Minerva, then began chivvying the little boys into a semblance of a line. She tucked in a shirt here, brushed back a curl there, took the pillow away before it was reduced to feathers.

"My niece, Martha," Mrs. Strickland announced. "She's come to help, thank goodness."

Mina smiled at the girl, who was whispering to the boys to be on their best behavior, for this nice couple had come to find a lad of their own to take home.

Now the boys got quiet, although some were too excited to stand still. Some of them grinned appealingly, or smiled pleadingly. Two looked fearful, and three seemed resigned to being passed over. One boy started crying, and another had to be rushed off to the necessary.

Lowell groaned from behind her. "No, you cannot take them all. We will send more help and get Mother to hold a benefit ball."

"I shall have Mr. Sizemore establish an endowment, and I believe I will ask Homer if he wishes to assist Miss Martha now and again."

"Lud, matchmaking for the boy already? You have been spending too much time with my mother." He squeezed her shoulder. "Now look carefully."

Mina did look. She studied each boy in turn, waiting for that burst of recognition. A mother would know her own son anywhere, wouldn't she? She had been dreaming of him for four years, wondering what he looked like, how tall he was, if he knew his letters yet. How could she not pick Robin out of this hive of halflings?

She could not. All of them played on her heartstrings, but none struck just the right chord. She felt tears of despair gather in her eyes. Without a word, but with his own eyes suspiciously damp, Lowell handed her a handkerchief. "We'll think of something else, then. Maybe your father's papers have the answer after all."

Mrs. Strickland had roused herself enough to count heads. "Fifteen, sixteen. There should be one more, I thought. No, not that plaguey Peter who can never hold his water. I counted him, did I not? Martha, how many are we supposed to have?"

Martha scanned the group that eddied around her. "Oh, dear, Bobby White is missing. He's most likely off playing with his wooden boat again."

"Bobby?" Mina and Lowell both asked. "For Robert? Robin?"

Mrs. Strickland frowned. "No, just plain Bob, that's all

he's ever been. The brat's never where he's supposed
to be."

He sure as the devil was not supposed to be in the
Strickland Charity Home.

Chapter Thirty

*H*e had brown hair, like Mina's, but blue-green eyes like Ninian's. He was slight of build, with a determined jaw. He clutched a finely crafted wooden sailboat, with the name Dorothea painted on the stern. Dorothea was Mina's mother's name.

She sank to the floor beside him, while Lowell stayed by the door of the now empty room where the child played by himself.

"Why did you not come down with the others?" Mina softly asked, clenching Lowell's handkerchief between her hands to keep herself from pulling the boy to her breast, frightening him.

He kept turning the boat, swooping it through the waves of his imagination. " 'Cause I didn't want to be 'dopted. I'm waiting for my own mama."

"How will you know her when she comes, though?"

"She's a real lady."

"I am a real lady. A countess."

He looked up for the first time, head cocked to one side, studying her. "She lives in a big house."

"I live in a big house. With a lot of other boys you'll like."

"No, this one has dogs and ponies and a tiger."

"Well, I have a dog, and the ponies are coming soon," she said, wondering where she could get a tiger. "But who told you about your mother?"

"My grandfather did, when he brung me my boat."

"It is a beautiful boat. I had one like it when I was a

girl, you know. Can you tell me your grandfather's name?"

"Grandpa, of course."

"Of course. How silly of me. But, Bobby, did he say why you were living here instead of with him, or with your mother in her big house?"

"He said he made a bad bargain with some bad men, but he meant to fix it soon. How long is soon?"

"I do not know, dearest. Did your grandfather say how he could fix the mistake?"

He shrugged. "One of the bad men got sick. Do you think he is in heaven with Mr. Strickland?"

Mina thought Sparrowdale was burning in hell, but she could not say so to her son. Her father must have stopped here on the way to the earl's funeral, disappointed with the lack of returns from his investment in Sparrowdale. His daughter was not a star in the social firmament; he had received no new government contracts; there had been no other grandsons to be lords.

With Sparrowdale and Viscount Sparling both dead, however, Malachy Caldwell saw another opportunity. A grandson who was earl was far more valuable than a whoremongering, titled son-in-law who was one. Malachy would have himself named guardian—who better?—and control the Sparrowdale holdings, including the pocket boroughs and their votes in the Commons. He could even persuade Minerva into a more advantageous match when she was out of mourning, by offering her the boy in return.

Her father must have had it all planned, Mina thought now, except for the rain, and the congestion of the lungs that carried him off within days of Sparrowdale's interment. He had never come back for Robin. She had to tell the boy that he never was going to return.

"I think your grandfather must be in heaven too, talking to Mr. Strickland about what a fine boy you are." And maybe her father's soul would not burn for eternity, for keeping Robin safe, at least.

"Did your grandfather ever tell you that you had another name?" Lowell asked now, coming from the doorway to kneel beside her on the worn rug. Robin let him admire the wooden boat. "Your real name?"

Robin looked up at the fine gentleman who was with the sweet, pretty lady. If his grandfather was not coming back, how was he going to find his mother? His lip began to tremble. "No. He said he couldn't, 'less the other bad man took me away where Mama could never find me." Tears began to fall as he realized she might never find him now. He wiped his nose on the back of his sleeve. "But he did say someday I could fly away with her. Like a bird."

"Like a robin, my precious baby," Mina said, lifting him into her arms at last. "Like a robin."

The dowager lowered her lorgnette. "I definitely see something of Sparrowdale about the boy, don't you, Dorcas?"

Mina's cousin squinted uncertainly, then borrowed the dowager's quizzing glass. "I thought he looked just like Minerva when she was younger, but, yes, now that you mention it, there is something different about the nose."

"He's got a beautiful nose!" Mina protested.

The duchess tut-tutted. "A mother never sees her children's failings. To me, Lowell is quite the handsomest man in London, except for Andrew, of course, despite his spectacles."

He was to Mina too, but what was that to the purpose? "My son does *not* have the Sparr nose."

Her Grace raised her lorgnette again, this time to scrutinize Mina. "If *I* say he resembles Sparrowdale, my dear, then the *ton* will see the likeness."

Mina had to bite her tongue.

The other children adored him. He was a good-natured boy, and let them take turns with his beloved sailboat, even blind Martin, who sank it in the copper bathtub. They did not call him Bobby, though, nor Robby, which was what Mina had decided on, nor Robert or Bob or Robin. They called him Sparrow.

"We need an earl," Perry explained. "I told the other

about Sparrows Nest, and we all want to live there, 'stead
of in Portsmouth. We can't, an' the crown keeps it.
Homer says they'll give it to one of the Royal Dukes,
who'll do nothing but keep his doxies there. 'Sides, it's
closer to Marcel.''

The mad artist and his sister had been good to Perry,
but Mina did not think they were the best influences on
the boy. The further away from them, the better. "I am
afraid we cannot be concerned about Monsieur Palombe.
Lord Lowell did pay him handsomely for my portrait"—
which he lovingly placed on the mantel in the library—
"and Westy, that is, His Grace of Westcott, mentioned
commissioning him to paint Lady Millicent." And the
Duchess of Mersford, but the dowager's girlish giggles
promised that would be a different kind of portrait.

Perry was still frowning. "It ain't—it isn't—right,
though, Granny staying on with her sister in Bath and
all of us stepbrothers going off without Marcel."

"All of you . . . ? Marcel?" Of course. M.P., the eldest
of Sparrowdale's misdirected dynasty.

"He'd be famous, though, were it known he had an
earl for a brother. Sparrow could see he had his pictures
hung at the Royal Academy, even."

"Sparrow, that is, Rob, is only four. And I have not
yet decided whether—"

"You could do a lot for all the other children we
couldn't take, being an earl's mother."

Harkness had served at Sparrows Nest his entire life.
His father had been butler there before him. It was not
an easy job, considering the nature of the preceding earls,
yet that was where Harkness wished to spend the rest of
his days, as senior servant of the Earl of Sparrowdale.
He told Master Rob about the ornamental lake there,
and the fountains and the fishpond. Lovely for sailing
small ships, Sparrows Nest was, with plenty of space for
a pet tiger to roam.

Once everyone else had retired, it was Lowell's turn.
The library fire burned low and only a few lamps were

left burning, so they sat close together, as if holding the shadows—and the world—at bay.

"No one will question Rob's claim to the title, you know," Lowell told Mina, as he gently stroked the back of her neck. "Not with my brother's backing and no other heirs crawling out of the woodwork. The word about town is that Roderick was capable of every kind of crime, including arranging for his cousin's death. Having someone kidnap Sparrowdale's infant son and replace the baby with a dead child would be just Roderick's style, not getting his own hands dirty. If someone should, however, challenge your son's right to the succession, I happen to have a half brother of my own, the best barrister in all of London."

"Your unacknowledged half brother. Her Grace told me how proud she is of him."

"As she should be. He would never let your name or the boy's be dragged through the gutters, I swear."

"But I cannot lie!"

"You will not have to. Did you know you were increasing at the time of your wedding?"

"I . . . I thought I might be, but I was not sure."

"Which means no, you did not know. Now I know this is personal, but did you miss your courses?"

Mina twisted the ribbons on her gown. "Yes, but . . ."

He brushed that away. "Bridal nerves. Now here is the only question that matters, my love. Did Sparrowdale consummate the marriage?"

Mina wished for still less candlelight so he could not see her embarrassment. How could she say such things and what if Lowell thought less of her because of it?

"My love?"

If she really were—his love, that was—he would understand. "Once. I was afraid and upset and feeling sick to my stomach. It was awful. Worse even than when Ninian . . ." She did not finish. "Sparrowdale tried again but . . . but I did not please him. Then it became obvious I was carrying a child and I was ill all the time, so he left me alone. That must have been when he took up with Wendell's mother, while he still could."

"Good, else he would have spread his vile disease to you. But the fact is, Rob could have been his. Declaring him so will at least preserve Sparrowdale's name and title, and keep his holdings intact for the other boys to know their heritage. You can guard it for them—and teach Rob to look after the land, and for his mother's wards."

"I don't think I can do it, Lowell. I do not know the first thing about children."

"You can do anything, Mina."

"Running Sparrows Nest, raising all those boys, looking after my father's business and investments, guiding Marcel's career—I cannot do it all."

He turned her to face him, on the couch. "You would not have to do it alone, you know."

Mina tried to find answers in his eyes. For once she wished his glasses did not hide so much. "Harkness?"

He laughed. "I had a bit more personal assistance in mind, my love. For you are my love, you know, and I would willingly share your burdens, yes, and your joys. At first I thought I was unworthy of you, a second son and all that. But now I would gladly die for you, and surely die without you. That has to count for something assessing a gentleman's prospects, wouldn't you say?"

"I'd say it meant more than any title or fortune."

"Then will you marry me, Mina, and make me the happiest of men?"

"Oh, Lowell, I do love you, but . . ."

He stopped her protests with a kiss. "If you love me, nothing else matters."

"It does, though. What if I do not please you, either?"

Since that one kiss had left him aching, Lowell had no qualms there. "I fear you will please me so well I shall die for it, or die without it." Which required another kiss.

"What if I do not like it, though?" Mina had to ask. "Sparrowdale said I was cold."

"Sweetheart, you are like molten lava. Trust me, you will like it. You already like my kisses, don't you?"

So Mina had to show him how much.

Then, even though her senses were spinning, Mina had

to make sure that he was sure, for she could not bear it
if Lowell regretted their marriage later, not when she
would love him until the day she breathed her last. "But
my birth is beneath yours, and my past does not bear
examining. All those children will keep the gabble-
grinders in grist, you know."

"What I know is that the boys deserve a chance at
happiness, despite their being born on the wrong side of
the blanket. Do you not agree?"

"Of course. That is why I want them here, with me
where I can provide for them."

"And they deserve the opportunity to better themselves, to be the best they can be, despite the stigma of
their birth?"

"Yes, but . . ."

"Then why are you any less deserving? Better yet, why
am I? Am I not entitled to find my happiness, to find
the rest of my soul, the part that makes me a whole man,
a better man than I could be on my own?"

"I can do that?"

"Let me show you what you can do, my love."

After a very informative interval, during which Harkness went off to bed, a satisfied smile on his face, Lowell
asked, "I take it that is a yes?"

Mina also wore a satisfied smile on her face, and not
much else. "Hmm."

Lowell covered them with his discarded coat, without
letting her out of his arms. He might never again, he
thought, she felt so good there. "You do know that marrying me will mean a step down the social ladder?"

"I do not care for that fustian, as long as I am with
you."

"Yes, but people are going to say I am marrying you
for your money, you realize."

"Aren't you?" she teased, knowing him for the most
admirable man in the world.

"No, I am wedding you for the boys, and your butler,
and your gorgeous little body, of course." Which he
paused to admire again. "In fact, I'd wish the money to
perdition, except that I could not keep you all in d

monds and furs and tigers and oil paints and ponies. But
I do intend to earn my keep."

Mina smiled and rubbed her cheek against his, loving
the feel of him, the scent of him, the closeness of him.
"How is that, Lowell?"

"Why, as a discreet detective, of course. I am the finest
around, you know. Just ask my mother. After the wedding, which event, incidentally, had better take place as
soon as possible so we do not add even more tidbits to
the scandalbroth, or another Sparrowdale surprise, I intend to find the earl's daughters."

"Sparrowdale's daughters?"

"What, did you think a man could have so many sons
without siring a girl? Highly doubtful. I'll find them for
you. But right now," he said, touching his lips to the
tender spot right below Mina's ear, "I think we need to
conduct a very private investigation of our own. What
do you say?"

Mina was already smiling. "I say you are hired, my
love."